Praise for *The Man in the Stone Cottage*

"I could not put this book down; and when I did, because it ended, I was crying because the writing was so beautiful. It was as though the Brontë sisters had walked out from the pages of one of their own books. Stephanie Cowell has written a masterpiece about the women who wrote masterpieces like *Jane Eyre*, *Wuthering Heights*, and *Agnes Grey*. I imagined I could reach out and touch them, feel the wind of those magical moors on my face, hear the love in their voices for each other, and believe in *The Man in the Stone Cottage*—who may have been in Emily's make-believe world, but who seemed so real to me as well as to her. This is surely Cowell's best book yet."

—Anne Easter Smith, author of *A Rose for the Crown* and *This Son of York*

"With *The Man in the Stone Cottage*, Stephanie Cowell asks what is real and what is imagined and then masterfully guides her readers on a journey of deciding for themselves. Along the way, her lyrical prose brings three exceptional sisters—Emily, Charlotte, and Anne Brontë—to vivid, aching life as they struggle to write the masterworks that will keep them from the poorhouse and to find the love that will mend their broken hearts."

—Cathy Marie Buchanan, author of *The Painted Girls*, *The Day the Falls Stood Still*, and *Daughter of Black Lake*

"A mesmerizing and heartrending novel of sisterhood, love, and loss in Victorian England. The author's lyrical prose, rich with period detail, invites the reader to lose themselves on the moors and amid the waking dreams of the Brontë sisters. A poignant and fresh take on some of the most famous female authors in history. I couldn't put it down."

—Heather Webb, *USA Today* and international bestselling author of *Queens of London*

"*The Man in the Stone Cottage* is an exquisitely written novel about the people, the events, and the lonely and haunted landscape that shaped the lives of the Brontë sisters. But it is much more than a biographical novel. The genius of the book lies in its dreamlike exploration of Emily and Charlotte Brontë's imaginations. I have twice visited the Brontë Parsonage Museum at Haworth, and even experienced the Yorkshire moors during a chilling fog; reading Stephanie Cowell's book was the best journey of all."

—Katherine Kirkpatrick, author of *To Chase the Golden Hours*

"*The Man in the Stone Cottage* is a luminous tour de force. The elusive man of Cowell's title may be part spirit and part flesh, but his presence adds mystery to this elegant, heartbreaking novel that sheds new light on two iconic literary figures."

—Susan Dormady Eisenberg, author of *One More Seat at the Round Table*

"Cowell breathes life into these two extraordinary Brontë sisters. The tone is bittersweet. The love and support of the sisters for one another is keenly felt. The novel provides a window into the hearts and minds of these brilliant writers and then expands upon what is known with an imaginative look at what could have been."

—Susan Coventry, author of *Till Taught by Pain*

"*The Man in the Stone Cottage* is yet another exquisite novel by the amazing Stephanie Cowell. The novel is the story of the Brontë sisters; who can resist? Stephanie tells their stories with fidelity to history, but especially to the vibrancy of the lives of this amazing family of writers. A novel to treasure. You will love it!"

—Sandra Gulland, author of *The Josephine B. Trilogy*

"*The Man in the Stone Cottage* is a passionate imagining of the complex relationships of the Brontë sisters, Charlotte, Emily, and Anne. Their devotion to each other and their elderly parson father contrasts richly with the secrets they keep from one another and even themselves."

—Judith Lindbergh, author of *Akmaral* and *The Thrall's Tale*

"Very few authors possess the magical ability of Stephanie Cowell to travel back in time and so wonderfully conjure up the past for us. The Brontës come alive in this beautiful, poignant, elegant and so very readable tale. Just exquisite."

—*New York Times* bestseller M. J. Rose

"A tender treatment of literature's most-loved heroines."

—Finola Austin, author of *Brontë's Mistress*

The Man in the Stone Cottage

A Novel of the Brontë Sisters

Stephanie Cowell

Regal House Publishing

Published by
Regal House Publishing, LLC
Raleigh, NC 27605

ISBN -13 (paperback): 9781646036240
ISBN -13 (epub): 9781646036257
Library of Congress Control Number: 2024951347

Cover images and design by © studiochi.art

Printed in the United States of America

Regal House Publishing, LLC
https://regalhousepublishing.com

For dearest friends and family

"Besides, I seemed to hold two lives—the life of thought, and that of reality."

—Charlotte (from *Villette*, 1853)

"But ever that man goes
Through place-keepers, through forest trees,
A stranger to strangers over undried sea…"

—W.H. Auden (from *The Wanderer*, 1930)

"I know that ghosts have wandered on earth."

—Emily (from *Wuthering Heights*, 1848)

Early Summer 1831

Yorkshire: The Stone Cottage

Emily

Twelve years old was too young to go wandering. Her aunt said this, knitting needles clicking indignantly. Heaven knew what would happen to young girls who dallied way out on the moors! But the girl always slipped away, ran, never minding being sent to bed without tea afterward, shouting through her closed door, "Don't care!"

Because if you wandered too far on the moor, someone might snatch you up, or you might snatch up something.

The stone cottage had been abandoned a long time ago, quite forgotten. The window had a broken shutter. The door which once has been painted yellow stuck when she opened it. She held her breath. She pushed hard. You never knew what you would find. And then she stood inside with light coming down through a broken place in the roof.

She walked about the single room. Ashes in the fireplace had fused together into a splayed lump and yet might be kicked a bit to fall apart. A rusty skillet, a broken kettle lying sideways. On what had been a bed, mice had long since partially devoured the mattress, but they were gone. It was more awesome than church on the holiest evenings or pagan rites under the full moon, where a washerwoman had once taken her.

She let her fingers trail along things. A shelf with nothing on it, a place on the soot-darkened stone walls where somehow something had hung. A pipe.

She came here again and again when sad or angry, crouching on the floor, making stories, feeling satisfaction that her ridiculous aunt would be so worried. She drew a map showing how to find the cottage, but sometimes she couldn't even find it herself. Emily Jane Brontë even visited the town registry, which listed dwellings on the environs of the moors, but could find no mention.

That winter when she was thirteen, she looked up to see a man at the door smiling down at her. Then he was gone and when she ran out to search for him, saw him far in the distance walking toward the grey blowing clouds.

She grew older; she ceased to visit. Other things filled her mind. Then one day she could no longer find the cottage. By the age of twenty-five, she had forgotten it entirely.

DECEMBER 1843

BRUSSELS: THE TEACHER

Charlotte

At ten in the morning, Charlotte Brontë whispered his name and with her bitten fingernails scratched at his office door in the school hallway. The door was locked. She tried the handle and called a little louder.

Monsieur Héger was not within.

She retreated to the garden in her long skirts. The church bells of Brussels rang out. For a time, she stood with her hand on the iron gate.

She lifted the latch; the sound scraped the cold air. From within the school, the Pensionnat de Demoiselles, she heard the young pupils speaking rapid French, broken by muffled giggles. Had they seen her leaving the school premises, her mouth pressed hard to contain her tears? She knew what they thought of her when she stood before them to teach them English: a dry young woman who never revealed her feelings. Did they know? She dared not reveal them.

Charlotte opened the gate and mounted the steps at the end of the street, which led from the medieval part of Brussels to the wide newer boulevard.

The bells had ceased to ring. The wind came rushing down the corner, blowing her plain dark skirt, thick shawl, and escaping strands of brown hair. Face obscured by her *bonnet anglaise*, she walked for some time on the broad street until she came to the Cathedral of St. Michael and St. Gudula, the great church that had dominated the city since the eleventh century.

To enter a Catholic church was forbidden to the daughter of an English Yorkshire parson. Yet this was the only way.

Charlotte ascended the cathedral steps.

She walked the nave with the stained-glass windows and apse above her. Pulling her shawl closer, she made her way down the long nave toward the carved confessional boxes.

A mild elderly priest in wire spectacles rose from his chair. He opened the door to his little space and motioned her to the door to hers. Charlotte entered, almost stumbling on the hassock on the stone floor. She knelt.

She had read about confession in a catechism in the school chapel and had memorized the French words. *"Mon Dieu, j'ai un très grand regret de vous avoir offensé. . . ."*

She spoke those penitent words and then added more toward the grille. *"Je suis amoureuse d'un homme marié."* (I am in love with a married man.)

Shifting in his seat, the priest muttered, "Terrible! You must erase this from your heart."

Charlotte was silent for a few moments. She thought of the oil painting, which hung in the school parlor, of the very much married monsieur with his wife and their several children, *au sein de la famille* (in the bosom of the family). Then, kneeling more upright and taking a breath, she shook her head. "But *mon père,* I don't want to give it up. I thought I did. *Excusez-moi.* I am so sorry to have wasted your time."

Even as his voice rose in protestation, Charlotte left the confessional and fled back down the nave to the church doors. She had sought absolution and found she didn't want it.

She wanted the schoolmaster's love. Yesterday when she and he were alone in his office, Constantin Héger had murmured the words, "I have a tenderness for you." His wide lips seemed wistful. Was it his poor English or did he mean it?

She ached with desire beneath her thick cotton mended undergarments.

A week before, when there had been only the desperate feelings she tried to hide, she had written home to her sister: "I'm returning, Emily." Then she had changed her mind. There was no life without him. But oh God! As she walked softly down the school hall, she noticed that his door was a little open. He was there.

Charlotte hovered in the doorway.

Monsieur stood behind his desk, so very slender, his trim beard brown and his complexion dusky. His thick jacket and vest were of soft brown wool.

Without looking up, he smiled slightly and said, "Mademoiselle Charlotte, *bonjour.* You were missed at dinner. Your place was empty."

She dared reply nothing.

He raised his eyes and looked at her, unblinking. "Do you hear from your sister Emily? Is she well?"

"She's quite well."

"It pleased me when you were both here last year to study. A pity she didn't return with you! Ah yes! She's the cleverest English girl I've met, so imaginative! Why do you look at me so? Eh? Mademoiselle, tell me. You can tell me anything."

"Because...because..." Surely his slight smile meant to come closer; surely his slowly extended hand meant, *Do you know how I lie awake and think of you?*

Dazed, she moved across the room. She had almost reached him when a knock at the door made her freeze.

Charlotte spent one of the worst nights of her life. At last, she rose and lit a candle carefully, hoping the light would not awaken her roommate, the woman who taught music and art. Hunched over the page, she wrote the words she could not speak. Then she tiptoed down the wide wooden stairs and hesitated a time before Monsieur's study. He was not there, of course; his manly weight lay beside his wife, asleep. Before she could lose her nerve, she slipped her letter under the door.

> Surely you know it, for I was just about to speak it. I love you. Had I said it, would you be indignant or amused? But tomorrow, having read this, how will you greet me? Now that I have spoken my truth, will you turn from me? If my master withdraws his friendship from me entirely, I shall be absolutely without hope—if he gives me a little friendship—a very little I shall be content—happy, I would have a motive for living—for working…
>
> No more do I need a great deal of affection from those I love—I would not know what to do with a whole and complete friendship—I am not accustomed to it—but you showed a *little* interest in me…and I cling to it as I would cling on to life.

Her hands and feet were icy when she retreated to her room. By this time, she felt she must retrieve the letter—but how could she with the door locked? What a fool she had been! He flirted with many. She could only flee.

By six in the morning, Charlotte had packed all her things. Only the cook was awake, banging porridge bowls in the kitchen, muttering to herself. The bowls would be laid at places in the dining room one by one. The heat of the fire rose from the kitchen. Soon the languid, nubile girl students would sigh and stir.

She unlocked the school door and walked down the path to the steps. A vagrant errand boy carried her trunk.

After a journey of several hours to the Belgian coast, Charlotte found passage on a boat in Ostend. The price shocked her. The sailors looked at her indifferently, a plain little woman not worth two stares. Then she was on the packet home to England, the boat plunging into interminable wild water, the sky threatening to fall and crush them all any moment. All around her was the sound of other passengers being sick into buckets.

Part I

January 1844—Yorkshire

1

I'm happiest when most away
I can bear my soul from its home of clay
On a windy night when the moon is bright
And the eye can wander through worlds of light…

—Emily Brontë, from "I'm Happiest When Most Away"

Emily

"Emily, where are you?"

Seven in the morning on this still January New Year's Day. The just-rising light was soaked gray and made dark shapes of the fence as Emily Jane Brontë stood with her hand on the moor gate behind the parsonage. The distant sheep formed faint lurking shadows amid the low, shrubby, bare trees. But she had only thought someone was calling her. No one was there; neither her brother nor her father had yet stirred from their beds.

Ancient drystone walls ran far into the distance on the Yorkshire moor, and now last autumn's heather and grass were covered with a light frost. A red grouse cackled from a wall and leaped into the air. She glanced back at the stone parsonage. Then, with a few strides, she was off.

Emily kept to the known path for a time, mounting steadily upward, then stopped and looked about. There had been rain yesterday; her hem was already heavy with wetness from fragments of thin ice, and her worn leather boots were mud caked. Laces frayed, the boots had belonged to her dead mother and sat forever in the corner of a wardrobe. When Emily discovered them last year, she claimed them. She alone of her sisters had such very long, slender feet.

"Where did you find those boots?" her father had asked, a

little alarmed, drawing his arm against his coat—a black coat as always, with the bleached bands of the clergyman about his neck. The coat was paler in the seams. He had looked at the boots and down the long corridor of his life.

Now, Emily breathed deeply, her chest rising impatiently beneath her wool vest and cloak. Her breasts were still small in her middle twenties, and her hips narrow like a boy's; she was strong, too, like a boy.

Everyone at home would know when they woke that she was out walking; it was her way. Sometimes she returned with a sick bird or baby rabbit in her cloak to keep in a warm corner in the kitchen. Later, she would have the baking and the cooking to do for the house, but now she was free.

From the hill, she looked over the few familiar stone farm cottages and the paths that wound up and down. Her father, the Reverend Patrick Brontë, used to walk this way and much farther; he was a strong man of sixty-six who trudged forth, his thick stick balancing him, to visit those in need for miles around. In all but heavy snow and fierce wind he went, his rough face burned and dried with weather, though his eyes were those of a scholar and his voice fittingly of the preacher who called the sinful to repent every Sunday from his pulpit. The same voice called his children to prayers or to tea. "Repent! Come! Eat bread!"

Emily walked more slowly.

Sometimes an uneasy sense would rise inside her that, while she was out walking, the parsonage and her family would fade away. Her mother had slept in the family burial vault within the church since Emily could remember. Her eldest sisters, Maria and Elizabeth, slept there as well. The girls had come home to the parsonage on the hill but died of sickness caught at their horrible school for poor clergymen's daughters, which most of the Brontë girls had attended for a while. Even after so many years, the two dead girls seemed to stir beneath the stone, murmuring things.

She, Charlotte, and their sister Anne had survived.

Emily paused to look about and down. Sometimes she found things like tufts of wool or strange stones.

Today there was something else.

In the slightly frosted mud off the path, curling up toward her, lay a man's heavy cloth work glove. She poked it with her boot, and it flipped over. The original color was stained with dirt in the inner fingers. She picked it up and dropped it inside the canvas bag she always carried on her shoulder.

By the pale sun shining through the graying clouds, she knew a few hours had passed and turned through the cold day toward home. Suddenly she was walking more rapidly, her cloak pulled tighter. Her sister Charlotte, who had been away one year, was coming home today from Brussels. With the canvas bag knocking against the side of her cloak, Emily walked through the moor gate and through the kitchen door.

The gray stone Haworth Parsonage, with its slate roof, which needed repair, and its weather-worn window frames, had been home since she had been an infant. Their family housekeeper, Tabitha, face lined like an old parsnip, sat on a bench before the kitchen table peeling carrots, which she had brought up from the cellar.

"Mr. Brontë's had his proper breakfast and is long gone," she said. "But that brother of yours is still sleeping. Supposed to be bad off, sick he says, but by my salvation, he was out with friends at an hour no believing soul should be. I left some food for you on the table, girl."

Tabby rose crookedly with a frown. Years before, she had fallen on the icy cobbles of the town's steep Main Street, and broken her leg; it had never healed right. She now lived with them, assisted by the sexton's young daughter, Martha, who was fast but clumsy.

As Emily dropped her canvas bag to the bench, the elderly woman glanced at it and asked, "What's here? Not another sick bird?" She peered inside. "What's this, a glove? Where's the other of the pair?"

"I don't know; there was just one on the ground. I should have left it there, and then I was too much in a hurry to turn back. I'll hang a notice in the post office for anyone who might have lost it and another on the moor post. I found it near there."

"The man who owns this has big hands."

Emily hesitated for a moment and slipped her right hand inside the glove, feeling the worn soft interior. She wriggled her fingers, as if she were about to find something. There was a lingering warmth. She said, "It's not Shepherd Peter's. His hands are like those of a child of ten."

"Then whose?"

"Heaven knows."

Emily tossed the glove on the table near the milk jug as her huge mastiff, Keeper, bounded toward her, and she dropped to her knees on the stone to nuzzle his brown face. Two cats purred around the table legs, assessing her with green eyes. Her sister Anne's spaniel, Flossie, rushed nervously in circles, as if looking for his mistress, who had also been away a long time.

"Rain will come. I feel it in my bones," Tabby muttered. "Hoping your sister isn't caught in it coming from the train."

A small fire burned in the parlor, but the breakfast tea was already cold in the pot and the toasted bread hardened on the rack. The table was piled with books and newspapers. The windows had no curtains and the floor no rugs; her father dreaded fire.

Emily ate half a piece of toast and listened to the sounds of Tabitha closing the front door and her uneven footsteps around the graveyard with the help of her stick. Suddenly, she missed both her sisters with a hollow, cramping place inside her. Christmas had been sad, cheated as she was of her usual cherished two weeks with her younger sister Anne when Anne's holiday had been canceled. At least Branwell had arrived a week early, coughing away, and Charlotte was coming.

Winter rain had begun to fall against the window. Emily thought of her father and hoped he would take shelter.

2

Charlotte

Charlotte's train drew into the Keighley station just before two that afternoon. The cold rain had ceased when she mounted into the open carter's wagon, which would take her the few miles to Haworth. Between her tiny height and her heavy skirts, it was always an effort to climb.

She felt for her glasses in her pocket. Without them, the houses of the town were blurs of brown and red.

As the horse pulled, her trunk shifted in the back of the cart. The wheels splashed mud, and the hilly farmlands of Yorkshire appeared on either side of the path.

Charlotte felt the damp between her gartered hose and undergarments making goose bumps on her thighs under her petticoats. She would have sent on her trunk by the wagon and walked the two miles to save the penny but for the weather. Still, maybe if she had walked, it would have helped shake her misery.

"We've not seen you in a time, Miss Brontë! Been away to foreign parts, have you?" said the driver over his shoulder.

"Yes, to Brussels," she murmured. "Across the Channel."

"Ah, so far! Myself, I've only been once to York. Your father must have missed you! I remember the very day he came to be parson here at St. Michael's, years ago. Your poor mother was alive then. What a good woman she was!"

"Thank you; that's kind."

It was useless to wish he wouldn't talk.

Charlotte gazed at the bare winter fields. West Yorkshire was old country. News reached here slowly, for centuries only by cart and horse and now by the trains, their heavy smoke ascending in the air and drifting over the fields.

A flock of sheep moved past, the wagon stopping for them. She looked down at the woolly backs. The cart was approaching her village of Haworth, houses stained dark with coal smoke. The horse slowed on the steep cobbled street. At the top, the lad Charlie, who worked at the Black Bull public house, came out to open the gates and carry her trunk up the path past the side of her father's church. One magpie crowed irritably. Back, are you? Nothing here for you.

Rain dripped from the graveyard trees.

But there was the parsonage, with its two stories of five windows each. Charlotte felt the house reach out to her as she walked up the few steps and through the door: her father's study to the right, the parlor to the left, candles and lanterns on the shelf, the draft from the hall; the heavy coal scuttle, the sewing box with the carefully hoarded bits of thread wound around papers.

She removed her spectacles just as a thin shape in a dark dress rushed down the hall toward her. In an instant, Charlotte was caught up in Emily's angular embrace in a rush of sharp elbows and the smell of baking and dog.

"Oh, darling, you all but knocked me down!" Charlotte exclaimed. "How are you? A year since I've seen you, a whole year! How I've missed you! But I wrote and wrote. Do you still have that odd beast?" She had heard Emily's rough brown mastiff barking ferociously from behind the house, where he was tied, and was glad not to have dog hair all over her new cloak.

"Yes, he's the better part of me."

Emily pulled back, her voice a little gruff. "Was the trip very tiring?" she asked. Within moments, she was turning into her old self, always a bit removed, a little wary of emotion.

Like brambles, that girl, Charlotte thought. And that she will not wear a single petticoat makes her look thin as a farm boy wearing his sister's frock at Christmastide revels. And her hair, all bunched with strands loose. Not that I have much glamour. The intellect is all that counts, yet all the men I know really want…though my figure is full and pretty. Still, men are… Oh, my love, who by now has found the letter I pushed under his door!

"The journey?" she replied lightly. "It took three days, but the inns were clean." Charlotte removed her bonnet. "Finding the train in London was confusing. I wished I could have seen more of the city. All those lovely theaters and concerts. Will I ever? I just hurried through."

"Nice news here, though! Bran's home for a few days because of a bad cough," Emily said. "He got to come home, and Anne didn't. At least working for the same family, she can watch out for him. Awful better-than-thou Robinsons! He's gone out now. We can carry this up the stairs ourselves."

The straps of the chest pulled and threatened as the sisters mounted the few steps and turned at the landing.

Charlotte's room was smaller than she remembered. There were her books on the shelf as she had left them, but some flowers in a vase that Emily had likely gathered in the autumn were brown by now. Dry leaves and petals had fallen on the oak washstand. She could have been away a minute, not a year.

She knelt on the floor and opened her trunk to unpack. "I've brought presents," she said as cheerfully as she could. "Rose soap for Anne. Here's a French novel and a cravat for Branwell, very smart…tea for Tabby…"

She looked down at her dull work frocks and continued to speak more quickly, hoping to outrun other feelings. "How are Anne and Branwell getting on in their tutoring work at the Robinsons'?"

"They both loathe it, but she's more patient with the two daughters than he is with the lad," Emily replied. "She sends letters all the time. I've saved them for you. She wrote you also."

"A great deal, the darling. And Papa?"

"The same as ever. If you went away a hundred years and came back, you'd find him still at his desk writing articles and sermons."

"Yes, the same as ever…and I'm the same too. I thought by this time I'd…" Tears pricked Charlotte's eyes, though she tried to force them away. Her voice broke. "I suppose I should be grateful," she managed, "that I was asked back to the school to teach. I should be, I should be...but now after what happened..."

Kneeling on her bedroom floor by the unpacked trunk, her dark skirts pooled about her, she covered her face with her hands and let her sobs come. "Oh, dear Lord, Emily! I wrote to you about my feelings, and here you are, not saying a word. It's just like you! You never answered my letters about him. You'd be happy that it never happened."

"I didn't know what to say."

"I couldn't help how I felt."

Emily replied stoutly, "You're wrong about that. Everyone can help how they feel. And that pompous Monsieur Héger! He was flattered that a lonely English spinster was so in love with him. And still are, by the look of you."

Charlotte's voice rose a little bitterly. "I'm not like you, totally happy alone! I must have someone to love. He feels so much for me but won't say it."

Emily jumped up, tall and thin as a tree on the winter moors before the window. She muttered, "Does he indeed? I saw what he was when I was there studying with you. It's lovely for him being married with so many children and also having you adore him."

"Next thing you'll tell me that no good woman is in love with a married man."

"It's not that he's married, it's that it's not worth your tears. I wish you'd stayed in Brussels and become his lover. Perhaps he'd leave his wife for you. You're nicer."

Charlotte stared at her. "What, are you mad? She owns the school! And I would be entirely turned away from good society."

"The devil with them."

"The truth is, I'm nearly twenty-eight, and no one I want wants me. I wrote him a letter. A desperate, emotional letter. I couldn't retrieve it. I had to go." She began to cry.

Emily knelt and put her arms around Charlotte, rocking her a little. Charlotte's weeping eventually softened. She said, "Emily, no one speaks more clumsily than you do when you mean to be kind. Oh, dear Lord, I hear Papa's voice below from his study. I must run down. Does it look as if I've been crying? He mustn't see it. He mustn't know I went into a Catholic church to pray."

"You did what? That would shock Papa more than pulling up your petticoats for Monsieur. Not really. He expects virtue in women."

Charlotte walked slowly down the steps past the tall standing clock on the landing, which read half past three. As a child, she had believed God lived somewhere inside her father's study on weekdays and hurried off to the church in time for Sunday service.

No voices came from within. The Reverend Patrick Brontë was alone.

That was unusual. Many parishioners visited him. They crept up the walk past the church, caps in hand for the men, looking ashamed or purposeful. From behind the closed door came muffled confessions, women's tears. What had Patrick Brontë not seen in his work on the poor farms on the moor and the rotting houses of the factory workers? But he knew of poverty; he had been born in Ireland, the eldest of ten.

She called out his name and opened the door.

He came toward her with arms spread wide, long straggly white beard, fingernails needing trimming. As always, he wore his white silk stock wound several times about his neck against drafts. The study was unchanged: the small desk and two large bookshelves, each filled with mainly religious volumes, their centuries of writings weighing down the shelves.

His face looked more worn, engraved with holiness. He bumped into the table edge as he came and held her. She kissed his knobby hands.

Does he see my face clearly? she wondered. I think his sight's worse than when I left. There's still that large magnifying glass on the desk. And he's grown older in my year away. Emily said nothing of this; she doesn't notice things. Except for household tasks, she's in a world of her own.

Charlotte scolded, "I'm afraid you were quite wet in the rain before, Papa! Your shirt's still damp."

Her father's voice was low, the Irish inflection never lost entirely but mingled with the purer English he had learned at St. John's, Cambridge. "It's nothing," he said. "Your brother's still here on an extended Christmas holiday, recovering from a fearsome cold. My son's delicate, not like his strong sisters. My darling, I'm so glad you're back! Now, you mustn't look for other teaching work again for a time. You need rest. Lie on the sofa and read long afternoons. My brave Charlotte."

"Yes, I'd like to stay home for a time."

She glanced at Emily's cabinet piano, which sat against one wall with an overflowing wicker box of music on top. Even here, she remembered Monsieur's presence close to her, how he'd say her name ponderously with his French accent as if giving it serious thought.

The letter! After he found it, what then?

Charlotte gazed at the open book on her father's desk and the huge, heavy magnifying glass. Yes, Papa's eyes were worse.

Patrick Brontë lowered his voice. "I'm glad to have you home. Emily's a good daughter. My boots are polished, the meals excellent, the floor swept. But what does she think? She can spend a meal not saying a word, and when I speak to her, she starts as if I've come from another world. She walks out alone in all weathers. I shouldn't allow it."

Charlotte barely heard his words. "She loves the moors, Papa."

His voice darkened. "Long ago there was a man roamed there, ravishing girls."

"Most people say it was a legend." Oh God, *the letter!*

"Perhaps, but legends are based on facts. Do you remember I told you of the mill workers' riots of many years ago in the towns about here? There's anger seething, believe me. Emily trusts everyone. I recall that time she brought home a tramp for a meal, and we found him at our kitchen table enjoying soup. And that sick hawk she found and nursed it to health? It bit her hand until it drew blood, but she wouldn't turn back. My unique children. All four of you. But what place is there in the world for you without money? Alas, we prevail. I wonder at times if she remains a true Christian. Moor spirits...only a legend."

"Yes, of course," Charlotte replied without thinking, vaguely taking in his rambling. If Monsieur wrote her kindly, she might go back. Perhaps he never found the letter, or he'd forgive it as part of her intense nature. Until then, she must make a place for herself here once more. The rooms were so small; the family rubbed elbows in the hall. Everyone knew each other's griefs and joys. How could her passionate thoughts remain hidden? "Good women are virtuous," her aunt used to say. "If a woman falls once, she is lost forever, and no good man will ever marry her. Concentrate on your samplers, girls."

The ghost of her long-dead aunt moved away, pattens clicking down the stone hall.

From the adjacent kitchen came the smells of leek pie and apple cake. "Tea, my darling Charlotte?" her father asked.

Though they often ate in the kitchen, today they gathered around the parlor table. Bookshelves hung on either side of the fireplace, and a small desk sat between the windows.

Charlotte lingered after tea was cleared away. Only one candle remained lit, though darkness had fallen, and she heard the wuthering of the wind. She remembered herself and the others as children, kneeling on chairs around that very table, printing imaginative, voluminous stories of brave heroes and lovely heroines in tiny letters on brown parcel wrapping. Three little girls in plain dark dresses and one boy with a bright, shy, mischievous face and wavy red hair.

It was all long ago. No one had written fanciful things at the parlor table in many years. Anne, Charlotte, and Branwell were teachers in the world, and she could not recall where anyone had put that box of their writing.

She felt so alone.

Walking down the hall and looking through the kitchen window, she made out Emily in the stone-walled backyard, where they did household washing. Her sister was kneeling and reaching under a small bare bush, lantern at her side. Charlotte drew her shawl about her and came outside, asking, "What are you doing?"

"Looking for a little gray kitten."

"Emily, when were you going to tell me how bad Papa's eyes have become this past year? Suppose people notice it?"

Emily shook her head. "They won't. I was going to tell you at once, but we haven't had a chance, and I didn't want to write."

"You ignore important things! We aren't children anymore. What if Branwell loses his job again? Even if he's not drinking, his money disappears. And we can't discuss it with Papa; we never could. We have to protect him. We simply don't have enough money. Anne must stay at her work, and I have to find something else, while you…"

Emily's back stiffened. "Don't," she said.

"It's true," Charlotte persisted, trying not to let her resentment fill her voice. "You're too sensitive. You hated studying French in Brussels. And I remember what you were like in Roe Head School when I was a young teacher there and you were a pupil. Even though you had a scholarship, we had to send you home before you fainted from not eating. And the school was lovely."

Emily remained kneeling by the plants. She muttered, "I can't help the way I am. I hated to be away from home. And I couldn't bear to speak to others."

Charlotte remembered that night years before, in the frigid school dormitory when Emily was fifteen. Her sister's back had grown so thin that every vertebra seemed to push through the flesh when she changed into her nightdress. Charlotte had managed to coax some broth and a fragment of bread into Emily, who had opened her lips like a small bird.

Now Charlotte asked, "Why must you be so different and strange?"

"I don't know. Why don't people leave me alone? Why don't you? I don't want to talk about it." Emily bent her thin shoulders. "Now you've come back, you'll be directing us how we should have our lives. You've done it since you were a child."

"I had to…Mama died. I was the oldest. I still am responsible."

Emily was still. She knelt in the shadows, shivering from the rising January wind, which came over the stone wall around the kitchen garden. The stalks of dead flowers quivered.

Emily said, "I just want to be here. I want all of us here. I'm awfully glad you're back."

3

Emily

After the kitten had been fed milk and fallen asleep by the dying kitchen fire, Emily and Charlotte retreated to the parlor for their mending. The mending basket was full to the brim with their father's shirts and trousers and socks needing darning. Charlotte began on trousers snagged by a bush, looking stern, as if it could have been helped. They bent close to the light of two candles that reflected in the wood of the table. The spines of the shelved books were too dark to make out.

The tall clock on the stairs had just struck ten when Emily heard someone at the parsonage door. Branwell's tenor voice from the hall called mildly, "Hello?"

Their brother appeared in the parlor, breathing as if the short walk from the pub down the path had tired him. His red unbrushed hair stood on end. His narrow, bony shoulders sloped to a rounded back. His spectacles were dirty. He smelled of pipe smoke. His long brown muffler draped to the floor. And yet, as always, he bore himself as if he were the son of gentry.

Charlotte rose to kiss Branwell's cheek, saying, "Darling, it's been a year! How have you been? You don't write much."

"Not much to write," he muttered. "Want to hear all about Brussels. Too tired now. Wretched cold for weeks. Nearly ended me. Glad to see you, dearest big sister."

But when Emily took his arm to mount the steps with him, he muttered under his breath, "Oh, now we'll have no peace! Charlotte and I haven't seen each other in a year, and what her eyes ask me is how I'm conducting myself. She starts badly. Misery for me. Days of peace fled."

"She's tired; she just returned."

"She minds I was out for an hour with friends at the Black Bull. What's a man supposed to do?"

"How much did you drink?"

"One glass. I'm moderate. So she's up and quit her work? Now she's free. I wish I were, but I'm the only son. It's my job to make our fortunes, though I'm still not quite sure how. You girls have all the freedom."

"Freedom! She works very hard for us."

"Yes. And then tells us all about it."

Through Branwell's open door, Emily glanced at the dirty socks and shirts heaped on the floor, accumulated in the days since her brother had returned. Her candle shimmered on the battalion of wooden soldiers their father had given him as a boy, which came alive for them when they used to play secret stories with their battles and seductions and haughty women and daring men.

"Goodnight, dearest dear," she said. "Bran."

Emily closed her bedroom door and turned the key. She set the candle on the table, hearing the creaking and sighing of the house and the wind howling in the chimneys.

She walked toward her wardrobe drawer, which was locked by the key she always wore on a ribbon around her neck tucked under her dress. The drawer held her poems. Of course she was writing, but she wouldn't tell Charlotte or anyone.

Now she unlocked the drawer, arranged her little box desk with its small supply of ink, pens, and paper on the table, and bent over a clean page, biting her lip.

Yes, she loved her brother so much. In some way, he was deeply pure. Perhaps in another country, he would have been a brown-hooded monk, walking chastely to the sound of Catholic church bells. Where did he belong? A woman could always bake and sew for someone no matter how her thoughts went, but a man had to make something of himself in the world.

Branwell was too fine for ordinary life.

They had all gathered behind him when he had decided to

become a portraitist; he had gone off whistling to study with a master in Leeds and then attended the Royal Academy in London before coming home to build a portrait business. He had painted his three sisters and himself in one portrait and after had painted out his own face because he didn't like it. Little work came with portraits, and their father had found him a job keeping railroad accounts. That position was also somehow gone. Now he was a tutor.

Sometimes I seem to see thee rise,
A glorious child again;
All virtues beaming from thine eyes
That ever honoured men....

She wrote across the top: *A Wanderer from the Fold.* For no one to see but me, Emily thought as she slipped it unfinished into her drawer, which was already stuffed with poems in various stages of completion and some notes for a novel about a lost homeless boy.

She locked the drawer and then lay down, staring at the dark night outside her window.

Later she heard footsteps on the stairs and knew Branwell had gone out and come back again; still, his were steady steps. He was well. Even if she quarreled with her family, she would give her life for them. That love was so intense that anything else was as inconsequential as dry leaves blown down a steep street.

Another thought came to her. She needed to put a sign up in the post office and on the moor post to find the owner of the lost glove. What a nuisance! Emily was sorry she had not left it on the moor.

She lay still, listening to the wind rushing about the stone parsonage, and felt she had lived a long time.

Part II

January 1844–November 1845

4

We wove a web in childhood
A web of sunny air;
We dug a spring in infancy
Of water pure and fair....

—Charlotte Brontë, from "We Wove a Web in Childhood"

Emily

Doors creaked, voices rose and fell a few hours past sunrise a week later. An old man's laugh came through the churchyard: poor Jack, whose mind was feeble. Emily watched from her bedroom window, kneeling on the blue quilt of her bed.

"Emily, where are you?" Charlotte's voice broke into her dreams. "Really, don't you want to say goodbye to our brother?"

Emily walked reluctantly down the stairs, her hand grasping the banister. The longer she took, the longer she could keep him. In the hall, Branwell was manfully lifting his bag to his shoulders. It was the same brown canvas bag smudged with his efforts that he had carried to embark on previous jobs. His father and Charlotte waited anxiously near him.

"Do you have your bread with ham?" Emily demanded. "And apples from the cellar? Bottled ale? And the new scarf I knitted for you? Maybe you'll find the other one. Behave, at least!"

Wool was ten pence a skein, and that had been more because of the burgundy color. She felt the skill of her efficient hands that had made the scarf in such haste, longing to keep him close and safe.

"Yes, of course!" was her brother's impatient reply. "Goodbye, darlings." He hardly met their eyes as he kissed them and walked off down the cobbled path by the side of the church, calling, "The wagon will be by in a quarter hour to take me to the carriage to my work. Do wish the train went there; it's more comfortable. Don't work too hard, pater! I'll give your love to Anne." His look said, *By God! I'll try to be what you need!*

Charlotte called shrilly down the path, "Give her the cake we baked her and our letters and a hundred kisses!"

"Yes, darlings!" he called, not looking back again. Last autumn's leaves whirled in a frenzy around his footsteps.

Emily looked steadily after him, a slight figure swaggering a little, down the path past the sexton's house and to the town, disappearing when he descended the steep street to his carriage stop. The sandwiches would not last forever, nor could she be there with him in the house where he and Anne now worked for affluent strangers and their demanding children.

"There goes my son," her father said. He stood like the stalwart man of God he was with arms folded, shivering a little. Wind nipped his great long white beard. "God, keep him from all temptation. I hope they pardon he's been gone two extra weeks for his illness."

"What illness?" Charlotte asked sarcastically, but Emily was silent in the missing of him.

Later that day, Emily walked down the path and across the street to the tiny post office. There she gathered letters to her father and glanced at the notice of the lost glove, which she had hung last week.

"Nobody's responded," the postmistress said, "but many people around these parts never come through this door. Why should they? No one writes them. People only write when someone dies if they can. Shocking how many about here can't even read. They mark their name with an X."

"I'll call again to inquire," Emily replied. "I need to bake for tea."

Charlotte

Upon moving back home, Charlotte had taken on the dusting, ironing, and sometimes cooking, helped by Tabby and Martha —one old and the other young—who were really part of the family. Still, her heart was heavy. By fleeing back to Haworth, she had lost the chance of even friendship with her master. She could not wait to escape upstairs to her room to write to him. She sent two letters, carefully pruned. She dared not include much of her sharp, bitter longing, her desire, her aching breasts. Those bits she burned.

I left in too much haste. Perhaps I was not clear.

When in my bed quite alone, thinking of you… (She had the prudence to not send that.)

Each day, she waited for his reply. He was, of course, *très occupé.* Dozens of girls clustered around him, all lovelier than her. Rising one night from writing a letter by her candle, she confronted her face in the mirror: severe, no charm, too small, too timid, murmuring her feelings to the floor. A back tooth had been painfully extracted one day in Brussels. No one could see the empty space if she refrained from smiling too fully.

As March progressed, she continued to wake in the small hours, staring into the darkness, listening to the wind that wound around the parsonage. She drew the bedclothes higher.

She should be married now. Two men had asked for her hand; both were dull clergymen. The thought of sleeping in the same bed with either of them appalled her. The French schoolmaster was all she desired.

That was it, she thought. I must go back and speak with him again. I must make things tidy here and say goodbye.

Her father's church, St. Michael and All Angels, where she went to dust the following morning, lay some steps from their house. With a slated limestone roof, it had developed water leaks over the years that stained the walls. Some pews were unstable. The flagstones and memorials in the nave had sunk slightly, and the stained-glass windows needed new leading.

She had finished dusting the altar and rolling the cloth to be washed when she heard voices. Two gentlemen were walking briskly toward her down the nave. "Good morning, Miss Brontë," one called, removing his hat. "Just the good daughter we hoped to find!"

Peering through her spectacles, Charlotte recognized the church wardens in their buckled shoes, close-fitting coats, and silk cravats. In the small world of Haworth, these men—the solicitor Mr. Smith and the grocer Mr. Lockley—were important. As elected church wardens with the vestry, they were responsible for the church property, the financial stability, and the competency of its priest. Not that they knew much about anything.

She said with a slight curtsy, "Good morning, gentlemen."

The men inclined their heads. "We came to look at that leak in the wall. Pity, it's worse since the last rain. But how fortuitous to find you! May we have a word? Sometimes your saintly father is a little loath to take suggestions, and we know he listens to you."

She thought, Of course. I am home and it is always the same. When my father won't heed them, they come to me.

Her head had begun to ache before they left. Her father was not in his study, and when he did not answer her knock at his bedroom door, she lifted the latch and walked inside.

She had been here little since she had come home.

The air was heavy with memories.

The bed's blue hangings were tinged with the dust of coal fires. Charlotte felt the creak of loneliness in the silent bed ropes, in the closed wardrobe door, which still held two of their mother's dresses, in the oval framed drawing of her on the wall. Here many years ago, when Charlotte was only five years old, her father had knelt in sobs at her mother's deathbed, clutching the sheets in his fists. Charlotte had never seen him cry until then, and the hoarseness and the hugeness of it terrified her. Her two elder sisters, Maria and Elizabeth, had wept by the bed as well, golden brown hair loose and tangled. In that hour, three-year-old Emily had cried out, "Wake, Mama!" and shaken her unmoving mother. And in terror, they had heard her father shout, "God, from this time forth you're nothing to me!"

Of course, he denied ever saying such a thing. And they never mentioned it because he was a holy man, and his faith was solid in the earth. But Charlotte recalled him and four-year-old Branwell that night, and the baby Anne, clinging to each other. A few years later, when both her eldest sisters were dead also, merely damp motes in the air, someone at the second funeral had bent down, saying, "You're the mother now." Her soul had recoiled in terror, but she had heard it and nodded. She was not yet nine years old.

Nothing had changed.

No, she couldn't stay. But first she had to speak to her father.

The Reverend Patrick Brontë had returned to the parsonage toward the one-o'clock dinner. His study door was open, and he was already at his desk, raising his heavy magnifying glass above his reading. By the tension of his shoulders and the seeming greater sharpness of his beard, Charlotte suspected something had angered him. Social injustice, she thought. Perhaps a reply to his latest article in one of many obscure journals that would print them with his proud signature: *The Rev'd Patrick Brontë, Haworth, Yorkshire.*

"Papa, the wardens were here today," she said slowly. "They wanted me to ask if you'd thought about hiring a curate to help you. They say the work is too much for you at your age. They are also worried about your eyes."

Her father brought his fist down on the table. "If they come again, tell them to jump into a sheep bath. How many times do they ask that? I will not discuss my eyes. I will not discuss a curate. And I will not discuss my fitness to do my work when the pews are full every Sabbath. Tell them whatever you wish… more discreetly than my words, perhaps, my darling girl."

"They also want the church repaired."

"Ah, that. Put it from your mind. Come now and let me kiss you. I want you resting here without a thought in the world. I shall be wealthy one day, when our inheritance comes from our cousin. Then I will call back your brother and your sister Anne to quit their work, poor darlings, and come home. All of us around the table! Again! There's nothing I want more. I will repair our beloved church. Until then, our Lord will not fret over a few leaks. The bastards blame me that I'm not wealthy. They dislike my social conscience. Look at your worried frown."

"Suppose you should have an accident?"

He smiled benevolently. "Lotte, my darling girl. The Lord takes care of everything. Nothing will ever happen to me while you need me."

There is nothing I can do with him, Charlotte thought as she left the room. Still, I can't stay here indefinitely. I'll write my master and ask if the spring would be convenient for my return.

Over the next few months, she spent her days reading to her father and writing his letters. She dusted the rooms and tried to conserve the tea leaves in the caddy. From the parsonage door, she watched him walk slowly with his cane down the path to visit a sick person. They needed much more money than they had. He would not discuss it. She didn't want to write Anne worried letters. Emily was always in her own dream.

And there was only silence regarding her last letter to the French master.

5

Emily

Emily felt the moor calling to her a little past dawn. It was all she could do not to run out with a cloak over her nightdress. She could not. This morning, in the yard washhouse beyond the kitchen door, would be the first big spring washing and she was needed.

After some quick bread, she ran out to join Tabby and Martha in their heavy aprons. Emily tied hers on as well. The two other women had been working for a time. Already soapy water bubbled in the huge tub, causing arms of shirts to rise to the surface as if trying to escape until they poked them under again with the long wooden paddle. Meanwhile Tabby gossiped about unmarried girls swollen with child from years before. Her tales were lascivious. Babies were abandoned.

Emily and the women hung socks and undergarments on the rack above the kitchen fire and the huge wrung sheets on a strong rope stretched from wall to wall outside the back of the house, where they flapped as they dried. They had been waiting all winter to wash the bulk of things until the sun stayed long enough to dry them.

Drying her hands on her apron, Emily found Charlotte in the parlor, sewing a new hem on a dress by the window. She said eagerly, "I'm going for a walk. Do you want to come?"

"No. I didn't sleep well last night. Take bread and cheese and be home for tea."

Emily nodded solemnly, concealing her relief that her sister had decided to remain behind. Since Charlotte had returned, she was such a help reading to their father and taking his dictation for articles and letters. And yet Emily could hardly be peaceful with her about. On walks, Charlotte seldom saw the strange beauty of the moors in all seasons: the hills, the dips, and the birds. Emily suspected that silly infatuation with the married professor was not yet over, or perhaps Charlotte was making plans for something else. She had been making plans since her girlhood. They seldom came true.

Emily shrugged and whistled for her dog.

Near her village, the smoke of the new textile factories rose in the sky. Gasworks emitted a foul odor. All the factories had been built within the last fifty years. They were huge brick buildings, and each rang a morning bell summoning women and men to their labor. Twelve-hour shifts, day in and day out, in those dusky rooms with faint light from high, dirty windows, hot in summer, cold in winter.

Emily breathed more easily when she reached the barns and stone houses of the farmlands. The moors were full of sheep; ewes swelled with young. A fine light mist now hung in the air. Sheets would dry more slowly.

For some time, she climbed hills and walked over stone bridges. If she listened, she always felt she could hear the land back to the time of the Celtic heathens who gathered here to worship the stars and strange gods.

Keeper bounded, large tongue hanging, eyes adoring. One night some years before, the family had heard whimpering behind the house and found the strange bony dog starving. Emily had lifted him in her arms and settled him on a blanket before the fire; she'd warmed that day's leftover porridge drizzled with milk and honey and spooned it into the dog's mouth. She lay down near him, her arm stroking his straggly fur. The whole family gathered around in their nightcaps and gowns and shawls.

"He'll die, poor thing," said Tabby.

"He'll not."

Within months, Keeper fattened and smelled of all the things he loved: winter grass, leftover mutton dinner, and sheep dung.

Now they crossed the moors together. When she stopped, he stopped as well, ears back, awaiting her next footfall.

Emily felt the earth beneath her mother's boots as she turned toward the hilly and rocky section nearing the Pennine Hills. She heard the rustling of the breeze in the new and old grass. Would the mist hold? The sheets needed to dry. Still, the sky was not dark but for clouds in the west.

Then through the fragrant air came the insistent bleating of a lamb. Emily saw nothing but rising earth and stunted trees. Keeper barked, poised on top of a boulder, looking down. She climbed up to join him.

A newborn lamb lay below in a narrow muddy hollow, breathing in sad little gasps. Oh dear Lord, thought Emily. Just born…a young thing, an abandoned thing. Thoughts came to her of her poor dog found in the cold, the birds, the rabbits, all the little things she took into her room and hid in baskets and biscuit tins lined with straw, and fed through droppers. And here, another one.

Her heart beat faster. She looked around. There was no ewe. Some disdainful sheep had birthed her lamb and walked away. She knew farmers and shepherds; she had heard ewes sometimes rejected their little ones.

But it would die if not fed, and she had nothing to feed it. Broken biscuits wouldn't do or the apple core in her pocket. She only knew she must carry it to help, for it belonged to someone. She slid down and used her handkerchief to clean its nasal passages of mucus remnants as she had seen farmers do, stroking the wet body. Some of the sac remained, and she peeled it away. Carefully she lifted the lamb, long legs sticking out at odd angles. She felt the heartbeat through her fingers.

It was so new: maybe less than an hour.

She must find the mother.

Emily walked downward by instinct, singing lullabies from her own childhood under her breath. And when she had come a way whispering soothing things to the lamb, she saw the ground rising again. For a moment everything was still.

Somehow, she knew this place.

Keeper growled.

Through the wild grass a tall stranger somewhere above the age of thirty was striding sternly toward her, wheat-colored hair to his shoulders under a squashed-brimmed hat. His hands and clothes were encrusted with dirt, and the trousers ragged over his muddy boots.

Keeper growled again. "Down, boy!" Emily said.

The man's face softened when he saw what she carried. He walked more slowly toward her and spoke tenderly to the lamb in strange words. Then he raised his face to Emily. "I knew the dam lambed," he said. "She's off with the others, I wager. They do that at times, do not want the lamb. I've another dam who lost hers. Maybe she'll mother it. This little one must drink milk. Hold her if you will. I'll clip short the cord."

His rolling accent had the same softness as the words he'd spoken to the sheep. She watched, fascinated, as he clipped and clamped. She said, "It was good fortune I found her. I was wandering and heard her cry."

"Give her to me. The ewe who might have her is by my house." He took the lamb and looked at Emily. "Have you seen it done? The little one to a new dam? If you want, I will show you. And you can wash before you go your way. I owe you much. The little one might have died before I came."

He looked down at her closely. "But we have not met. Whose are you, lass?"

"I'm the parson's daughter from St. Michael and All Angels in Haworth."

"An hour's walk, three miles or more."

She looked down at his big hand, which he had slightly extended, and remembered the notice she had hung in the post office. "Did you lose a glove some months back? I found it."

"Why, lass, I did! I looked everywhere."

"Had I known I'd see you, I would have brought it." She also recalled standing in the parsonage kitchen slowly inserting her hand into the soft cloth. It seemed too intimate, the sort of thing he might know by looking at her. She withdrew into the parson's inscrutable daughter, tall and private, and a silence fell between her and him. It was the lamb that held her interest, not him. She would see it with a foster mother and then go.

They began to walk.

Houses were sparse here. Soon they climbed a steep hill with no trees to grasp. Emily stopped walking, for down the slope was the very same stone cottage she had created secret worlds in so many years before. But that cottage had been derelict and slowly falling to pieces, while this dwelling was in good condition. The roof and shutters were perfectly mended, and yellow celandine gathered cozily near the door.

It could not be the same one.

The shepherd had turned to the left toward the field where there were several sheep. How many she could not see in the mist, for they receded. But he brought the little one and let the dam sniff it. With some reluctance and then fondness, the mothering sheep allowed the lamb to feed from her teat. The shepherd's shoulders had been tensed, and now he slumped a little. "Good, good," he said. "Sometimes it does not go well."

They passed the open door of the barn, where an old mare watched them from her stall.

The shepherd looked down at Emily. He said almost shyly, "Come inside my cottage to wash."

"The one with the celandine?"

"There is no other," he replied with a slight, crooked smile.

Emily did not like strangers, yet she was curious. She knew Keeper would attack if he sensed danger, but he merely trotted pleasantly after the shepherd, sniffing his hand. She joined them as they climbed over the pale green moor grass to the cottage door. It was not proper to enter alone the house of a man not known to her family. Charlotte would not approve. That gave her satisfaction.

Then she was inside the cottage.

On the ceiling among the beams was the one crooked, narrower one she recalled. So it *was* this same cottage, though the damp spots that had splotched the wall were gone. Everything was neat and dry. There had been no furnishings when last she had visited. Now a plain table with two chairs sat by the wall under a framed sampler, with embroidered words in a strange language, and the new, narrow bed was covered by a quilt. A few trousers and coats draped on wooden pegs; dishes and cups filled a shelf, and two pots for cooking hung over the hearth by chains. Near the bed, affixed to the wall, was another shelf, which previously had been empty and now held books.

So many books! Most people around here could not read.

She blurted, "I know this place! I found it as a girl, but it was almost ruined."

"Aye, it was a poor hole a rabbit might scorn when I came."

He smiled a little, and his softly rolling accent was stronger. Some part of Scotland, she thought.

Emily studied him as he knelt to stir up the fire. The elbow of his shirt was patched, and his nails were cracked and dirty. A week's dull golden stubble roughened his cheeks. He was taller than she. His eyes were a little sad, and a thick scar ran from his mouth to the side of his chin.

He roused a small fire, then hung the kettle and poured more water from a large bucket into a basin. "Make free to wash your hands and face, Miss… Your name I don't know."

"Emily Jane Brontë," she replied.

"They call me MacConnell—Jonathan it is."

"Jonathan MacConnell."

"Aye."

Emily washed and then, at his bidding, carefully perched on one of the wobbly chairs. Two chairs. There was no sign of a wife. No dresses hung on a hook, no smaller female shoes in a corner.

On the table, however, was a letter addressed to him in care of the Haworth post office. So he came to the village to call for his post, though she had never seen him there. She asked, "How long have you been here?"

He said, "A fortnight before Christmas and then buried in snow at once. I walked to the post office last week."

"I'd hung a sign about your glove."

"Very kind! I didn't see it. Tea. Will you have some?"

She nodded because she was curious enough to stay a time more.

Over his shoulder, he said, "Your father's the pastor at Haworth? I'm not a man for church services."

"Likely he'll come knocking on your door. It's been winter, so he hasn't gone this far, I suppose. You may be between parish boundaries, so another parson may come."

"They will not gain much with me. Are you his only lass?"

She sat back a little more on the unstable chair. "I've two sisters and a brother. Anne and he are away to work. I always walk the moor; I know it well." Now she had to say it. "I used to like to be here in this cottage alone as a girl. It was desolate, but I liked it."

"That it was, being empty for many years. A friend from Glasgow had inherited it and lent it to me. Tea's ready! I've only one good cup—the other's cracked. I've sheep's milk but not a bit of sugar."

They drank their tea in silence. It was odd to sit so close to him in this place, but it seemed he was not one to start a conversation, and neither was she. His clothes smelled slightly of sweat, soap, and moor grass. After a time to make up for the lack of words, she turned her head to the bookshelf.

She asked, "May I look at your books?"

"Aye, look away! Every time I have a few pennies, I buy another one. Some I brought when I arrived. I thought surely they had perished in all the water."

There was an intimacy in other people's books. She opened the first one carefully, as if words might fall out. Turning to others, she discovered a few poetry books and an almanac, a few novels by Sir Walter Scott, and a book on the stars with fascinating charts. Some bindings and pages were indeed water stiffened. But what water had they survived?

She said, "You have a lovely book on the heavens."

MacConnell remained at the table. "I like to study them," he said. "I lie outside and look up for hours when the sky's clear. I think how small our lives are and how great eternity. I think sometimes the stars know the thoughts I send them."

She raised her head from a book. "What thoughts do you send?"

"Good wishes to some I've left behind."

"You're not from these parts?"

"No indeed, lass! Far away."

"I sometimes watch the stars at night too and think I hear voices from centuries ago. My two eldest sisters died when I was young."

"Ah, the pity if it!"

"Your speech sounds a bit Scottish."

"Well then. We spoke mostly Gaelic where I came from."

"And where is that?"

"Far away off the coast of Scotland in the Outer Hebrides islands, difficult to reach for that the sea's so rough. St. Kilda, our group of islands is called. We lived on Hirta. The sea cliffs are so high, it's said they touch the edge of heaven. There's but a few hundred people who live there."

"I've heard there were islands, but I know nothing about them."

MacConnell rubbed the wooden table and frowned. "Wild places. I in turn knew nothing of this land across the sea. We had only the Bible to read, those boys who were taught it. Not all learned their letters. I did, and then a wonder came to me."

"A wonder?" she asked, now more curious.

His large hands moved through the air as if to paint the picture. His face burned with memory; he stammered a little. "An empty dingy drifted to us one day. No sign of men but a chest of books. No one wanted them, so my father took them for me. They were mostly in the English, as you see, and I could make nothing of them, but the parson taught me. He knew your language. My kin say that was the beginning of my downfall."

A breeze blew through the window carrying the smell of sheep. She asked, "How could it be a downfall? Books are good."

He passed the back of his hand over his stubble and laughed wryly. "Books make us want new worlds and leave us discontented with those we have. That book is my oldest, verses in Gaelic and old English, some of them written almost nine hundred years ago. Hand copied on vellum, sheepskin."

"I know what vellum is. Who copied it? Monks?"

"I'm supposing. The papers tucked before some poems with translations are mostly mine, but my friend Michael, someone I've known forever and hold most dear, made the others. Take it away for a time, if you like. You'll bring it back."

"Such a rare book! You'd lend it? You don't know me."

He sat back in his chair and smiled a little. "I trust you."

"My family loves books. I write a little, or I used to." Her hand went without thinking to the ribbon that hung around her neck.

There was a smell of rain in the air. He laughed a little and almost flushed. At that moment she was aware of every sound within and without the cottage: her dog sniffing a corner, MacConnell's shoes scraping the stone floor as he shifted his weight, a coal dropping in the fire, and somewhere a lapwing and sheep.

Perhaps she ought not be here.

She said, "I should go."

He stood as formally as if he were gentry. "My thanks for saving the lamb, Miss Brontë. When you come this way again, stop by and see how he grows. And bring back the book and my glove."

"I shall," Emily said. They shook hands, and she felt the roughness of his skin. She looked back as she left him and found him standing there watching her go.

Keeper bounded by her side as they climbed the hill. She clutched the book, which was bound in brown stained leather, and once stopped to open it, taking in a few of the foreign verses and their clumsy translations. Warring kings and girls betrayed and the sea, always the sea. She had never seen the sea. The wind rose; a loose page of translation blew away and settled in a thicket of last year's heather. When she hurried after it, it lifted once more on a gust and floated far away.

The sky was darkening; the clouds were rolling in. There had been a great storm once when she was small. Rocks upended and flew into the air, mud sprayed up and descended, struggling through the rain to find its place again under the heather. But the heather could not receive it because it also flew in the air until sky and air and moor rolled around and around each other.

Emily and her sisters and brother had gone walking with Tabitha who was the new housekeeper at the parsonage then. When the storm began, they escaped into a deserted house.

"The world is ending," Emily had told her siblings with a certain calm. She moved away from the window, whose shutters had torn away as the storm hurled through it. Her white pinafore was brown with mud and her hair was wet and plastered.

The storm quieting, they perilously had made their way home. Several times they slipped to their knees, and Tabitha pulled them up. Through the rain they saw their beloved parsonage and even a candle in the window, and their father running down the path toward them with his beard quivering, shouting their names.

His beard had been dark then.

That night when the rain stopped and the earth no longer shook, stars tried to find their right places in heaven again. The parsonage smelled of ashes and melting butter; flour hung in the air. There was apple cake, of course; she devoured two pieces. There was a bedtime story, read by her father in the parlor.

She was almost sorry the world had not ended; it would have been so very interesting. Would the dead arise? Would things that had occurred in centuries past return? But that was years ago, and now she was hurrying home for their six-o'clock tea.

Keeper ran ahead.

Why have I borrowed the book? she asked herself, now

impatient. I'll send it and the glove back by the boy Charlie from the Black Bull. I have no use for strangers. I need to help Charlotte at home.

But as she approached the parsonage, she stopped, startled. What was this now?

More candles and lamps shone from the windows than was their habit to burn. She quickened her step. Through the curtainless windows, she could see people walking back and forth agitatedly within: Martha with her sloped nose; her father's bluff sexton, John Brown; and a few parish women.

Then the house door was flung open, and Charlotte stood in the doorway, waving her arms, crying shrilly, "Thank God you're here."

As Emily ran closer, she could see that her sister's face was splotchy under her little spectacles. "Oh, come in, come in!" Charlotte cried, seizing Emily's arm with her little tight hand. "It's Papa! He was bleeding awfully when they brought him in! He fell. Oh, a terrible fall and where were you?"

The small parlor was crowded with people. Past them she could see their father on the sofa, one arm in a black coat sleeve trailing to the floor. Emily dropped the book on the chair and shoved her way to him, gasping at the deep, bloody cut of a few inches on his forehead below his hair. His eyelids flickered.

A cry rose in her as if she were a terrified child again. "Papa!"

The voices around her muttered information and suggestions. "Fell on the path from the moor behind the pub!" "Someone left loose stones! He was barely conscious when found." "Where's Dr. Gregory! Send for him. He's the man."

"John Brown's done it. He's coming up the path."

Emily and Charlotte knelt before their father. Small moans came from him. John Brown lumbered above them. Emily took her father's hand and kissed the risen veins and dark spots, murmuring, "Glorious Papa, beautiful Papa!"

She knew it; she had always known it. She must not go far away, or something would happen in the fragile thing called home. In one moment, all might have been lost to her because she had not been close. But where *had* she been? An abandoned lamb that had left its newborn mucus on her skirt. A stranger whose name she could not recall. Garments on pegs and a large old teacup.

Dr. Gregory huffed toward them, leaning over to examine the bleeding cut. "Hmm," he murmured. "Parson, can you hear me? He's dazed. This may be bad. Let's have him upstairs in his bed, more comfortable."

Huge John Brown lifted their father with a grunt and steadily carried him up the stairs. Emily took her sister's hand and followed the men up the stairs. Quarrels were forgotten. They did not release each other as the doctor washed, bandaged, and settled their father.

His eyelids flickered; they opened. "Nasty fall," he murmured. "Need no fuss. Was walking and then fell… No need…"

Dr. Gregory's stern voice rang out to the windows overlooking the darkening moors. He said, "All work canceled for a week at least. I doubt there's brain injury, but rest is imperative. I'll be back in a few hours. Don't let him sleep."

6

Charlotte

How slowly the hours passed as she and Emily sat by their father's bed! Time played with them; it seemed like an hour and then a week, and dusk seemed like dawn, and they were children in this room again and it was their mother in danger. Footsteps sounded from years past: their toddler brother climbing the steep stairs with difficulty. All the times of their lives hung in the room.

She and Emily huddled, saying every silly and important thing in the world to keep her father awake. "You never fall," they said. "Do you remember…do you recall…do you recall how little the Harrow baby was when you baptized her! She grew to be six feet before they moved away. Ah, and our John Brown. Papa, a miracle! He's not had a drop to drink this week, so effectual were your prayers!"

"Silly of me to fall," their father said, putting words together. "Stumbled on a stone when I am needed. Not a drop, you say…?"

Emily murmured, "Glorious Papa!"

Days seemed to pass, and darkness had long fallen. The doctor's steps and huffing breath sounded on the stairs again; he spoke kindly to their father. The church wardens slid into the room, grasping their hats in their hands. Charlotte felt her blood stop in her veins as she imagined that when they heard the news of the accident, they would have said contentedly among themselves, "Ah, the pity! We must look for another priest now." But they only approached the bed humbly, murmuring, "Patrick, how are you, good man? Don't worry about a thing," and the doctor turned to Charlotte and pronounced buoyantly, "He'll be well. Go down and have some tea. You look like to faint yourself. I'll go fetch Martha and tell her what to watch for. Go down, my dears."

"I do not faint," Charlotte said coldly, but she stumbled going down. Once in the little parlor, she dropped onto the sofa and broke into sobs. "Suppose, suppose…"

"He's well," Emily said. She had now appropriated the role of the elder sister. She sank beside Charlotte, trying not to look at the darkened blood on the floor, her stomach tight with fear. After a time, the wardens and doctor passed down the hall, looking into the dark parlor at them, touching their hats again.

The parsonage door closed softly.

Charlotte hunched, both her hands now on her skirt over her hidden knees, rocking a little. "But don't you see?" she gasped softly. "The wardens are kind now, but soon they'll say this fall is proof that Papa's too old for his work. They and the vestry will call some other priest to take his place, and we'd have to leave our home."

Emily's voice rang out to the portrait and bookshelf. "Shut up!"

But a dark spirit in Charlotte would not let her words cease. "Suppose they made us? When the vicar of St. Mary's in Keighley became feebleminded, they gave his family a month to leave. They're in a barn somewhere perhaps, or the workhouse."

Emily jumped up. "You heard him speaking clearly! Papa will be fine."

"Come, sit closer."

They were silent for a time, holding each other.

"Brown was decent," Charlotte said reflectively. The big, bluff man of middle years had been sexton here all their lives. At times his heavy drinking had encouraged Branwell, and for that she loathed him. Now she was so grateful to him.

She looked about at the dove-gray walls, at the portrait that Branwell had drawn of them hanging over the mantel, and still held Emily close. Ours, she thought. This has just been a bad moment. They would never leave this place where they heard the creak of the oven door, the wind against the stone walls in winter knowing they were safe, hearing their footsteps from long ago. But how could she ensure that?

Two days following, the bill from the doctor arrived, dropped off by his pimply young assistant. Charlotte, standing in the vestibule, saw the relatively small sum due. Even with her father much better, worries for their future were never far from her thoughts.

She walked with rapid little steps into the kitchen, where Emily was elbow-deep in kneading dough. Keeping her voice low, she said, "Come, we must look. But be quiet, or Papa will hear us."

Emily washed her hands and arms, nodding seriously.

They opened the door to their father's study down the hall and quietly lifted the cashbox from the bottom desk drawer. They had long since taken on the responsibility of knowing their resources. Of the family, they were the most practical, and their little money upset their father too much. He saw his inadequacy in contemplating his modest reserve.

Heads together, they studied the three small books in which the banker had written their investments in blue ink. This was the inheritance left to the three sisters Anne, Emily, and Charlotte from their late aunt. Its' combined interest was perhaps fifty pounds a year.

The additional large, soft banknotes, each limp and worn in their fingers, were from the salaries Branwell and Anne sent home. Their father's quarterly stipend would not come for some weeks.

Emily counted twice. "Surely there's more," Charlotte said. She wrote the sum of their worth and stared at the figure through her spectacles.

Emily folded her arms across her chest. She said, "I invested the money. It's done as well as it could."

"Oh, you did brilliantly, dearest!"

Charlotte touched the banknotes again. She closed her eyes for a moment and then forced the words out. "We must look at realities. If we had to leave the parsonage for any reason, the principal of our money would sustain us three years, more if Anne and Branwell kept their work. We'd never end up in some horrible workhouse where they'd separate us and make us wear workhouse clothes and feed us gruel. But we would lose the house and Papa's wages, and his position, which is his life."

She was silent for a few moments. Then she said, "There are four things we must do. First, Papa must take a curate to help him. Second, our brother simply has to stop wasting his time and find a good profession."

"Charlotte, I should have been born the boy."

"It wouldn't do you much good if you didn't leave the house, Emily! Third thing to manage is Papa's eyes. It's imperative he have surgery for his cataracts. Lastly, I must find some sort of income. And there's always Papa's distant cousin…"

"Oh, Charlotte!" Emily said. "Sometimes I wonder about him. How would we know that he will leave his money to us?"

"Because Papa has always assured us that he's very old, sickly; and we're all he has. Now, let's tuck this all away and bring Papa up a tray of cake and tea. I don't want him trying to get out of bed alone just yet. We are reprieved for now." She thought of how welcoming the wardens and vestry had been. Surely they would not urge Patrick Brontë to leave just yet. But when would they?

And how would she move him to do even one necessary thing? To solicit the services of a curate? To address his failing eyesight? Or to seek news of the cousin, who he mentioned had not written for a year?

For some time, Charlotte had been reluctant to go farther than the village shops in case the still-awaited letter from Brussels arrived. She hoped. She cried a little. She was embarrassed by her complaining letters to her sister Anne and her old school friend, Ellen Nussey. But she was lonely. Once the immediate danger to their father was over, Emily returned to her old self, sometimes spending days saying little.

Charlotte turned to poetry and reread a great many of the household copies of Shakespeare, the lauded eighteenth-century poets, and the romantics. Wanting more, she put on her gloves and bonnet one morning to walk the two miles to the larger town of Keighley and its Mercantile Library, whose stone engravings of ships above the entrance doors had always fascinated her. Years ago, she had hurried over with Emily to take part in the Shakespeare readings.

Inside, down the long hall, hung portraits of famous men who had made their marks on English literature. That opened to a large room with aisles of wrought-iron shelving heavy with thousands and thousands of books.

"A good day to you, Miss Brontë," the librarian said. Mr. Howard was a bachelor of some forty years who easily found each book's card in the tall cabinet with its dozens of drawers. For some time when not yet twenty, she had hoped to attract his attention, but he was or chose to be oblivious.

He added, "The weather is fine."

"It is indeed." (He always said that except in the worst of it, when he remarked sadly, "The weather is not fine.")

Now he asked, "How is your father enjoying the book he borrowed on Plato? Dear man, he must have one of you girls read it to him with his sight!"

Charlotte bit her lip. Did everyone know what they were keeping a secret? What did anyone else have to discuss in these towns but the price of wool and wheat, the baker's unmarried daughter swelling with child, the cataracts of the priest, and someone's misfortune? Haworth! She loathed it.

She turned to the oil painting of London's St. Paul's Cathedral, which hung above Mr. Howard's desk, recalling how she had passed through that city when she'd returned from Brussels. "Have you visited?" she asked.

"Once with my brother. Oh, the theaters! And the writers! Hundreds, they say."

Charlotte walked down the aisles between the stacks, turning to the poetry section. She chose volumes of Tennyson and

Rossetti and a seventeenth-century collection from the shelves.

The librarian smiled shyly as he wrote the books' titles in his ledger. "In my youth I wrote a poem or two," he confessed.

I did as well, she thought, but said nothing. Still, walking slowly down the hall again to the great library doors, she remembered herself at seventeen, writing poems privately, huddled over the page. It was when she was first teaching at that English school, hardly older than some of her students. She had so much inside her that she could barely express. Most of the poems were not good; she had thrown almost all away. Finally, she had produced a handful she thought were not too bad and, one morning, posted them to the great late poet laurate Robert Southey to ask if he saw the possibility of a career in letters for her.

His reply was crushing.

> Literature cannot be the business of a woman's life & it ought not to be. The more she is engaged in her proper duties, the less leisure she will have for it, even as an accomplishment & a recreation. To those duties you have not yet been called, & when you are you will be less eager for celebrity.

She had cried; she had raged; she had retreated in shame. So, there was no way out of the only careers that lay before her, either schoolteacher or governess. By duties, he meant those set aside for women's lot to keep her hands busy: sewing, cooking, dusting, laundry, nurturing of weeping children, until the woman herself was lost under all this detritus. Were women supposed to have a self, something they did not hand over to a man? Did they never not have soup that needed stirring?

She had walked halfway home from the library when the baker's boy, passing in his wagon, asked her if she wanted to ride. She climbed up beside him. Only the dim glow of their lantern shone on the darkening path, and wet leaves squished under the wheels. In the distance, thunder crackled. Above, a needle-thin bright bolt of lightning flashed above the trees.

Rain poured down. She had drawn the oilcloth the baker kept over their heads and held the books protectively against herself. The wagon now rattled on the wet cobblestones. Shopkeepers huddled in their doorways, shawls about them, looking gloomily at the rain. Charlotte kept her hand on the side of the wagon to steady herself.

As she rode, her mind was working fast.

The devil with the poet laureate! Suppose she took up her poetry again? She had lived more now; it would be better. Perhaps she might publish something so acclaimed that great people who now did not know of her existence would write her ecstatic letters. She would send her poems to the man she loved. Those he would receive.

For the first time since she could remember, Charlotte felt absolutely happy. Even the thick drops on the puddles about the cobbles seemed lovely to her.

She was so full of thoughts as she rushed inside the parsonage that she hardly heard Martha's words, "Miss, you've a letter in your room. I found it when I fetched the master's post. It's from foreign parts."

She ceased to walk.

After a few moments, she slowly climbed the stairs.

On her bed lay an envelope. She knew at once both his handwriting and the new, exotic Belgian stamp. But the letter she extracted consisted of only a few lines, filling but a small portion of the page.

> Mademoiselle, sadly my wife found your recent letters and the one I believe you slipped under the door some time ago. For you to return here would not be possible. You have misinterpreted my feelings.

So, he didn't love her at all. He never had. She knew in that moment that it had all been in her mind. Yes, this was the way it always was! Men had the love and approval to give and withhold. They owned the world. They beckoned to a woman with a smile, promising interest, and then turned away to better things.

Charlotte was crying. She looked across the room to her mirror at her pale face. She needed love, she always had. Of course, she had fallen in love with him. There was no one here but farmers and shopkeepers and the celibate librarian to choose from, whereas she had always longed for a brilliant man. But what had she to give Monsieur? She was plain and poor without a shilling for a dowry, a highly educated woman in a world that wants no such thing.

That late afternoon, rain pounding at the window, despair and longing began to form. Lines grew into poems, though they came roughly. Most of her deepest feelings were hidden too far inside for her to reach them. All her life she had had to hide them, and now perhaps she had buried them so deeply, she could not access them.

She crossed out much, beginning again and again.

She thought, The devil with Monsieur as well. I will put love aside. I will not be obscure. I will rise above the others. My poems will be famous throughout England. If I cannot have love, I will have renown. I will make the fortune of the house. I will bring everyone here happiness and save them.

7

Anne and Emily and Charlotte

Thorp Green Hall
Little Ouseburn, Yorkshire
17 July 1844

Dearest sisters,

I am overjoyed that Papa has recovered completely.

I finally had a serious talk with Branwell. You know how he is: he sees great things he could be but has no idea of the patience it needs to get there. Men he knew as boys have all entered some steady work. He wants to step into greatness as if he opened a tower door. This is his only character flaw, and he can't quite see it. He feels he ought to be above such mundane clambering. But Father's accident has shaken him, and he promises he will start working toward a career that will provide for us all. He talks of the law. It's a direction, at least!

I loathe being here though I try to be patient. The house is grand and cold. Mr. and Mrs. Robinson see the world through their wealth and are only satisfied if it is more than their neighbors'. Mrs. R. is unhappy. Her husband is much older, quite dull, and cerebral. But her daughters are fond of me. And Bran likes it. He likes what money can buy.

Oh, Charlotte, I do agree the best way to earn enough and stay home is to publish our poems together. I have been writing a lot! It keeps me sane. I wish Emily would join us, for hers are the best, but she says she doesn't write them anymore, which we know is untrue, for I do believe there are some locked away in a drawer in her room. Will you try to persuade her?

Yes, we need a curate and Papa should think of cataract surgery. With those things, he should prosper for many more years.

Your loving sister as always (and lonely for you!),

Anne

17 September 1844

Dearest Anne,

After several weeks of disputation and Papa showing his intractable side, which quite shut us down for a while, we have his final decisions. He adamantly refuses the surgery. He knows a scholar who was left blind from it. I don't know what the truth of this is, but fear is stronger than truth. It creates its own truth.

But he has with some reluctance agreed to employ a curate. He says he will only have a plain dull man with nothing but scripture in his heart. Since most men are plain and dull, that should not be a problem. So as Papa says he is too busy, I am off to advertise for a curate at slave's wages. The wardens and the vestry will pay.

Emily is now her old distant self. Oddly, she takes few walks these days and seldom far. I wonder if she saw something on the moor that disturbed her. Or Papa's accident made her uneasy. Needless to say, she says nothing.

Many kisses, dearest Anne!

Charlotte

19 September 1844

Very dearest Emily,

I miss our writing tonight and the worlds we created. Do you think this is what books do, make places and worlds for people to live? Do you think that once a character is created, if it is real, it can walk out in the world among us? Because sometimes the worlds we created as children were realer to me than this one.

I suspect you still live in those worlds. You know we intend to make our fortune as poetesses, and beg you to join us, for you are our most rapturous writer. Where do you keep your poems? I can't believe you destroyed them. Can you reconstruct them? Didn't you once mention you were thinking of a novel?

This is my plan: first the great successes as poetesses, and then to write novels. What do you think?

Why have you stopped your long walks? Charlotte said. You hardly seem yourself without them!

Always, your sister Anne

28 October 1844

Anne, my love,

I am planning to write a love story as well but not a happy one. I don't believe in fulfilled or redeeming love. If such existed, there would be a prince come to take you away. Then I would not hear Charlotte crying softly over that wretch she made so much of. One day we should tip our crate of childhood writings into a fire (where did it go?), but you are sentimental about it. I miss you with all that is in me.

But I burned all the poems, so put that from your mind. And the story is too undeveloped to share.

I am the one who loves you best because Charlotte doesn't (she can't).

Emily

8

Emily

The first curate came for his interview in October. Emily heard his high, nervous voice from behind her father's study door when she passed with her coal buckets.

Then the wind rose sharply, and the second applicant arrived half bent over and clinging to his hat with both hands. Others who followed simply would not do. And what did the position have to offer? Few applied. "No one wants to live in this dull village," Charlotte said, rolling out dough for pie crust. "No concerts, no literary societies."

"Winter's coming indeed, miss," a farmer remarked when he arrived for Sabbath church. The horses and carts of some parishioners waited outside the church gate, crowded together. She could hear the restless animals neighing below the singing of the service hymns.

Another applicant was coming today.

But he'll not be what Papa wants, Emily thought as she closed her hymnal. Winter will arrive, and Papa will trudge out into the snow ten miles or more again and come down with pneumonia.

She was reading in her room that afternoon when from her window she saw a tall, dark-haired man approach the parsonage. He was a long time behind the closed door of the study for his interview, and when her father called her name, she hurried down curiously.

The young man rose from his chair. He looked like a sturdy farmer with his short, thick beard and sideburns that made his serious face seem longer. His arms hung cautiously at his side. He was far from handsome; in fact, he was homely. He measured his words carefully when he spoke, as if there were few in his supply and had to last until he could find more.

Her father said, "Emily, my dear, this is Mr. Nicholls, my new curate. Sir, my second eldest daughter. Nicholls is a countryman from the Irish soil, are you not?"

"Life is hard for many there," the curate said.

Later that day, Mr. Nicholls was established with his few possessions in the damp room on the second floor of the sexton's stone house, a handful of steps from their parsonage. Emily brought him bed linens. When she told him how to respond to her rough dog, he smiled narrowly and said, "I like dogs."

Ah, poor man! Emily thought. He'll last the week!

But Arthur Bell Nicholls settled down, working with her father as if he had always been there. At least there was that, even though the Reverend Patrick Brontë's declining vision made him cautious with stairs and he kept his magnifying glass close. Then all was quiet, and nothing much happened but the usual weddings, baptisms, and funerals of the life of a country parson.

December had arrived almost unnoticed when a letter was slipped under the kitchen door with no envelope or return address. Emily, who was preparing tea, thought at first that it was from one of the few girls to whom she gave piano lessons on the piano in her father's study.

Then she understood.

She was not sure she wanted to open it; after all, it was a time ago, indeed early last spring, that she had found her cottage again and been startled that it was restored and inhabited. She remembered her secret girlhood afternoons there and felt somehow the stone dwelling had been wrongfully claimed by this shepherd from the Outer Hebrides, a gift to him of someone else she had never heard of in Glasgow. For wasn't the cottage really hers? For that she could not like him.

And then once or twice, she wondered if she had merely imagined him as she might have done with the people who came in and out of the cottage when she had played there as a child, or one who wandered in and out of her poems and the new bits of a novel, and in the middle of the night when something whispered, *Emily…*

No, this was a real letter set before her.

And the book and glove upstairs hidden in her closet were real.

She propped the letter on the kitchen table against a bowl of potatoes in the afternoon sunlight. The meat pie was baking, and she set about snipping open the seams of one of Charlotte's oldest dresses to turn it inside out so the stains would be hidden.

Keeper snored by the fire.

The letter was closed with a thorn. She remembered coming home to all the candles and lanterns and the bloody gash in her father's head. She had always dreaded that something would happen to someone in her family if she was away too long or far. Recently, she had gone to the waterfall and no farther. It was a much closer walk than to the stone cottage and more familiar as she and her sisters had wandered that way since small girls.

The words were written in pencil.

Miss Bronty, a few seasons have passed since you stopped this way. Would you return my glove when you can, as I can't say when I'll be in Haworth again? Also bring the poems, unless you want to keep them longer. Your lamb's grown to a sheep. I still thank you for your kindness.

Yours, JCM

The handwriting was more uneven in the postscript, as if he had pressed the paper against a stone surface to add it.

I knocked at your door this morning, but no one answered, so I am slipping this letter inside.

Emily stroked the dress that lay across her knees. It was strange to see his handwriting, which she knew only from the inserted pages of translation in the book. Now she recalled the way he turned his head and his full, deep laugh. I liked him, she thought.

But why should I? What is he to me?

She glanced through the window. The season of high wind–snowstorms was coming, and sheep would lose themselves. With the internal shutters latched, his stone cottage would be utterly dark inside unless he lit a lantern or candle. If she was going to return his things, it was best to do it now.

In her room, she took his heavy poetry book from the shelf. She had looked at it only a few times before forgetting it. The binding was cracking leather over boards, and water had stained the edges of some pages. Again, she turned back to a poem that had first drawn her. The language did not look like anything she had seen before. There was a loosely inserted page of translation, written in two different scripts; the other she supposed was the shepherd's friend. Even in his English translation, she had to study it to make the meaning clear. The theme of the poems returned time and again to a haunted, regretful man roaming the cold seas and paths of exile. Then he was at home again, lord of some huge drafty feudal hall.

But wasn't that oddly like part of her?

One Emily was the mystic who stalked for miles following souls blowing across the moor, while the other Emily darned stockings, baked pies, aired bedding, and worried for her loved ones. The second was strongest these days. Now she disliked the other part of her. There! She was resolved.

Emily tucked the book and glove into a wicker basket. Tabitha, whom she could hear coming slowly through the hall below with her cane, could watch over the baking leek-and-potato pie. Emily stuffed the letter into her pocket and threw on her winter cloak. She wouldn't be done with vague thoughts of the stranger until she had given him back his things.

The December wind was rising; the sky darkened to the west, and the last leaves tumbled down. Keeper bounded by her side as they started down the path.

And there she stopped because her sister Anne was hurrying toward her, past the tombstones and the church. Emily dropped the basket and rushed to throw arms about the slender and beautiful young woman.

Anne said in her light, clear voice, "Oh, darling, I hoped to surprise you. I did."

Pulling apart a little, Emily saw her sister's pale face with the faintest freckles across her nose. Strands of Anne's hair, the color of diluted brown watercolor in a glass, blew from the edges of the blue bonnet. She smelled both of old velvet tucked away with lavender and the sweet scent of a newborn.

Emily cried, "Oh, darling, is it you? We weren't expecting you until next Thursday for Christmas holiday! I'm so glad to see you! Keeper, no!" Emily's voice was fierce. The dog, who had tried to lift himself to Anne, hung his head and whined.

"Let him!" Anne said, kneeling down to draw Keeper to her.

"Long ride? You look tired."

"Yes, a little. The public coach was crowded with large men, and I barely found space between them. They were drinking, too, and slept and snored and fell into me. They left us an hour ago and I could breathe. Fifty-five miles of such bumpy travel, and I counted the hours by my watch."

"If I'd been riding with you, those men wouldn't dare…"

Anne had risen and Emily drew back, ceasing to laugh at the thought of the men examining her sister's pale, sweet face. Suddenly Emily's mood fell. She mumbled, "Oh, dearest, is something wrong at the Robinsons'? Is our brother well? Why isn't he here?"

Anne shook her head, and the faded bonnet ribbons swung back and forth. "Oh, he's very well! The Robinsons are traveling with the girls, and they said I might go home early. Poor Branwell had to remain with the son until next week, and then he'll come, and we'll all be together again! How are you, darling? How's our Charlotte? And Papa? And the new curate?"

A moment's sullenness passed through Emily, as if now that Anne was here, she could allow herself to feel the weight of many months of missing her. How close they both had always been, hiding in corners of the house, writing their stories, sharing secrets! She felt like a child again, sitting wretchedly in the kitchen corner, crying out to all her siblings both living and dead, "If you loved me, you wouldn't go…"

A magpie cawed. Last leaves rushed about their feet and caught on dress hems as the winter sun glistened against the parsonage stones and windows.

Anne observed her gravely. "You're thinner. You'd fit through the eye of a needle! Heavens, it's cold!"

They hurried inside the parsonage, where Anne's spaniel, Flossie, rushed down the steps, squealing and tumbling. Anne lifted her, exclaiming, "Darling!" Flossie licked Anne's face, wriggling, barking in her high manner, again and again, as if to shout, *Then I am not deserted after all!*

Ridiculous mutt, Emily thought. A dog with no dignity. She said, "You have no idea how she missed you! Tea? Kitchen's so warm!"

"Yes, I'm thirsty! We stopped a few hours ago, but since then, nothing."

In the kitchen, Anne sat down on her common spot on the bench, spaniel in her lap. She gazed from the warm oven to the dishes and pots. Some stockings hung to dry, and Charlotte's half-altered blouse was bundled in a basket. "Oh," she said. "Home. The most beautiful place in the world."

"Except when the church fathers arrive to complain."

Anne bit her lip. "Have they recently?"

"Not since the new curate's come. Disgusting churchmen! They'll be round complaining of something else soon." Emily was putting on the kettle and counting teaspoons of tea, sifting them into the blue teapot, when she heard Charlotte at the kitchen door. Charlotte's small face was radiant as she pulled off her cloak and exclaimed, "Anne, darling! I was visiting the poor Holywell children. But you're home early! Is everything…?"

A bit of tea fell to the stone floor.

Why did Charlotte have to come in now?

Anne asked hastily, "Charlotte, dearest! How's Papa? Is the new curate some help?"

"Dull," said Charlotte. "He hardly talks to us. He might as well be a monk, the way he's so tongue-tied around women. He helps, though. Papa's not nearly as tired. So it's a blessing."

The milk delivered that morning was still in the covered tin bucket on the shelf. Emily hardly saw her own teacup for watching Anne. How could you yearn for someone when they were a few feet away? Emily wondered. She's all things I could never be. I'm not good and I'll never be beautiful. I'm stark as a bare tree.

Though Anne had lost weight, she seemed stronger than ever. Women passed through life, enduring things.

"Eat something, Anne!" Emily urged. "Early tea. Full tea later."

The three of them sat close around the table so that their arms touched and skirts overlapped, helping themselves to a bowl of Emily's blackberry preserves from last September, creamy Wensleydale cheese bought at the Keighley market last week, and leftover beef pie. Outside, December dusk was gathering, cold and damp.

Anne pulled her shawl tighter. Emily drank out of her christening cup, which the potter had painted a long time ago with the words *Emily Jane*. She held it in both hands.

"Papa's late," Emily remarked.

Lowering her voice, Charlotte murmured, "But tell us truly before he arrives, Anne! How is Bran coming on?"

Anne gazed down at her half-eaten bit of pie and murmured, "Oh, well enough. The other day he told me he was thinking of emigrating to America or Australia, but you know his moods. People make fortunes there, he said."

Charlotte exclaimed with an incredulous voice, "Emigrating! That's ridiculous! He was planning to be a barrister last month. He's been studying all summer. I sent him a book instead of buying one for myself. He's on a good path, isn't he? Well, isn't he?"

Anne hesitated and then laid her fork on her plate. "Yes, but the past few weeks he's been a little depressed. It *is* such a climb to enter any good profession—you know it. And when he's sad, he walks over to the pub, where he knows some fellows. A little of his wages goes there. If the amount he sends home is smaller, he feels he needs to calm himself this way. The boy he tutors was born wealthy, and Branwell, who is so much cleverer than him, remains poor. Bran is so sensitive, he can't not feel it. But we could talk the year about social injustices."

"Yes, so many…"

"…the poverty around here. Even that it could come to us. Our dread of losing the parsonage."

"Never say that!"

The gaiety of the twilight kitchen had somehow slipped away into the shadows. No one spoke, and then Charlotte said, "Well, Bran needs a bit more time, I suppose. As for life here, since the curate's come, the church wardens and vestry are delighted with Papa even though they would like a younger, wealthier man as parson. And then they'd make us go. Books packed in crates, the dogs' dishes too."

"Horrible thought!" Anne murmured with a shudder. "To have to leave forever; to leave Mama and our sisters alone in the church crypt. How terribly they would miss us! The dead feel cold; they feel lonely. I think they mourn for all they never were able to finish here. I think they long for us and new bread and preserves. Yes, truly, to taste things and feel the fire's warmth and be together. They know we're here. It comforts them. That's why we must become famous writers and save us all."

Emily cried, "Oh no, you've just come, and now you are on to that! I told you that my poems are gone. And the novel is a silly little thing, gone too…" Emily thrust her hand deep into her apron pocket, finding some nuts, a little bottle of her father's eyedrops, and the edges of the stranger's letter.

She sucked her finger. The thorn that had been used as a seal had pierced the tip of her forefinger. Then she hurried out into the dark to retrieve her dropped basket from the path, thrust the book and glove into her wardrobe, and threw the letter into the fire. For a moment she was still, filled with a sense of sadness and loss. *I am missing you, Emily Jane Brontë*, the letter seemed to whisper, until all was silent but the small flames.

He hadn't seemed real to her, and then he was so real she could feel his breath. *Speak of me*, he murmured in her ear. *You can't tell Charlotte of me, but you surely can tell Anne.*

As expected, when the house had gone to bed, Emily heard Anne's footsteps. As a young girl, Anne would often creep into Emily's bed, huddling under one blanket, whispering in the dark. Now grown young women, they lay close in their long wool nightdresses and bed socks, talking softly, languidly, giggling. The heat from Anne's body was gold as firelight.

Outside the window, the moors lay covered with night and fog. "How the wind cries in the chimney!" Anne said. "It's like souls caught there."

"Have you any new secrets, Anne?" Emily teased. "Are you in love?"

"A neighbor's son came to church weekly, but his family sent him up to London to study law. I think they didn't like how he gazed at me because I'm poor! I wish someone would come for me! Charlotte makes fun of any woman marrying a parson, but...don't look at me like that! Papa's new assistant Mr. Nicholls could never win my heart."

"You don't find him dashing?"

"Dashing! He hadn't two words of conversation through our whole dinner. I need a handsome, romantic man who'll sweep me away. Someone like Papa's former curate. Had he lived and asked me, I wouldn't have minded if we were poor and had six children. Nursing my babies, sewing clothes for them..."

"It's a terrible life, Anne. You know Mama..."

"I know you think Mama died because she worked so hard. It wasn't that; she was ill. Cancer took her. But it's likely I'll find no one and continue to work as a governess. We're not meant to have everything in life. I want to do good for people and be taken seriously."

"Stay home!"

"I can't without an income, and knitting socks doesn't pay. Tell me any secrets, Emily! You have one."

Emily hesitated. She asked cautiously, "How do you know?"

"Because a long time ago our souls melded. Does Charlotte know?"

Emily shook her head, hesitating a long time, letting a strand of her sister's loose hair run through her fingers. She felt her throat tighten and heard the odd voice from the letter, which had seemed to call her name from the fire. She murmured casually, "If you must know, then! I met a stranger on the moor who lives in a cottage quite alone. He asked me in for tea."

Anne sat up a little, her voice dry and cautious. "What? You went inside his cottage? Alone?"

"Shhh, it was quite all right. He just came about a year ago. He's from the islands off Scotland, way out in the sea. He lent me a book of poetry. He lives in one of those stone cottages, actually the very one I found years ago when I was young. I'd forgotten it until I found it again. It was deserted when I was a child, but he's changed it. It's a lovely little place to live now, quite snug."

Anne' stared at her, gripping the pillow against her body. "Oh, Emily!" she whispered in what Emily supposed was Anne's voice when speaking to a recalcitrant child. "Oh, I don't like the sound of this! It's not just one of our stories we made up together. It's real and you don't know who he could be! My very dearest Em, think! He might be a bad person. He might ravish women. He might be a murderer. You must send back his book by one of the boys around here and never see him again. Papa wouldn't like it."

"Murderers don't lend poetry books."

All the softness had gone from Anne's voice. It was stern and dry. "Promise."

"Oh, very well. I wasn't going to see him again anyway. Don't tell Charlotte. You know how she frets!"

"I promise on the moon and the stars. I'll never tell anyone."

Anne slowly lay down again and drew up the heavy covers.

"If only there were a way to stay here together! I don't think Branwell should go off and become a barrister; I think he should return here and take up his portraiture again. Soon."

But Emily was listening to the tone beneath Anne's careful words. She watched her sister's elusive face and asked, "Anne, is there something about him you're not saying?"

"I told you about his drinking. Only on his days off…and the Robinsons don't say much because he's the only one who can teach their son. It's just that…"

"That…"

Anne's voice was so soft, it would never move beyond the feather pillows or reach the boots in the corner. She said, "I think Mrs. Robinson likes him in a way a married woman shouldn't. When her husband's away, he goes into her room."

"Into her room? But why?"

"You know very well. Men are morally…well, not what we are. She and he are inside a long time. I hear them laughing. Don't tell Charlotte; she's so prim. I'm so worried one of the servants will find out and tell the master. I confronted Bran, and he denied it but then came back and said he was sorry, that he was ending it. He said she coerced him into her bed. So, the worst I thought was so. She's ten years older than him. But I think it's done with, please God!"

"Isn't he worried he'd be caught?"

"He takes chances."

Emily shook her head slowly and sternly. "It's disgusting in a way…a woman letting a man do that."

"Not if there's real married love. I think it must be nice."

"No, it would be horrid. If you marry, don't tell me please." Emily's words fell away. She thought, Anne won't confide in Charlotte about this. And it will come to nothing, anyway.

She suddenly wanted to tell her sister more about the stranger and the lamb and the cracked teacup and the shelf of books once wet by the sea, but Anne was asleep.

9

Charlotte

Snow clung to the parsonage roof and the church steeple. Branwell arrived home and at once took over the hanging of holly leaves and berries around the parlor mantel.

On Christmas Day, everyone exchanged small gifts of books or knitted slippers, wrapped in bits of fabric and tied with ribbon too worn to have any other purposes. Then the family sat down to goose and potatoes.

They spoke the way they had done in the best times. They talked under and above each other. They spoke of news from Parliament. They spoke of the polluted drinking water, which her father knew ran underground through the graveyard and sickened villagers (the village council wouldn't believe it and was against Patrick Brontë's idea to divert the water).

Branwell told stories in a loud voice, as if he were not in a little room. "Once I knew a fellow on the rails, rode all over England and never bought a ticket…" He drank whiskey and was merrier; he had two helpings of apple cake. Later, more solemnly, he spoke of his intention to do something good in the world.

Charlotte tried to focus on everyone's words. She looked down at her sweet and thought, *How I love them! How lovely this afternoon is, how happy we are together. But how to keep it always?*

Someone asked her a question, and she could not respond.

Much later past eleven, upstairs in her room, after all had said reluctant good nights to each other, Charlotte undressed to her chemise, pulled on and fastened her warm dressing gown, and walked up and down as softly as she could to keep the floorboards from squeaking.

She spread her poetry on the table and for a time read some

of it. It wasn't bad; some was very good indeed. The fact was, though, she needed some source of income now. Greatness in literature would come later. She needed to find something to make them all secure. What and how? That was the question.

The answer came quietly. In this moment, she knew. How could she not have seen it before?

"What, Charlotte? What strange impossible idea is this? You mean to open a boarding school for girls?" her father asked at breakfast in the kitchen the next morning when she told him in a breathless burst. Even as he bent to toast a thick slice of bread on a long fork over the fire, she poured out more of the plans she had lain awake half the night consolidating in a small notebook.

He carefully dropped the fragrant brown slice to Anne's plate and shook his head. "Twelve girls in this house?" he repeated. "How could I do my work? Where would we put them?"

He did not like change; he muttered; his eyebrows darkened.

Branwell mounted the cellar steps with the new jar of jam in his hand. "Twelve girls here?" he echoed. "What's this?"

"She wants to open a school," Anne explained.

Emily crossed her arms over her chest, frowning.

Charlotte rearranged the cups before her. "No, not here," she said. "I've thought of that! We'd rent a house. There's one in the village near the tailor; it's been empty a year, so perhaps they'd rent it cheaply. And I need all of you to teach." She tried to keep her voice calm in her excitement. "Papa could give religious instruction weekly. Will you, Papa? We'd earn plenty of money for all of us to stay home together."

Patrick Brontë was browning another piece of bread. He hesitated. "Well, my darlings," he said at last, "I do want you here about me. What do you think?"

Anne's voice was excited. She exclaimed, "I'd like it very much! Would it happen in the autumn? I'll stay at my position until then. Bran?"

Branwell cleared his throat. He spoke in the loud way he

often did, as if he were making a proclamation. He said, "Why not?" The more profoundly he spoke, the more Charlotte felt he was hiding something. Did her sisters know? She sat straight before her untouched tea and forced her mind back to the school.

She asked softly, "Emily? Piano and French?"

Emily remained in profile, her face rich with thoughts that no one could guess. She replied at last, "Yes, I'll help. Let me do that, Papa!" She touched his arm gently and took the toasting fork. "I think we are agreed."

Branwell said, "Yes, by God! There will be a school! Excellent plan! It will make our fortunes. Very good idea!"

Then the door opened, and Martha came in with the milk jug. "Still warm," she said. "The cowherd's lad brought his cow outside the church gates. The wind blows hard there, like it wants a bite of you."

Charlotte looked gravely down into the jar of creamy thick milk as if she saw her life change within it. This was it then; this was the answer. Her family had actually agreed. By next September she would not be a governess far from home but the director of The Misses Brontë Academy for Young Women at Haworth, Yorkshire.

Christmas ended, and Anne and Branwell departed for Thorp Green Hall to take up their work as governess and tutor with the Robinsons again. Emily disappeared into books, and their father worked behind his study door.

Wrapped in wool shawls, feet on a hot brick, Charlotte was left to plan for her school on the parlor table.

She saw herself as headmistress, stern in her small spectacles. Anne would teach general studies; Emily, French and piano. Branwell could instruct Latin and, if needed, Greek and painting, of course. Charlotte envisioned many girls, in pretty dresses and with long hair held back by ribbons, arriving in Haworth.

She rented the proposed house, and sometimes twice a day

she walked over to it and explored the rooms, thinking, "Here we'll have four beds and four in the next chamber. Martha will cook. And upstairs in the garret, which is quite light, Branwell will hold his painting instruction."

Charlotte found several of her brother's discarded framed paintings and hung them in the garret. She stood by the window, overlooked the roofs of the town, the street, the stone bridge over the glittering river, and felt utterly happy.

10

Emily

In early spring, Emily finally walked out on the moor to meet her shepherd again.

The winter had been bad, and she had not heard from him since his note under her door. Once or twice, she thought of visiting him, but she had promised Anne she would not. Greater than that promise was still some small fear in the bottom of her stomach that there would be a loss in the beautiful regularity of her parsonage life if she went too far from the house for long.

Yet all was well. Anne and Branwell had returned to work, Charlotte was happily preoccupied in arranging her school, and their father was no longer overworked with his distant proper curate. So Emily called for Keeper, and they went.

The moor was beautiful. Lapwings flew above her. The fields in the distance were green, though the heather would not bloom for a few months. After that, black currants would appear, which she would gather for jam to preserve and seal in jars and mark with her initials and the year.

She had no trouble finding the cottage this time and climbed up the hill to look down on it. For a moment, she expected it to be as derelict as in her childhood, but it was as neat as on her last visit. On her walk, she had remembered how much she had liked the shepherd. He was interesting, well-spoken, and a little mysterious. Men normally were dull; they didn't speak much of who they were or what they thought. "Have a pint?" "Wheat's too wet." "Wife's poorly." Curates pontificated and left. The current Mr. Nicholls had five words to say at tea. Almost all men paled next to the heroes in the stories she, and Anne, and Charlotte had created as children.

Walking around the cottage, Emily found Jonathan MacConnell on his knees, digging in the earth, wearing his rough brown shirt and pushing away his tangled wheat-colored hair from his face with the back of one hand. She watched him in silence for a moment and then called cheerfully, "Hello! Do you remember me, the parson's daughter?"

He looked up, startled, his hand on the trowel as if he might have to defend himself, but Keeper trotted to him and nuzzled him. "Affable creature!" Jonathan MacConnell said, smiling, stroking the dog and then raising his eyes to her. "And you're a very sprite of the moors. I was certain I'd never see you again or that I had imagined you. I'm delighted you've come. Did you like the poems?"

"So much! Ah, no! I forgot the book and your glove."

"You can keep them a time longer."

He rose. He was taller than she remembered and now self-assured. He planted his large feet on the ground.

She said, "Last week I noticed a letter to you at the post office; it looked like it had traveled long distances. It made me think of you."

"Ah, that," he said with a frown, rubbing his back a little. "I walked into Haworth few days ago and fetched it. I saw you then. You were strolling down the street with a small, serious woman wearing spectacles." He stroked her dog again.

Emily came a few steps closer over grass. "That's my sister Charlotte! We're opening a school. You could have greeted us. But then I'm glad you didn't. You're my secret. Everyone is always trying to find my secrets." She would not tell him about confiding in Anne, not just yet.

She went on, "I was too busy at home to come here. You could visit my father's church of a Sunday morning and sit in the back if you want to be private. I'm always there."

His voice was more serious. "I'm not a man for church, as I said. And I didn't know you wanted me to come."

"I don't always know what I want."

Keeper was sniffing happily about the sides of the cottage.

Still remaining several steps from Jonathan MacConnell, she said, "This was a harsh winter. How do you manage here alone?"

He frowned. "That snow in February almost buried me. I couldn't tell sheep from blinding snow until they bumped into me. I'd be lost without my new dog. He's out with them now."

She remembered, fascinated. "That storm! You couldn't see more than a few feet from the window. The wind howled so. My father talks of souls in pain."

He looked at her curiously. "Do you believe that? It occurred to me sometimes, especially when my candle didn't last the night after I had latched the shutters. Then I felt the weight of darkness. Hard to recall such thoughts on this bright day."

She did not like to think of her family so cozy and he alone. "My sisters and I used to hear the souls in the graveyard at twilight when the rooks and magpies called. But mine is not church theology. My father calls me his little heathen."

MacConnell continued to study her. "Do you really hear them?" he asked. "What do they want?"

"They want us to love them, to remember they are still there. It's the same as the people who lived here thousands of years ago. I feel them on the moor. I wish I understood their language—so strange!"

"I've heard them. They call us, but...to go to them, we must leave here. I like this earth. It's a pleasant place at least here. When I wake to the sun and birds and have food, I'm more content than I've been in a time. It's beautiful, your Yorkshire!"

He had seated himself on the low stone wall, and Emily also took a seat some way from him, looking at him closely. He had not shaved in days, but most of the men here didn't bother but for Sabbath. His hands were dirty with earth, and he kept them slightly cupped on his knees, as when a working man receives the holy bread at the altar in church.

She wanted to move closer; she forbade it. There was silence within her, and then he smiled as if to say, *Penny for your thoughts.* She asked, "Mr. MacConnell, does your family write to you from your island?"

"No, thank Christ! I hope to hell they never know where I am!"

"Why do you say that?"

"I never want to see any of them again. Particularly my wife."

So, he was married. "Why don't you want to see them?"

McConnell rubbed the loose dirt on his hands to the ground, calming himself. "It's a bad thing in life not to love anyone and bad to love too much. It all went wrong. I left my world."

"I would never leave here."

"You wouldn't want it, the life I fled," he said darkly. "The loneliness! I'd stand on the high cliffs and look over the endless sea and imagine a world beyond myself. There I climbed down the cliffs with my closest friend to find birds' eggs for food. I can still hear the cries of the gannets and puffins. It was dangerous work, but you know when a boy is young, he feels himself invincible. In my dreams, I am climbing those cliffs with the sea hundreds of feet beneath me. Every damn night of my life. So much for leaving it."

He fell silent and rose to his feet. Shoulders hunched, he walked away from the house along the edge of the stone wall.

Emily rose to join him. His story was so vivid, she imagined a fragile rowboat pushing into the huge waves waiting to smash it to boards, which would float away.

He slowed, for as fast as she walked, he was faster.

She felt his anger, conflict and sorrow. It was as if somehow things inside him were moving into her and she couldn't help it.

Kicking at a stone, she murmured, "I wouldn't ever leave my family, but Anne might leave if she marries. I'd hate it. Charlotte's opening a school here, so she'll stay. My brother will become something magnificent. On the other hand, maybe we'll all be four elderly people tottering around the parsonage. As dull as anyone in this world becomes. My father will be immensely old. And our curate will say one word at tea, no more."

MacConnell smiled a little.

She asked, "After you left your island, where did you go?"

"I went from island to island and finally reached the mainland of Scotland and made my way to Glasgow. It was a bad time for me. I didn't eat for days. I was jailed as a vagrant. Then I found a friend, a solicitor, a man much older than me who had also fled my island when I was a boy. He helped me. He told me he had the deed to a farm in Yorkshire, and I could have the cottage and land for as long as I liked. Here I am. A remote place where I could think, though I'm glad you've come again."

They passed several sheep munching the new growth of grass. He dug his hand so deep into his pockets, she wondered if the thread would give.

They had stopped walking.

Emily gazed over the farmlands far beyond, seeing the sun shining brightly on the winding roads uphill and down the fields. She felt the ground under her feet and heard somewhere from the left the sound of a stream.

When she turned back to him, he was smiling.

He said, "We talk deeply for strangers, Miss Brontë."

"It's because we're strangers that we can," she said. "If you know someone well, you worry how your words affect them. I only imagine other places, but I love my own too much to leave it. Even with that, I must have my own worlds, so I write them."

He looked down at her curiously. "What do you write?"

"Poetry and bits of a novel, but I doubt I'll finish it. They're locked in a drawer, and I keep the key on a ribbon around my neck."

He laughed. "No wonder you liked the poems! You strange girl! How old are you?"

"Twenty-six."

"Why have you never married?"

"There isn't anyone I'd have nor anyone who's come for me. I've no dowry nor charm nor beauty, and anyway, I'd never."

He frowned. "My family married me off when I was twenty. If you come again, I'll tell you more of the story, but you won't. Because we might become friends then—you might know me…and I you. And you might not like that. I don't think anyone knows you entirely, and you like it that way."

"Yes, I do," Emily answered intensely. "It's safer—then nothing I love will ever change."

"But, lass, time changes things."

"Not for me! Not my family."

He reached his hand to her, but she stepped aside. He said a little sadly, "Ah, of course. I'm a stranger. This is only the second time we've met. You don't know who I am, only what I tell you. Still, truly you can trust me. Do come again. Bring my glove…and the book."

She flushed. "I am sorry."

He said, "Watch out. Some of the poems will captivate you."

"They already have. I read your translation:

Oft to the Wanderer, weary of exile,
Cometh God's pity, compassionate love,
Though woefully toiling on wintry seas
With churning oar in the icy wave,
Homeless and helpless, he fled from Fate…"

She added, "I wish you had translated more. It breaks off some lines farther down. I memorized that bit."

"I did translate the whole. There were papers there."

She chose not to tell him they had blown away.

He said, "Never mind. Keep the book as long as you'd like. I can always come and knock at your door. Maybe I can write down the translation again. Keep ye well. Haste ye back."

Still, as Emily climbed the hill, she felt uncomfortable, as if he had not only held out his hand but somehow, in spite of her wishes, gently touched something she had never shown to anyone inside of her. I won't come back, she thought.

11

Charlotte

Eight on a September morning and Charlotte was still in her bed. She heard voices, doors closing, and Martha saying that the chimney was blocked.

Charlotte winced, and buried her face in her feather pillow. What did she care for doors or talking? Nothing mattered now. What months it had been! And what had come of it?

She buried her face deeper in the pillow, pulling the blanket to her ears. She would have liked to hide entirely.

No one could have worked harder to open a school, no one! That was the truth. She had advertised and replied effusively to inquiries, detailing the proposed instruction, painting and piano lessons included as well as healthful walks on the scenic Yorkshire moors. Anne was to give notice at her work and come home. Branwell would also join them. It was to be the best school. It was to lead all the girls' schools in England.

Only not one girl had enrolled.

Haworth was too remote, families said. They preferred to send their daughters to established institutions. Charlotte had to prove herself as a headmistress (they wrote), and no one was willing to give her a chance. And now September was here, and the dream was gone.

She rose at last, taking a long time to dress. Then she gathered the printed advertisements, the canceled lease, the lesson plans, the bills for desks and beds, and took them downstairs where she fed them into the kitchen fire. Dully, she followed the sound of Beethoven's *Appassionata* sonata to their father's study.

Emily was at the piano, her lean shoulders bent, thin hands flying over the keys. The piano tuner had visited last week while making his round of villages, and now all the strings were perfectly in tune except the rumbly lowest notes. Sensing her sister, Emily turned in mid-chord, her face full of compassion.

Charlotte blurted, "It's all my fault. Do you know the money we've lost in my madness? Our precious little store of money! I must find a governess position at once. Nothing I do is enough. Nothing. Nothing." Her voice rose to the piles of unshelved books and her mother's portrait in an oval frame on the wall. "No, don't try to comfort me. You and Papa never liked the idea of a school. Intrusive, you said. But it would have saved us. Dear Lord, I am so useless."

She fled to housework to soothe herself as she had always done, washing floors with the rag mop. Then she tidied the whole house, beginning with the cellar, where they kept old sketches, some childhood clothes, copies of the *Illustrated London News* and the *Spectator*. She straightened her father's room, finding her mother's fragile wedding bonnet in a trunk and the long-dried flowers her mother had carried at her marriage. Charlotte found cobwebs even Emily had failed to notice, a mouse hole, an empty bottle of some French brandy behind the tall clock. She could do nothing with her father's study; he would not let her touch it.

She turned to her own bedroom, starting with her wardrobe.

It was a slender but deep wardrobe, too tall for her to reach the top shelves. Only the sexton Brown could manage it. Still, Charlotte would not be deterred. She moved a chair to stand upon. What stuff was there! Unmendable childhood bonnets, a bottle of dried cough syrup, a tiny chemise, lesson books from schooldays. And then, behind a moth-eaten thick shawl that her aunt had worn, a heavy wooden box.

She simply could not believe it. Here was the lost box of their collected childhood writing. Because she could not manage to lift it down, she dropped it onto the bed below and climbed down after it. The box was now sideways on her quilt.

She made out the faint letters printed on the side, reading *Hair tonic for the gentleman, James Street, London.* There was a smell of orange and oil from the original bottles it had held long ago.

So her dead aunt's shawl had hidden their childhood work all these years. No wonder Brown had looked and reported no box was there. Her sisters and brother had been resigned that it had somehow been given to the junkman to cart away.

Charlotte lifted the lid and reached inside to lift the loose pages and small, handsewn books, laying them on the desk to look through. Here were all the stories she and her sisters had written after Papa had taken them home forever from that school for clergymen's daughters. Bran's prolific stories were there too.

Carefully, Charlotte sifted through the tiny handwritten pages. A whole little book, carefully stitched, was her creation. Oh, the worlds they had made up as children! On the top of the box was written in stern childish letters, *Property of the Brontë children, return if found or be cursed always.* Not that it could be lost then; it never left the house, and they were always adding to the papers.

How serious they had been, and what a struggle to find enough paper for their words! When they could find no more scraps, she and her sisters walked to the village shop that sold writing supplies, dry goods, and sundries. The stationer John Greenwood would stand up from his stool. His heavy whiskers were always wet from his saucer of tea.

A large, dusty bottle of ink sat on the shelf. Master Greenwood would lean over the counter to ask, "And what will the little misses Brontë have this morning?"

"A dozen sheets of paper, if you please."

"Third quality, as always?"

"Yes, sir."

He would slide down the paper box and place it on the counter. Little Emily would raise herself on tiptoe. The quantity of paper there in the box, hundreds and hundreds of sheets, pale brown like wet, newly cut wood! Greenwood would feel for his handkerchief, find a clean place to blow his long nose, and then resume counting. "Twelve pence then," he would say. "What will you do with all this paper?"

They would not reply. She and her two sisters would mount back up the steep hill, Emily protectively holding the rolled pages in both hands. People would call out to them; they would curtsey. They were the serious little Brontë children, terribly thin, noticing everything with their large eyes, always wary of anyone but each other.

What will we do with this paper, sir? Why, we'll write great books. We'll grow up and never marry, but always stay together in this house.

As Charlotte stood laying out the single pages of childish writing and the little bound books on the bed, a joy filled her that had not come in months. Of course, she thought, God has shown me the way. He has not formed me to be a teacher or a governess or a headmistress. I am a writer. I was never meant to be anything other than that.

That day she took out her small portable writing desk again, found her adult poems written over the past several years, and began to revise them. All day she concentrated with such intensity that everything else in her life had a quality of unreality. I am a writer, she thought again, pressing her lips together hard. Anne is as well. This is how we will make our pathway in the world.

She felt happy that autumn the way she always did during the short periods in her life when she wrote uninterruptedly. She also dusted and ironed, singing as she worked. She floated down to dinner and, after, washed the dishes and joined the musical evenings with Emily at the piano. She was a second soprano who did her best to sing the higher notes when Anne was away. Emily sang a rough contralto. The curate Mr. Nicholls shared a music sheet with Charlotte's father. His voice was true bass. The piano was still in tune.

Anne and Branwell would be home in a few months for vacation at Christmas. They'd all be together then. She and Anne would write.

But Anne came home more than six weeks early, in November, flustered, wretched, tearful, bonnet strings tied too tightly, dragging her carpetbag behind her.

Part III

November 1845–December 1846

12

The house is old, the trees are bare,
Moonless above bends twilight's dome;
But what on earth is half so dear—
So longed for—as the hearth of home?

—Emily Brontë, from "A Little While, A Little While"

Emily

Emily was trudging around from the coal room at the side of the house carrying two heavy coal buckets, when she saw Anne making her way from the street past the church, walking as if every step were an effort. Charlie from the Black Bull followed her, pushing her two trunks on a wheelbarrow.

Emily dropped the buckets and ran, crying, "Darling!" She caught Anne to her, then looked at the wheelbarrow. She exclaimed, "You've brought all your things home? What can it mean?"

Anne murmured against Emily's hair, "I'm home for good. My work's ended."

"What do you mean it's ended? Oh dear God, what happened? Are you well? Come inside.... What is it? What can I do?" Emily put her arm around her sister's shoulders and drew her into the parsonage.

Once inside the hall, Anne began to gasp with sobs, glancing at the door of their father's empty study. She wept, "It was horrible, horrible. I can't bear it there anymore, but Bran's remained, not enduring to leave that wretched Mrs. Robinson. He's staying in the stable, bribing the stable lad. Branwell and his love were caught by the housekeeper."

Charlotte was coming down the stairs with a small basket of

laundry. She dropped it, saying, "Anne, my darling! Why are you here? How was he caught? What did he do?"

The three of them gathered at the bottom of the stairs while Anne muttered the story again. Then Charlotte asked sternly, "You both knew about this involvement? Oh, how could you hide it from me? Anne, you're trembling!"

They were still huddled there when their father came in, wearing a warm vest and muffler. At the sight of their faces, his mouth turned old like wilted fruit. "My darling Anne," he said, pulling her to him and kissing her forehead. "What's happened?"

She looked away from him down the hall. She said, "My brother will be home tomorrow as well."

"I fear some mischief, some fault on his part." Patrick Brontë's voice rose at the sight of his daughters' averted faces. "Tell me," he demanded, his voice finding its full power as when he preached his best. Then not one person in the pews did not hear him. "Tell me."

At times in their childhood and sometimes even of late, Emily felt as close to her brother as if part of her were in him. In her thoughts, she imagined his disgraced journey home that autumn.

She felt him rushing from the great Thorp Green Hall with what Emily feared were violent words and the threat of a pistol; eleven miles to York, then climbing aboard the larger coach from that great cathedral city; traveling more than forty miles more to Keighley. Onward then with horse and cart two miles past factories and farms to little Haworth on the steep hill, the plodding thick horse pulling him and bumping up Main Street to the parsonage, his thin body thrown about in the cart by the wheels jolting on the cobbles. She imagined scribbled drafts of protests of love and innocence in his vest pocket, words of defiance on his lips. He would insist he was right; more and more he did relentlessly as he grew older.

Emily envisioned her brother's whole journey and his coming home. He would walk up the path past the church and knock on the door like a supplicant. Or perhaps he had lost his own key. Three days had passed since Anne had come home, and every hour since then they had expected him.

As they were sitting down to dinner in the kitchen, Branwell finally arrived.

He came humbly toward them, gazing at them as if wondering if anyone in the world loved him. Emily saw with a pang that his hair was thinning on the top of the head. His lips when he kissed her were cold and damp. "Wretched weather," he muttered. "It will only get worse."

He stared at her through his spectacles, thin and eager, and then at his two other sisters and father who sat before their plates, regarding him coldly. There was an empty chair, and he took it. "Hello, dearest family," he said. "Here I am. Dearest Anne! Your pupils were crying for you: the darling girls you taught and who love you so much. My fault, of course. Is there a cup for me?"

Charlotte poured. His tea sloshed in the saucer.

Their father said coldly, "Your sister Anne has told us of these matters. You no longer have employment because you allowed your employer's wife to seduce you. Her husband dismissed you; it's a wonder he didn't shoot you. The woman is a wicked woman, but you're to blame. A man can say no."

"But I didn't want to say no," murmured Branwell with a slight smile.

"No, you didn't, Bran," Anne said, her voice tremulous with anger.

In her mind, Emily felt the little god who was her brother tumble again. He was nothing more than broken bits of a tiny statue to sweep up, and yet she knew she would work to put him together once more. Already she was trying. From the time she was small, trying to mend his hurt feelings, his insecurities, while at the same time, convincing him of his greatness.

Bile rose in her throat. She had played her part, but he hadn't played his. His hair was thinning. His youth was slipping away.

That was his fault. Where was the invincible boy of seventeen who she wanted to be more than anything in the world? Now she could see him nowhere. She didn't give a damn about weak women seducing him. She wanted him just sixteen again, barely beginning to shave, ready to take on the world as far as the stone walls went and beyond. Glittering Branwell.

"It's a scandal." Charlotte said. "If her husband took this to the law, it might jail you for life. They might deem it just cause to strip this church from Papa, and where would we all go? Now, not one of us is working. We can't survive. I need time to do something. How could you?"

"Children, we will make the most of what we have today and hope for a better morrow," said her father, putting down his napkin. "I have the living the church pays me and we have the house for now. Let's hope the church wardens and vestry don't hear of this."

"Papa," Charlotte said. They all watched Branwell's thin back as he walked from the kitchen.

13

Charlotte

Charlotte remained alone after the meal was done, drying and redrying the same plate as if she would rub the pattern away, holding her bitterness against her. She thought, The reprobate! The ingrate! I was in love with a married person. Still, he didn't take me to bed. How could Bran do such a thing so coolly? Even I…

But the subject was not her but him.

In some way, she had failed him.

Did it begin that day when she was teaching at the private girls' seminary Roe Head, a cheerful, roomy country house, standing a little apart in a field? It was there she had studied and, only a few years under twenty, returned as teacher. Emily had been a pupil for a time, fallen ill of homesickness, and returned to Haworth. Charlotte, hardly more than a child herself, was proving herself every day.

Washing a pot in the deep washing pan, she recalled.

She had been instructing a class of students only a few years younger than herself one day when the headmistress opened the door and said, "Your brother's here to see you."

Charlotte had hurried down the hall. It was a dark day with leaves hurling about the stone schoolhouse. More leaves rushed against the windows.

Branwell was waiting in the parlor looking through the dictionary on the stand, one hand turning pages, the other stuffed in his pocket. He had taken off his hat, and his dirty red hair rose in several directions. His throat was thin and his clothes a little too small. He has no mother to notice, she thought. I'm supposed to manage these things and can't be in two places at once.

She exclaimed, "Why, dear Lord! Why are you here, eighteen miles from home?" (When she looked back on it, she felt bad she had not said, Oh, darling, how heavenly to see you!)

"I missed you," he muttered. "There's no one home but Papa. You're all gone." At sixteen he sounded like a hurt little boy.

"You've come all this way to say that…"

"I know I'm supposed to save the family, and some days I think I can and some days I think I never will."

"You must just do the best you can," she had said in that parlor of dark furniture with the stuffed robins under glass and portraits of school founders on the wall. She had spoken between stiff lips. "*You* have a fortunate life. *You'll* go up to Cambridge. They don't allow *women* there. Does Papa know you've come?"

"I left him a letter. I miss you. I miss Mama. I had to come to make sure you were still here. You don't write me much."

"I'm working," she said flatly. She did not say, "I'm unhappy too; I haven't an hour that's mine."

Even at seventeen, Charlotte was already a person who needed to tidy things. She tidied her drawers, folding her clean hose and chemises just so. She folded linens at home and alphabetically ordered the jars of preserved vegetables in the cellar. She tried to tidy the people around her, inside and out. All Branwell needed was a bit of sorting.

So she had hurried forward and pulled him against her.

"I'm seeing you have supper and a bed here," she said firmly. "And then I'll pay your fare home in the public carriage. You're shivering. I'll come home when I can. Dearest, I promise."

Tears filled his eyes. He muttered, "Oh God, I wish we were little children again all together. The soldiers…how we played! The stories we wrote!"

Years had passed, and she had not come home for long because of her work; and he had grown up but never gone to university as expected and instead had tried a few careers. And now they were both home, and all she could think of was that lonely boy in the dreary parlor who needed her, not the man whose shoulders were bowed and defeated at the age of twenty-six.

I must look for him and speak to him, she thought.

She did not have to look far. When she emerged from the parsonage kitchen the next morning after again washing up, he was standing in the hall waiting for her. He smiled at her in his old boyish way, and within that smile he was her adored younger brother again, holding her hand. Her brother who had made her a crown of flowers and told her that when he was a man, he would always take care of her.

"We need a walk together," he said.

They set off on Main Street side by side down the cobbles; the first snow of mid-November was gone, but there was always the threat of icy rain.

Charlotte held her brother's arm delicately. She said, "We've missed you when you were away. We need you."

But he had changed overnight from the repentant boy to the secure man. His thin, wide mouth opened in a smile. "Oh, you can depend on me, dearest Lotte!" he said. "I may have fallen down here and there, but you know in the end you can count on me. I intend to apply for work. No more tutoring lads."

She looked straight ahead at the descending rows of familiar shops—tailor, bakers, grocers—and said as cheerfully as she could, "That all sounds quite promising! But to proceed well, dearest, you must forget that woman."

"You needn't worry; Mrs. Robinson and I have a future. Her husband's sickly; he'll likely die within the year. Then we'll marry. She'll have a great deal of money. You'll all be provided for. Meanwhile, she says she'll send me a few pounds sterling every now and then until I find work. And I will find work. I am a man of many talents."

Charlotte ceased to walk before the shop where they still bought their paper. "But this is madness," she exclaimed. "You can't wait for some poor man to die to shape your future. These are dreams."

He lowered his head and poked the toe of his boot into the space of a missing cobble. "I can't live without dreams," he said. "I suppose the rest of you can, but I can't."

"How dare you say we don't have dreams! Bran…suppose she doesn't love you!"

"Of course she does," he snapped. "But I may have to wait a time for her. I know that. So I am going to find work. I am here for you all."

Over the following days, Charlotte sometimes passed the parlor to see Branwell sitting at the table studying the employment notices in the newspaper, circling a few solemnly. He raised his eyes to her and smiled, and she caught her breath. She thought, Maybe he will come through for all of us! Surely he will forget Mrs. Robinson.

"We must not push him but coax him," Anne said. Charlotte nodded. We have a little time, she thought. Papa's work is secure.

In church on the Sabbath, Charlotte stared at the glittering stone apostles in the reredos, their serious expressions never changing year after year, the brass candlesticks holding the wavering candles, the holy vessels on the fair linen altar cloth. As she stood there, she heard the explosion of music from the small organ console in the choir loft and then her father's holy words. "O rest in the Lord…and he will bide with you forever." Forever was a long time. No one has forever.

Then coming down from the pulpit, his vision faltered, and he stumbled. Nicholls ran up the steps and took his arm. Turning, she saw one of the wardens staring at her coldly. When she nodded at him, he did not so much as touch his hat brim.

From that time, there were two things the family did not speak of: Branwell's adulterous lover and their father's vision, which had deteriorated to the point where more people wondered if he could continue his work. Instead, at mealtimes they talked about the great royal and parliamentary doings from London.

Letters from Ireland were dire. With the strange and dreadful potato blight, people had little to eat and no crops to sell to pay their rent.

Then Branwell found a portrait commission or two and the family felt once again that he had a chance to become a great painter, a Gainsborough, a Reynolds, a Constable. He would do something. They knew it.

She and Anne worked on their poetry book. It did not seem unreasonable to think they would soon be ready to find a publisher and receive a commendable advance.

But sometimes at night Charlotte woke sobbing, feeling their time was running out. She had dreamed that the little family had been made to leave the parsonage, leading their now entirely blind father down the path, walking behind carts loaded with boxes of books, made-over dresses, family letters, their childhood writing, and, packed in soft linen, their father's precious now useless magnifying glass.

14

Emily

Emily's nights were full of another sort of dreams. She dreamed of the stone cottage quite mended and Jonathan waiting across the room for her.

Then she was standing on the cliff's edge of his remote island as he was rowing out to sea far, far below, and she felt she was losing him and leaped, brown dress and unpinned hair floating out, until the sea took her. The waves pushed and pulled; salty water filled her mouth and drowned the calling of his name.

Emily woke not in the cold sea but in her bed.

Suddenly, she missed him. Why had she stayed away?

It was one of those February days when a strange warmth breaks through the winter, when suddenly you wake and find yourself in another season which has come out of place. Emily left the parsonage. She went on her ordinary way, skirting the small cottages, incredulous with the weather, feeling the pale warming of the sun. Keeper leapt by her side. She went by instinct as she had gone as a young girl, both anxious and happy. She hurried as she had done then, having scribbled her lessons and hidden away any unfinished sewing, as if she was running happily toward the center of her most secret dream.

She was not halfway through the old path when she stopped at Keeper's sharp barking. Jonathan MacConnell was coming toward her through the old high grass in the light, which shone on water and rock and dry grass. He wore a patched coat of thick wool. His beard was scruffy, and he smiled, showing his uneven teeth. The scar on his face was stark as if etched anew.

Keeper took off to him joyfully.

MacConnell held up a leather pouch. "I'm come from the blacksmith's," he called, smiling at the sight of her. "I needed nails. How strange and beautiful to find you here, Miss Brontë. I was just thinking of you."

For a moment he seemed part of the light on the grass, and she had no words. Finally, she asked, "Are you real?"

He laughed. "What a question! Should I ask that of you, who disappears for a year? Here's my hand. It's real enough."

She touched the palm of his open, extended hand and felt within it the things it had held from time to time: a hammer, a bucket, an oar. She felt also bits of all his thoughts which startled her. He closed his fingers lightly over hers.

"Don't," she said sharply, pulling away. "I don't really know you."

"If you came more often, you would."

"I'm odd about being touched. And touching others."

"But you touched me. I am sorry to offend you."

A cloud moved across the sun. All that had glittered ceased. The moment became ordinary and the question she had asked him ridiculous. He was so ordinary, too, with his squashed brown hat and strands of his wheat-colored hair blowing about his ears. He was any man who you passed who tipped his hat to you, and you said, "Good day, sir."

He repeated more seriously, "If you came more often, you'd know me. You take a time to come. Perhaps the second letter I slipped under your door for you was found by someone else. I drew a sheep on the outside."

"I received no letter. What did it say?"

"That I hoped you'd visit. You have the book still? Good. And your brother's come back after all? And your sister as well?"

"I wish you didn't know things about me."

"I hear it spoken."

"There's a large stone by our Moorgate. Brown with silver in it like a star. You could leave a letter there if you ever write another. My sister Anne's returned. She's an angel…too good for this world, but my brother's lost his work. He's drinking again. I have no peace when he's like that. He had a very good portrait commission, and he slashed it up."

Why did she tell him such things? Perhaps he knew them. He was looking at her kindly, and now she made out his scar even more clearly. Perhaps he had fallen near the rocky cliffs of his home. The thought of his falling as she had in her dream, tumbling down to the sea, made her draw her breath hard with loss.

"Were you coming to find me?" he asked.

She was evasive. "Perhaps."

"Then perhaps you will tell me how you've been. Shall we walk? Such a mild day. It will not last."

They began to walk, she cautiously keeping some distance between them, followed by Keeper, who was more interested in what he smelled in the earth than in them. There were no houses near, only stray sheep. She heard wild birds and then they fell away, and she heard only her breathing and his.

It was not comfortable that he knew things about her.

What else did he know?

On a sloped hillock, she saw rabbit holes. One brown rabbit ran as low to the ground as possible. "I suppose they were here with the Celts," she said. That was a subject that interested them both, and they spoke of those ancient people with some respect and wonder. For a time, they speculated what might lie beneath the moors. Broken earthenware or an old coin? She had found one once.

The time they had been apart fell away, and it was as if it had been only the week before that she had seen him. She recalled he was married. It seemed so strange.

She asked, "Do you mind if I ask: What was your wife like?"

He stopped, his face becoming solemn when men must think of what they do not wish. He said, "My marriage wasn't happy. My family arranged it when we were young. We never loved each other."

"Do you have children?"

"I wanted to go for a long time but I hated to leave my friend

Alex. He was unhappy on the island too and wanted to escape with me, but it's so long a journey to the nearest larger island. At the last moment, he was afraid to go. The sea was rough."

"Ah," she said. "But you didn't talk about…"

"I did not. I don't wish it."

"I feel I've known you somewhere before. Could that be?"

"You might have seen me in Haworth."

She shook her head. "No, long ago. I think I saw you one day in your cottage when it was deserted and I was a child. You waited at the very door. Then you were gone."

He looked down at her, his face bewildered. He said, "How strange, when in truth I was on an island far away! But how did you see me? Was I younger, as you were then?"

"No, you looked as you do now."

"Dear lass, that's not possible."

"You looked at me and were gone. Yes…you had the same scar."

He was silent for a time as they walked. Then he said, "At home, when I read or remained on a cliff's edge overlooking the sea, I knew that what I dreamed was realer than where I was. I felt this place."

"At your home on the isle of Hirta in the archipelago of St. Kilda? You told me. But I looked in our atlas, and it's not there."

"Sometimes atlases omit it, it's so far out to sea and so small. As a boy, I thought it was the entire world."

"Your mother and father must miss you."

"Not after I left my wife. They wouldn't allow me in their door, but they may be dead now."

"Don't you care?"

"No."

"You do, you must. Why do you say other than you feel?"

"Ah, dear girl, why do you also? I have to guess at you." He reached down and touched a strand of her hair. She backed away. "Well, I won't," he said, but he looked uncertain. That shut down words between them. Without speaking, they turned to sit on a rough stone wall. Jonathan MacConnell looked up at the sky.

"A storm's coming from the north," he said. "You'd best be on your way. Don't take so long to visit me again. I'm likely not staying here past summer's end. You may find my cottage empty."

She exclaimed, "You're going away? I like thinking of you here."

His face was shy now; he bit his lip and rubbed the palm of his hand over his knees. After a time, he began to smile. He said, "Since I will likely go and we won't see each other again, may I kiss you?"

"No, certainly not! But don't go."

His face darkened and he stood. "I will likely," he said. He stood, thrusting his hands deep in his jacket pocket, looking wistfully down at her, adding, "I did not flee the island as much as my loneliness and that, it seems, has followed me here. I leave you now, parson's daughter."

She walked away through the dry grass which pulled at her skirts. When she looked back, he was gone.

Keeper bounded toward her, but her mind was rushing so, she hardly noticed him. What had happened? She couldn't remember half of what they had said. And now he had walked away keeping something of her as a small stone you slip in a pocket.

Emily stopped, folding her arms across her chest. What she was feeling she did not know. I'll put it in a poem, she thought. And then it will be clear to me. Yes, that was what she wanted: to be in her poetry.

Only this past week, she had gathered many of her poems from loose bits of paper, some written in faint pencil, some on the backs of bills for ale and candles, and copied them into two new, thin notebooks she had bought at the stationer's in the village. They were hidden away in the wardrobe drawer locked with the key she wore around her neck. They were the realest things in the world to her near the sound of rain on the window.

It was only coming close to the parsonage door, wondering if Anne had baked a tart for tea, that she reached for the key and found that it and the ribbon were gone.

The storm broke, rain pelting the back of her dress until she was running through the moor gate and through the parsonage door. No one seemed to be home though someone had been here recently. The kitchen lamp still burned dimly and cold tea sandwiches and some cake lay under a cloth. By the lonely chiming of the tall clock, she knew she had been away several hours. Where had the hours gone? She had missed tea. Had she baked her own cake this morning? But that did not matter. The only important thing was to find that key.

Lighting a candle from the lamp, Emily searched under the table and then in the hall. She mounted the steps, looking near the banister. By the clock hands, she made out it was six in the afternoon. But where was the frayed violet ribbon?

Then she knew she was not alone in the parsonage. Light shone through the open crack of her bedroom door. She saw the yellow flame of the oil lamp shining on the cup of pens on her table and Charlotte standing by it with the secret poetry books in her hands.

Emily shouted fiercely, "What do you think you're doing, you thief?"

Startled, her sister stepped back a little, grasping the table edge with one hand, saying, "You told me you burned these. I found the key on the floor outside your room."

"Well, I lied, and you've no right to look at them!"

At this moment, all the vague memories of the afternoon disappeared. Emily knew only how she loathed her sister's conflicted face. Charlotte, who always knew the best, Charlotte, who should have stayed in Brussels as that teacher's mistress and left them to bumble on somehow here in the parsonage rooms. Ordinary, stupid Charlotte.

Her sister replied stubbornly, "Anne and I share our poetry. These are brilliant. What kind of person are you that you lock them away?"

"Don't you understand anything? The key at once!"

"Take your wretched key and books then! God only knows why, of all the sisters in the world, I was given you!" Charlotte dropped the key and notebooks on the bed, and Emily locked away her work. Then she fled down the steps.

Charlotte followed her.

They passed the clock.

Emily hissed over her shoulder, "I don't want to talk about the poems. If you insist, I'll burn them."

"Be quiet—Papa may come in. He's gone out with Anne."

"He ought to bring the neighbors with their staves since we have a thief in our house!"

At the bottom step, Emily felt Charlotte's hand on her shoulder and stopped. "Listen to me, you foolish girl!" Charlotte panted. "I've a plan. We must have a plan. Anne and I have been writing a lot of poetry. The three of us must publish our poems together. We'll become famous; we'll earn our fortunes. We'll be as famous as Lord Byron. We'll never have to worry about anything again."

"You and your bloody plans! The answer is never."

"Why won't you publish with us?"

Emily hunched her shoulders. "Because," she mumbled slowly, her fingers feeling the polished banister, "the poems are from the inside of me. What all of you see isn't the real me; it's a shadow. If I don't hold on, what's real will be taken from me. Who I really am would be thrown away."

Charlotte took the candle. She walked through the kitchen, opened the cellar door, and descended the stone steps. Emily followed.

The cellar had been the dungeon in one of their childhood games. Anne had come with a stick as a sword when they hid and shouted out as fiercely as a little girl can, "Prisoners! Are you there?"

About them boxes and beer kegs were strung with abandoned spiderwebs. She heard mice behind a trunk.

Charlotte was looking over their jars of preserves on a shelf. "Blackberries half gone," she murmured. "I don't understand the consumption of preserves in this house. It's months until we can put up more. No one considers, no one cares. Least of all you. Why are you here?"

Emily dropped slowly to a trunk and clasped her knees. "It's cold," she said, still clutching the key in her closed hand. "I want to be with you." She rocked back and forth a little.

"You love us."

"I do, endlessly. And no one else ever."

"Including me?"

"Yes," Emily replied grudgingly.

Charlotte sat down on a box, putting the candleholder on the floor between them. She had removed her spectacles, and her delicate, anxious face was a little gold in the light. "Emily, Anne and I are going to publish our poems," she said seriously. "Yours are the best. With yours included, we would do brilliantly. Please share them. We'd make our fortunes. We'd never have to be apart."

Emily shuddered. In her mind, they were at school again where she was small. The teacher had slashed the switch across her bare legs, and she had not cried but later she had hurled herself into Charlotte, clasping her about the waist, butting her head into Charlotte's flat chest, sticking her tiny fingers in between Charlotte's dress buttons to get closer to flesh and bone. Between the taste of rough cotton and the strong angry beat of her sister's heart, she knew she would be all right someday. "You will not touch my little sister!" Charlotte shouted later to the teacher. Charlotte was two years older. Such a big girl then.

After that, when they came home, they had begun to write their tiny chronicles. In them they were not little girls but captains in armies from imaginary countries. Branwell formed the battle plans. He'd lead them out, their little feet in imaginary boots trampling foreign bloody mud…safe, safe in their minds, always able to return in a word to their parsonage.

Emily rose from the trunk. "I'll think about the poems," she said.

The storm was over as she walked through the graveyard. Her palm knew the worn curves of some stone tops. The church was the best place when she needed to be alone.

Emily lit a candle by the church door and walked down the nave to the family vault. There were the stairs to the bell tower. Years before, she had climbed it and stood with her feet balanced on a catwalk, her little hand flat on the huge, silent iron bell.

She had been almost seven then, the year after she was taken home with her two dying eldest sisters. Their loss soon had set her running, stumbling over the moor, trying to discover what she could to persuade the pale bodies lying so modestly in their coffins to rise and play with her.

If they could fly, they could fly away from death. Death couldn't grab your skirt and pull you down then. She was certain that under her childish bodice she had secret wings.

Weeks after the last funeral, the certainty grew within her that she could bring them back. And so she had dropped all her clothes but her worn underdrawers and climbed to the bell tower window. Any moment, wings would appear and lift her into the air. She needed only to leap first for her sisters Elizabeth and Maria to rise from their tomb and follow her.

By this time, many people had gathered below, shouting at her, some crying. She had gazed down on them, mortal as they were. Only to have faith; her father said that was the important thing. There! She felt the wings coming.

Now her father was below, quite young and strong then. "What are you doing?" he had cried, and she called down to him calmly, "I'm going to rescue the dead."

But she had hesitated. The wings, sensing her lack of faith, retreated into her thin bare shoulder blades. And then the sexton John Brown, who was still young himself, had crept behind her, capturing her easily with strong arms, and that was the end of it.

Now quite grown, tall and lanky and earthbound, she waited by the church tower door, remembering.

Behind her, someone stirred in a pew, but it was only the homeless vagrant who came to the church to shelter in storms. She felt for the broken biscuits in her pocket and put them down near him, seeing his shining, sad eyes. Though she felt the child she had been, she was reconsidering.

If she had leaped, perhaps the wings would not have come. Death then would have taken her too. If she had failed. There would have been for her then no more baking of bread, no more her living sisters' laughter, no more discussing books. Ghosts did walk the world, but sometimes the living couldn't see them. She might tap on the window saying, "Let me in, let me in," but they wouldn't hear her.

Emily hesitated at the church door. Rain still dripped steadily from the trees. She looked across to the parsonage, making out candles burning behind the window.

Walking down the path, Emily found her sisters in the parlor, bent over some embroidery.

"I have decided," she said coldly. "Include my poems. To earn enough to keep us here, I'd do it. But my name mustn't be on the book. If you reveal who I am, I will never speak to you again."

Charlotte exclaimed, "Oh, thank you, dear! Of course, we'd never use our real names! It would have to be a secret! We've already decided on men's names. Currer and Acton Bell. We like Mr. Nicholls' middle name so we borrowed it. He'll never know. We're keeping our initials. You could be Ellis. You look like an Ellis."

"We should include Branwell's poems as well. He's had some published in the local newspaper," Emily said. "They're very fine."

Anne shook her head. "He mustn't hear about it. He'll try to lead it, and I don't think he could now. He'd tell his friends about it in the pub, and the whole village would know."

Emily brought her two notebooks of poems down to her sisters at breakfast, took a slice of toast and a cup of tea, and retreated to her room again. She felt empty with the poems gone.

Days later, she remembered she had hidden the pages of her incipient novel under the cloth that covered the bottom of the drawer. Fortunately, Charlotte had not noticed this. At first, Emily stared down at the words, while they seemed to gaze at her in silence. She rested the edge of her hand on them and felt some movement. Finally, the voices of the characters began to whisper. Then they reached up and pulled her into the pages.

The clock from the stairs below struck the hour of two in the morning. She heard Branwell climbing up slowly, negotiating every step. She wanted to run out to him, but she could not put down her pen.

Where did this story come from? She thought of leaves against a corner of the church, a homeless boy she had seen once with huge dark eyes. And there was that ancient book of poems, particularly the poem about a wanderer. He was exiled from all he loved and roamed the cold seas and walked the paths of exile, just like the man in the stone cottage who had aroused such strange feelings in her.

Emily heard the branches bend and brush against the roof. She dipped her pen in ink. In her mind, it was deep winter and the world heavy with snow.

> "I don't think it possible for me to get home now without a guide," I could not help exclaiming. "The roads will be buried already; and, if they were bare, I could scarcely distinguish a foot in advance."

Sometimes over those next days, she wrote so fiercely, she wondered if she would fall into the story and never come back again. She drifted downstairs, ate in silence, brought in the coal, forgot to say goodnight, and then tapped on everyone's door very late, asking, "Are you well?" She was afraid something dark had swept them away. The ghosts she had always heard in the wind were tapping at her window.

> "I'm come home: I'd lost my way on the moor!… It is twenty years…I've been a waif for twenty years!"

It was her elder sister Maria's voice she heard. Maria, into whose bed she had crawled those last few days to keep her sister from death. Emily didn't dare turn to the window, because she wanted her sister there and she might not be. Oh, come once more, my darling!

For a time then she sat motionless while the ink dripped from the pen and made a blot on the paper, and she felt the grief hard in her chest and tears on her face.

The late spring of 1846 was rainy and damp, and events of the outer world came from the newspaper, letters from family and friends, and people her father met on the street. The potato blight in Ireland was a disaster. Countless people faced eviction due to the inability to pay their rent. Many took to the roads, including some distant relatives who attempted to get to Liverpool and from there to America. An elderly cousin trying to cross the sea had died on the voyage. Someone wrote to Emily's father, and he prayed and then kept the letter about her in a box on his desk.

The Reverend Patrick Brontë had always intended to visit the county where he had been born, but there had never been time or money.

More of the world pressed against the gray stone walls of the parsonage. The bad water brought cholera and consumption into the village; more plain wooden coffins sat in the church, where families kept vigil for their dead. John Brown's hands were dirty from his grave digging and his palms calloused. He pushed down on the shovel with his cracking boot.

Slate tiles fell from the old church roof.

On good days, Branwell was moderately drunk; on bad ones, someone had to bring him home. They had faith that one day he would shake this from him and go forward again. He always had before. Besides, he was loved by that strange Mrs. Robinson, adulterous as she was.

Through all of this, Emily hid away and formed her story; she took the dull brown of the moor in winter and the endless loneliness of the exiled and dead and blended them in ink and paper.

A man found a homeless boy in the market and brought him home to raise among his own two children. He called the child Heathcliff. After the man died, his son made life a hell for his foster brother. Then the daughter, Cathy, who first loved the boy, turned from him and married a wealthy neighbor; and Heathcliff, now grown, disappeared for three years. He returned a gentleman with the bitterness of her rejection still in his heart, to fester there.

He returned, yet he was always a wanderer.

Often in the daylight hours, Emily walked to feel what warmth she could from the occasional sun on her hair and smell the heather and earth. The characters followed her, arguing with her. When she lay in bed at night, she could feel Heathcliff near her. If she put her fingers out, she could touch his warm hand.

15

Charlotte

When the poems for their book were finally selected, Charlotte and Anne closed the parlor door to put them in some order. Candlelight flickered on the pages strewn over the table. They spoke of their hopes in hushed voices. They kept the book secret from their father and brother.

They copied the poems into two notebooks. They had found the address of a London publisher who had advertised in the papers that he was looking for poets. Charlotte wrapped the notebooks in butcher's paper, enclosing a note: "My dear sirs! We are three brothers from the north who are so very pleased to offer, for consideration of publication, our first volume of collected poems."

Weeks followed. The struggling rosebush in the garden bloomed and then faded. A cat ran off and was lost. Their father walked into a box left in the hall and his foot swelled. Emily cooked. Charlotte dusted the house.

Calling at the post office, she at last found the packaged notebooks returned to her, some spill of greasy pork chop or a stain of beer on the reused butcher's wrap, the broken twine re-tied. Inside was a letter of one sentence refusing the collection.

Charlotte crossed out the name of the publisher and addressed it to another one. It was returned in only days. Several more rejections followed.

"But it's the wrong publisher," Anne always said patiently.

I cannot give up, Charlotte thought. I will not give up.

She sent the collection out again.

For a week she avoided even raising her eyes to the post

office when she made her way down the street past children playing in the gutter and shopkeepers standing with arms crossed at their doors.

At last she gave in and opened the post office door. She took in the boxes of letters waiting to be collected, the box of precious stamps and the notices tacked to the walls, some so timeworn that nobody recalled who had written them. She dared not look at the pile of unsorted mail.

"Fancy you've come!" said the postmistress. "A letter from London just arrived."

For some moments after she read the missive to her sisters in the kitchen, the only sound was the kitten licking up the milk. Anne who was seated on a bench at the table then took up the paper. "But I still don't understand," she said, raising her face after reading it. "He will publish our book if we pay for it. Dear Charlotte, I'm confused. Wasn't he supposed to pay *us*?"

I must make the best of this, Charlotte thought. Confidently, she said, "It's the way it is before you're famous. Unknown authors must supplement the printing costs. It's only thirty-one pounds, ten shillings."

"But, Charlotte, darling!" Anne answered, biting her lip. "That's nearly what I earned for a full year's teaching. What if we never become famous? Mr. Tennyson doesn't pay, surely, to have his poems printed."

"Perhaps not. But I am convinced that as soon as ours is published, people will flock to read it and we'll earn a great deal."

From outside the house came sexton John Brown's bass voice speaking about drafts in the church nave. Emily began to slice turnips. Without looking up, she asked challengingly, "How do you know we'll be popular in months? Some writers never become popular. They die in obscurity."

Charlotte dropped onto the opposite bench, hands on the table. She said, "Our aunt would surely want us to spend some of the money she left to put ourselves forward."

Emily sliced precisely and hard, the heel of her hand on the knife's back.

Charlotte raised her voice. She said desperately, "We must take this chance, sisters."

Anne stood. She exclaimed, "We might as well pay the fee and publish since we've gone so far. If it fails, I'll look for another governess position. My dearest ones, let's agree. Don't you know this one simple thing? All that we have in the world is each other!"

Charlotte collected the check drawn from their account at the little bank in the village and mailed it to London.

A parcel finally arrived addressed to the Bell brothers in care of the parsonage. When they untied the string, they found the book of their poems bound in green cloth. Their pen names were on the pale spine. Anne wiped her hand on her apron before taking it up.

A few small reviews subsequently appeared in newspapers, mostly complimentary. Eventually, they received their first sales statement noting that the poems had sold two copies.

"You must want nothing from the world," Emily said that evening as she stopped at Charlotte's door. She pulled her shawl tighter.

"Perhaps not," said Charlotte as she stared at her fierce face in the mirror. "I want such huge things I dare not list them. I'll find another way. I will always find another way."

In the weeks that led into Christmas of 1846, Branwell was changing. He was as devout as he had been in periods as a child. He stood and knelt and sang reverently at the service. As they sat around the parlor table at dinner together on Christmas Day, he mentioned that he was considering going to divinity school and entering the church. Dr. Gregory privately told them, when he came later for a holiday glass of punch, that he was relieved; Branwell had been compromising his health.

The family made music together again. They gathered

around the piano singing Handel's "Art Thou Troubled?" Anne sang the higher part. The curate Mr. Nicholls filled in the bass notes. Branwell had dusted off his flute which he had not touched in years and played it moodily, a light obbligato above them, dipping his thin body to the notes.

Outside the window, the long cold night hung about the stones of the church.

Art thou troubled?
Music will calm thee,
Art thou weary?
Rest shall be thine.
Music, music every divine…

The day following, a letter arrived for Branwell.

The husband of his love had died at last.

Part IV

February–Summer 1847

16

Riches I hold in light esteem,
And Love I laugh to scorn;
And lust of fame was but a dream,
That vanished with the morn…

—Emily Brontë, from "The Old Stoic"

Emily

The rest of the winter brought awful weather. It was too cold to hang wash outside, so chemises and underdrawers and petticoats and shirts were draped on ropes stretched across the kitchen to dry, steaming slightly from the hot fire. Outside, snow covered the fences and the high grass while the sheep seemed like ghosts as they moved in the blizzards. Even the curate, Arthur Bell Nicholls, with a new horse and cart allotted by the church vestry to the parsonage clergymen, did not visit the moorland habitants too often.

When Emily raised her face from the pages of her story, she finally allowed herself to think of Jonathan MacConnell in his small cottage, likely half buried in snow. No, likely not for she recalled that he said he might leave before this winter.

She sat up alert, hand resting on her manuscript.

Had it been a year since she had seen him? Yes, he said he'd likely go. The stone cottage would be empty, as it had been when she first discovered it. She put her fingers to her lips which he had wanted to kiss. But perhaps he had packed but not yet gone. Perhaps he was even now standing by his door surveying his cottage, making sure the fire was out and the shutter fastened.

Emily pulled on her warmest cloak and laced her mother's

boots, which could hardly be mended anymore. Within minutes, she was through the moor gate and plunging into the icy snow against the sadness which rose in her breast. He is gone; he is gone, she thought. Suddenly, what she had ignored was very important. Once she had kept a wounded bird in a box and had neglected to feed it. Oh God, when weeks later she recalled and ran up the steps to look…

She was panting by the time she saw the familiar hill before her which she had first climbed as a girl. I am always too late for everything, she thought. How could I forget to come?

Breathless she made the hilltop.

Her hood fell off, and the snow flew in her face. For a moment she could see nothing. She wiped it away with her glove, looked down. Below her, in the icy piles around its foundations, the stone cottage had returned to the ruins in which she first had found it so many years before. The roof was half gone, and the door torn away.

Then he's left for certain, she told herself. I have missed him because I forgot.

She covered her face with her gloved hands.

But when she took away her hands, the house was whole again. The icy snow was dying down, blowing away. She heard the sound of scraping and climbed down to the cottage, reaching it and laying her hand on the cold stone. Following the sound to the back of the house, she saw a ladder and Jonathan MacConnell standing on it, wearing a squashed hat on his head, scraping the snow from the roof. His face lit up at the sight of her and he called, happily, "Can it be you? I almost left, a few months ago before Christmas. I had sold my dog and sheep. How glad I am to see you! Wait, don't disappear. I think the spirits of the moor hide you and bring you back again."

She picked up his fallen hat and gave it to him. He brushed it off with his bare hand, leaving sparkles of ice in the strands. She could find no words to say but that she was very glad to find him and she would not say that. Her throat swelled.

The snow had entirely ceased to fall.

Finding her voice, she asked him, "Why didn't you go?"

"I almost did, but I wanted to see you first. I waited, willing you to come to me. One Sabbath between storms a few months ago, I rode my old mare to your church but remained in the back. You were with your sisters, singing hymns from the book. Three charming girls in bonnets. Was the preacher your father? I saw another clergyman guide him to the pulpit. I didn't realize he was nearly blind. I was ill on and off then, so couldn't return but I decided not to go away. I couldn't go without seeing you again."

She said uncomfortably, "I wish you had spoken to me when you came to the village."

"I know you a little and you didn't want it. I'm your secret. I sensed it. It gets lonely being a secret, lass."

"I think of us as friends."

"Strange friends indeed. 'I won't come to you, and you may not come to me.' 'I'll see you in a year, maybe not.'" He smiled, teasing. "And where are my book and my glove?"

She thought of his glove, thrust so intimately into her drawer with her shifts and petticoats and the book on her shelf whose strange writing she could see in her mind. She blurted out, "I suppose I wanted to keep the poems."

He smiled and held out his hand. "Come inside where it's warm," he said. When she did not take the hand, he shrugged and opened the door to his cottage. Fire warmth pulled her. Avoiding even brushing his coat sleeve, she passed him and sat down carefully on the wobbly chair near the burning logs.

He took the other chair, removing his mufflers. She said, "I did stay away a time. I've been writing a book. It so possesses me, I forget the world. I forgot everything. Even friends...you."

His face softened. "Friends indeed then?"

"Why yes, of course."

"A whole book! I cannot imagine writing so much."

"I think my sisters write books, but they aren't very successful. None of us are. Perhaps it was meant to be so."

She looked around carefully. The blue quilt, the sampler, the bindings of his books, the brown of the ceiling beams seemed so comforting that she was happy to be here. Some warmth crept into her old boots, though they were wet. She thought of taking them off and then did not feel right about it.

It made her flush the way he looked at her. Finally, he tossed his head as if discarding what he was thinking and asked, "Is it a novel?"

"How did you know? Sometimes it seems realer than my own world."

"Can it do that?"

"Oh yes! It makes me forget things I can't manage."

"Do you mean your brother? I've been thinking of him. Last month after seeing you girls in church, I had a mug in the Haworth pub and heard talk that he fell in love with a married woman who's widowed now and who'll marry him soon and solve your family's financial needs."

"Is it the general talk?"

"It is and I see you don't like it. I like the look of your father, very much the old prophet. What would he think of me, I wonder?"

"I don't want him to know yet. He's ill at the idea of us being hurt or taken in by a stranger."

"Am I still a stranger?"

"Not anymore, but my family mightn't understand, because you're a married man run away from your wife from a place no one has ever heard of. And we met in such a strange way. And you may disappear from my life as abruptly as you came. With my knowing nothing of it."

"I won't," he said. "I'll stay a time if you will continue to come to me."

"I'll always come," Emily said. Rising, she walked around the table and bent down to press her lips against his. He touched the back of her head to bring her closer. His lips were warm and slightly chapped, and she lingered a time before springing away. All the way home, she ran over the sopping ground as fast as she could.

That night her novel woke her like something shaking her arm. She stumbled to the desk. She had some attempts to light the lamp. The words came from nowhere, rushing and pushing. The scenes were still coming out of order. She remembered how years ago, in the marketplace, she had seen a boy about five years old, staring after her.

> "These things happened last winter, sir," said Mrs. Dean; "hardly more than a year ago. Last winter, I did not think, at another twelve months' end, I should be amusing a stranger to the family with relating them! Yet, who knows how long you'll be a stranger? You're too young to rest always contented, living by yourself…"

The clock on the stairs chimed two in the morning.

She forgot everything but her book.

Emily wrote for a long time, trying to make her penmanship legible, catching the words as they came. It was not until dawn began, slowly lightening the sky, that she felt too tired to continue. She locked everything away and lay down again. The whole story was gray, like the light, but she felt its edges, its middle, its muddled endings, the many of them.

Emily pulled the pillow over her head against the strange people in her room and whispers from corners. We have always been here, they murmured. We are more real than you are. We are more real than he is, your man in his stone cottage, and he is dangerously real.

Live for us alone.

> I know that ghosts have wandered on earth. Be with me always. Take any form, drive me mad, only do not leave me in this dark alone where I cannot find you. I cannot live without my life! I cannot die without my soul.

17

Charlotte

Charlotte had not let her sadness over the poetry book silence her for long. She was writing a novel. Anne was as well. They worked in the parlor and sometimes shook their heads over what Emily could be doing in her room above. She was writing something; they could not say what. There was no use being maddened over it. She would either tell them eventually or she would not.

As her subject, Charlotte chose an earnest young Englishman who goes to teach in a girls' school in Brussels. Walking up and down the parlor, she read over her scenes under her breath, beating the rhythm with her little hand moving through the warm air from the hearth. She wanted to do better. Inside her body, she felt such intensity. It was there like her poems, beyond her reach.

Charlotte mailed her completed novel *The Professor* to a London publisher, bound in the ubiquitous butcher's paper and twine. Within a week, the refusal came. She sent it out again. More refusals followed. Sometimes they didn't even include a letter. No one told her what was wrong, only that it did not suit their needs.

The last time the book was refused, she carried it up the stairs, where she threw it and herself on her bed.

Then she cried for everything: the lonely years of teaching and schools and the way she was not treated as an intelligent woman when a governess ("Sit in the dark hall outside the dining room in case you're needed, Miss Brontë!") and still that work did not pay enough.

All her dreams had come to nothing: the diligent planning of the school, the failed poetry anthology, the novel.

And of course, love. There would never be love. She was merely one of three spinster daughters of a parson in a little village, growing older until she was wrinkled and stooped. Her lovely brown hair, her one beauty, would never be loosened from its pins and kissed by a husband.

In the end, she had no purpose in this world.

Charlotte slid from the bed to the floor. She drew her knees up and buried her head in her arms. She was sobbing so hard, it was some time before she heard the repeated knock on the door and with a mortified start, made out her father's voice. She stood, wiped her face on the quilt, and tried to smile clumsily.

He was at the threshold, green glasses in his hand. His smile was as querulous as hers.

"I was reading a sad story that made me cry," she mumbled. "Do you need my help, Papa?"

In the past weeks, the family had noticed that Patrick Brontë held the banister even more tightly when he descended the stairs. He walked touching the wall with the edge of his hand. Now, as he appeared at her door, she thought, How could I have been so self-centered, supposing I have struggled through so much, when it is nothing to what he endures?

"What is it, darling?" he asked. "Your voice is worn."

"A small disappointment. Nothing much." He knew nothing about her novel. She wanted to bring him only successes after the failure of the school, and there were none.

She helped him sit in the one chair by her desk.

He looked about at her room, squinting to make out her pen cup, which he had given her for her tenth birthday, and the portable writing desk, another gift. He turned his head to where watercolors of her sisters hung framed on the wall and one of Branwell as a young boy, so straight and intelligent.

He spoke slower than was his habit. "I can't see it," he said bleakly. "I can't even see your beautiful face clearly. This is not endurable. I need you, my daughter."

"Whatever you need, Papa! Truly!"

"I must have my cataracts removed. Will you go with me to Manchester for the surgery? Then I can remain here always as vicar and keep you with me."

She threw her arms around him. Why do I want love and renown and to study in Cambridge? she asked herself. I have everything I need in this house: my sisters, my father, even my wretched brother.

"I will be at your side, Papa," she said as a new calm filled her. Her spirits rose. I do have a purpose, she thought.

They took the train to Manchester and then a carriage, passing streets of offices for lawyers and doctors and arriving at the boardinghouse where they had taken rooms for the three weeks of surgery and recovery.

She was moved by the love she had felt for her father and held on to his arm. Yet now she was also afraid. Suppose this surgery left him blind? If only the operation went well, she would never ask for another thing for herself in all her life.

Two assistants held Patrick Brontë still in his chair during the surgery. Charlotte stood with her hand on his shoulder as she prayed. Then the surgeon and his assistants were gone, with instructions that her father lie still in bed for three weeks as the wounds healed. The surgeon would come each day. The room was kept dark, the heavy curtains closed.

It was done; it was done.

How brave he was, she thought. Today and always since he was a boy who could not afford shoes. He had left his father's Irish cottage as a lad wearing his only coat and, some years later, had matriculated in divinity at Cambridge. She remembered how when she was small, he would ride her on his shoulders, galloping through the house as she cried in her imperious five-year-old voice, "Faster, horse!" and he had asked, puffing, "To where, my princess?" and she had replied, "To the very end of the world."

For the first few days of her father's recovery as he slept with bandages across both eyes, Charlotte often lingered at the slit of curtain at the window, which overlooked this street of stone houses. She had a great deal of time to think.

She remembered the years when all her siblings were still alive and that dreadful school that she and three sisters had attended. There had been a small, damp room high in the school building with a deep windowsill hidden by heavy curtains. There, when she could, she would hide away to read alone, thin legs in scratchy black wool stockings drawn up against her flat chest. She never knew when anyone would find her and punish her. It was the beginning of the fear that if she were not careful, all she cherished would be taken.

Standing in that room in Manchester, a few words came to her.

There was no possibility of taking a walk that day.

Something touched the small of her back and gently pushed her into the chair.

Her hands were cold as she opened her portable lap desk by the meager light from the curtain slit and leafed through her bound notebook to a clean page. A few of her unfinished poems were stuffed in the back, along with a letter from Emily that had arrived this morning saying the roof had leaked again in the last storm and Keeper was out of sorts.

Her father murmured her name, and she put down the pen and hurried to him. "Water," he rasped. Charlotte tipped water gently into his mouth, keeping his head steady so that his stitches would not pull beneath the bandages.

They would not know for a time if he would be left blind.

He slept, and she returned to the little notebook.

Her mind overflowed with words.

A small breakfast-room adjoined the drawing room, I slipped in there. It contained a bookcase.

As the days went on, she never stopped unless her father needed her. Sometimes she wrote half the night. She hardly knew how much time had passed. In three weeks, the surgeon removed the bandages and her father struggled to sit up, looking around the room. "The curtains are blue, daughter! They are deep blue! And outside there's a brick dwelling," he said, shocked, triumphant. She knew then how greatly he had feared and how much he had hoped.

They returned to Haworth by train with her father wearing his new heavy green glasses. She had three hundred pages of a novel, tucked in her carpetbag.

Mr. Nicholls had managed everything in the parish admirably while they had been away, but Anne had been ill with a bad cough and fever caught when she was visiting friends. Martha had been called away to take care of her elderly grandmother, so Tabitha had managed the house, which meant dirty laundry overflowed the wash baskets.

And where was Emily?

"Ah well, something peculiar," the old woman said. "She comes in late, and I think she didn't come home at all for two or three nights."

"How can this be?"

"Ah, child, dearest Miss Charlotte, my memory's not what it was, but I swear on the blessed spirits that her bed hadn't been slept in."

Anne would know nothing about it, as she'd also been away.

Emily arrived home a few hours after Charlotte, and when Charlotte asked her where she had been, she replied with a shrug, "Old Mrs. Hawkins, who's alone, felt poorly, and I stayed. I've done that before. You know I have. Why do you bother about me when Bran's drinking is the talk of the village again? How's Papa? That's all we need to think about."

Charlotte walked slowly upstairs. All the enchantment, the spell under which she had written, had faded to words on a great many pages. Who would care about the story of a penniless governess? What on earth had possessed her? Her life was for her family. Anne was weak, and Emily was concealing something that Charlotte must discover. She couldn't allow herself to have great dreams that would fail her again.

Her father called up sharply from his study and, terrified that he had fallen, she thrust her notebook deep into a drawer under her clean chemises.

Rain fell almost every day that early summer. There was a new leak in the roof. They could hardly bear to read more news of the homeless in Ireland trying to find ships to take them away. Men, women, and children died on the road. Now a priest wrote her father about two young cousins, not ten years old, who were no more. Patrick Brontë hadn't seen his family in nearly fifty years, but he put his hands over his face and softly muttered the prayer for the dead. "May the souls of the faithful departed by the mercy of God rest in peace." Again, for that moment, his voice was that of the young Irishman who felt by faith he could make everything better.

They sent what money they could. They managed.

On a chill morning, a stranger knocked on the parsonage door.

The gravestones behind him were darkened by the rain, and under its patter she could hear bits of the children's choir practicing hymns in the church. Charlotte took in the man's grizzled beard and the paunch that strained the buttons of his coat.

"Excusing the interruption, miss," he said "Mr. Holmes, bailiff from Halifax, at your service."

She knew no one from Halifax, a town an hour away filled with large industrial buildings for carpets and cotton. At first, she thought this stranger had something to do with Emily's peculiar behavior.

She asked, "Do you wish to speak with my father, Bailiff Holmes?"

The bailiff took off his cap, rain wetting his thin, graying hair. He said, "It's Mr. Branwell Brontë, to whom I am here to serve notice. Or if he's not home, would your father be within?"

Charlotte ushered Mr. Holmes inside the parlor and gestured to a chair. He sat heavily, ineffectually dusting raindrops from his hat. He glanced at the piles of books and papers on the table as if they were an oddity.

Just across the hall, she knocked on the study door. Her father's eyes were healed now, and she knew he was writing a condolence letter to a friend. His lips were pursed as if bitter sorrow had been rubbed on them. Since he had returned, he was busier than ever in the parish among weddings, baptisms, and funerals. Though he still depended on his curate, he made sure all knew that he was in charge of the parish.

Without looking up, he said, "Don't disturb me, child, not now." Then, feeling her silence, he added, "Who knocked?"

"It's the bailiff from Halifax," she answered, staring at the stone floor. "Concerning my brother."

Patrick Brontë pulled himself up from his chair. "Well, let us see what he wants," he murmured.

Charlotte nodded. Branwell was so drunk last night that he had dragged himself up the stairs. She had wanted to kick him until his spectacles fell off and broke, glass shattered in splinters on the floor.

Her father murmured, "We must always trust in God. Where's your poor brother?"

She kept her voice low. "Hiding in his room. I heard him in the upper hall."

Her father found a clean place in his handkerchief and blew his nose. He muttered, "What have we done to make him bring us trouble? Only loved him too much, perhaps. Did we do that, my darling? Now we must face this thing down. We must protect him."

The bailiff was still seated in the parlor where Charlotte had left him, hat on his knee. Small puddles formed by his shoes. Anne had come in from shopping with her umbrella dripping, her wicker baskets smelling of cold waxy candlesticks and washsoap and bacon. She looked at everyone.

The bailiff got to his feet slowly in the presence of the parson of Haworth.

"Pardon to disturb you, sir," he said. "It's your son I've business with. He owes money in Halifax to the innkeeper for drink, and if he don't pay, he must stand trial in York and be sent to prison for debt. Seven pound and sixpence. I am very sorry to tell you, sir, that I must have it all today. I must take it in my pocket here."

Anne's eyes widened as she waited in her dripping cloak. Staring at the man, Patrick Brontë said in a soft, clear Irish inflection, "My son's…health is delicate, and he would be very ill if sent to prison, nor could we bear it…my daughters and I. He has not been working, you see, and has no readily available money."

"If I may say, sir, less carousing would let him work."

"I am aware of that, sir. We must pay the sum."

Emily, who had come from the kitchen, remained motionless with her arms folded tightly across her chest. Charlotte carefully walked past her to climb to her father's bedroom, where he now kept the money box hidden, and carried it down the stairs, placing it on the table.

No one moved as he opened the box. "Seven pound, you say?"

"And sixpence, sir. Your son drank a great many nights there with his friends. He acted like a lord. The innkeeper thought he was a rich man."

Patrick Brontë counted the banknotes and the coin. Charlotte's rage rose until her vision blurred. There went Anne's new dress. It was only when the bailiff bade them goodbye, bowing and a little ashamed, that Patrick Brontë covered his eyes with his hand.

They heard the hesitant footsteps on the floor above them and on the stairs. Charlotte felt her brother's slight presence behind her. "I should go away from all of you," Branwell mumbled. "I should go to the river and throw myself in. I swear this is the last time. Not a drop more."

Emily, who was looking at her brother with violent loathing, cried, "Swear before God that you'll change. Swear! Swear on peril of your immortal soul. Do you want to bring us all down to ruin? Dogs and hawks will be tamed with kindness, but not you."

She pushed him.

Their father said weakly, "Don't."

Branwell was crying and raised his hand to protect himself. He murmured, "I swear…" And quietly Mr. Nicholls appeared with a tray of tea and milk and cake. How he had done it just when needed, she never knew.

When Charlotte opened the house door later, she heard the high voices of the two little boys who sang in the choir drifting through the wet air as the rain ended. In the weeks following, she watched as her brother trudged daily to the post office, hoping that his beloved Mrs. R. would write to him and call him to her arms. He walked unsteadily. Everyone in the village knew of his drunkenness by now. The pharmacist sold him little pellets of opium or the occasional bottle of laudanum, which he tucked inside his coat. Charlotte and her sisters heard him mumbling nonsense in his room.

Part V

Summer 1847–February 1848

18

I've watched thee every hour;
I know my mighty sway,
I know my magic power
To drive thy griefs away.

—Emily Brontë, from "Shall Earth No More Inspire Thee?"

Emily

> I sought, and soon discovered, the three headstones on the slope next the moor: the middle one grey, and half buried in the heath… I lingered round them, under that benign sky: watched the moths fluttering among the heath and harebells, listened to the soft wind breathing through the grass, and wondered how anyone could ever imagine unquiet slumbers for the sleepers in that quiet earth.

Emily slumped in her chair, staring at the sheets of paper on the desk. She did not move for a time as the voices within the pages grew softer. At last she rose, locked away the manuscript, and walked downstairs. She would not share it. This made two secrets. One was now locked in a drawer. The other was in a stone cottage on the moor.

The truth was that when her father and Charlotte had been in Manchester some days, Emily had walked out toward dark, and that night until the morning she lay next to the man from the island of Hirta in the St. Kilda archipelago in the Outer Hebrides. She did it because she wanted to; she never did anything without wanting it.

His bed was narrow, and she did not remove her chemise and thin petticoat; she slept with her face to his broad back, nose against his undershirt. Her little breasts had pushed against her chemise buttons to his back. He turned, his arm around her.

She had stayed two nights and yet they had done no more. She had said no. Sometimes she kissed him, but only when she wished. She was wary that she would give something of herself that she could never entirely take back. She was already so taken with the loneliness, pride, and mystery of him that she could no longer stay away. There had been this strange transference of caring. She now shared his sorrows and hopes, keeping them within her, fastened there, unshakable.

And yet she had said no and at sunrise had walked home aching with unfulfilled sensuality. She was wary of sensuality. From what she heard from other women in cottage gossip, the more it was fulfilled, the more it turned to disappointment and regret.

But her time alone with Jonathan was the loveliest she had known since she had sat as a child writing at the parlor table with her brother and sisters. There they had created worlds and known they could do anything while they huddled together.

During those two nights in the stone cottage and a few after, she and Jonathan had spoken of things that they had been reluctant to speak of before. Darkness allowed it. He had told her that he had two children and how he missed them. She felt tears on his face and was awed. With every confidence exchanged, she felt she was becoming him and he her. She trusted him; she knew he would stop when she said no.

And yet there was always the possibility she would say yes. She liked having that power.

Emily returned to him often in the lovely late summer when her father's eyes were newly good, and when the bailiff had come to arrest her brother, and she had finished the novel.

As this was her first novel, Emily did not expect all the things she felt when it was done. First, of course, there was relief; her body ached with so much writing and her mind was tired. Then came grieving the loss of the daily world of the people within it and hearing them talk. It was as if she were in the wrong body and time, for she had lived through all the characters for many months. She felt so close to them.

Eventually, the need to share was greater than her need for secrecy. One evening, as she sat with her sisters sewing in the parlor, she asked, "Did you know I've written a novel?"

They both turned their heads to her.

"It surely must be compelling," Charlotte said wistfully, "but we of course will never know, as it's likely to remain hidden in your room until we and everyone else in this world are ghosts."

That did it. Emily bolted up the stairs and seized her manuscript from her room, rushed back, and dropped it on the dining table. "Read it and do what you like with it!" she said. "Maybe it will be worth a few pounds, though it's very strange and who knows who will buy it! No one is buying either of yours. All three novels should perhaps languish together."

"It's brilliant!" Charlotte exclaimed on an early evening two days later, when Emily came in from the rain. "We passed the pages on as we read." Anne smiled at her happily. Then silence fell upon the room.

Charlotte dusted a speck from her skirt, eyes cast down, and said gently, "Brilliant but…one quibble, dear. The ending."

Charlotte was wearing her darkest brown dress, worn at the bottom from sweeping over cobbled streets and the rough floor of the cellar. The hem had been replaced several times. Staring at a loosening thread, Emily asked, "The ending? What's wrong with the ending?"

She suddenly disliked the parlor.

Charlotte looked at Anne as if for support. She said softly, "I so hoped the lovers could marry happily in the end when Heathcliff finally repents! Just that, dearest."

Emily could feel a hard stubbornness forming in her stomach as if something would not agree with her. She said, "But he doesn't repent. And neither does she."

Then Anne rushed forward and took Emily's arm. "Lotte,

shush. Darling Emily, don't change a word of it. It's wild and wonderful."

The lump inside Emily hardened more. "Well, I won't change a word," she replied coldly. "Send yours out again with mine, if you're not too ashamed of it, but this is how I write, how I am. Anyway, it's not mine anymore. The minute I gave it to you, it wasn't mine."

19

Charlotte

Now there were two novels in one packet wrapped in butcher paper: *Wuthering Heights* and *Agnes Gray* were sent out together, offered as a set. And because Charlotte bothered to take them to the post office, she also one last time sent her novel *The Professor* to a new publisher. The effort this cost her was great; she tried not to care, which was not possible. Coming home, she fell into a bad headache.

"I knew it," she said when, a week later, her novel was returned to her.

But when she tore open the paper, a letter fluttered out. Sitting down by the bowl of apples in the kitchen, she read it breathlessly. It conveyed that though the reader for the London publishers Smith, Elder & Co. had declined *The Professor,* the firm would be happy to consider another work. Charlotte bit her lip. What other work? Stories did not grow as easily as apples.

It was then that she remembered the chemise drawer in her room with the well-washed private garments and, under them, the unfinished story that she had written in that room in Manchester while her father's eyes were healing. It was the story of an orphaned girl who finds work as a governess in a gloomy mansion, where she falls in love with the master and he with her. There was, however, an impediment of a mad wife hidden in the attic.

He might like that or the devil with him!

Over the next few weeks, Charlotte finished her book.

Enclosed in her room, she wrote. She came down to meals and crumbled her bread, or she did not go and woke famished in the middle of the night. The dogs sniffed at her at the bottom of the stairs. Faint moonlight came through the bare window.

Her sisters and father slept. Her brother crept in late like a guilty ghost, falling against the banister, muttering, "Damn, damn…" Once he fell against the clock, which rocked. For days she watched it warily, but it ticked on.

September arrived. The heather was hot and sweet, and the wild high moorlands grass thick. Charlotte still worked in her room. In her mind, she didn't live in a small parsonage but in a great house. Upstairs was the madwoman in the attic, and the bitter man who was her hero was walking in the door. She heard his boots on the floor.

And then Branwell's defensive voice rushed through her dream, and her father coming down the steps with his broken shout, "What are you doing to me? Why do you bring ruin about my life, my only son?"

Charlotte hurried out with the lamp and threw herself between them. Anne ran down crying, her hair all loose, her slender feet bare.

A few weeks later, with things hardly calmer at home, a sleepless Charlotte made her way to the post office, her new novel wrapped in brown paper, knotted with twine, and addressed to the London publishers. The accredited author on the title page was Currer Bell.

Someone (halfway across England, in London, in an office up narrow steps) would receive it. He would perhaps be standing, his top hat not removed, untying the twine, unwrapping the brown paper. He would leaf through the first few pages. Perhaps he would take them to his chop house and read them there in a booth that was centuries old. And he would send it back again.

As she came home from shopping one morning, the postmistress's nephew trotted toward her with a letter. "For you, miss," he said.

By midafternoon she cried into her handkerchief. He said he loved the novel and thought it was extraordinary; he had read it in one day, he said, canceling any plans. It was going to press at once. But maybe that is how he felt yesterday, not today. She was not calm.

Five weeks following, she received a package from London with the printed copy of her book in green cloth covers and took it into the parlor.

She lifted it to her lips and then held it against her heart, feeling how it moved with her breath, though she held so tightly that no page could open, no scene escape behind a chair or in a sofa cushion.

Going to the door, she whispered loudly, "Emily! Anne. Oh, darlings, come!"

They emerged from the kitchen with dish towels and a half-peeled apple. She put her finger to her lips and drew them inside and closed the door.

Charlotte said, "Look," and set the book on the table.

They gathered around.

"It is real?" Anne asked. She opened the cover and looked down at the title page. She squealed, hands to her mouth. The apple rolled beneath the sofa. "Your book...your name! Assumed, but yours."

They whispered and hugged and read and reread the title page. They leafed through the pages. All the scenes were there; every word she had written. Emily had tears in her eyes.

Silence fell between them. Charlotte walked across the hall to her father's study and knocked on the closed door.

Patrick Brontë was at his desk, wearing his now customary dark glasses. Beneath them, his mended eyes seemed to say what they often did when he was working, that time was short and yet he loved her very much. He had marked his daily diary with appointments; it had not a free hour in it to drink an unrushed cup of tea.

"My dear girl," he said.

Charlotte held out her novel. She said, "I've written a book, Papa. I wanted you to know."

His eyes under the heavy brows crinkled with concern. "But dearest girl! Have you indeed? Why, it's printed and bound! What an unusual title. *Jane Eyre.*" He took it gingerly, as if it were fragile. He frowned. "But how will we pay for this expense?"

"They're paying me, Papa. I haven't taken the check to the bank yet. See, here it is."

He took off his glasses to study it. "What a huge sum! Is it really so? My brave, wondrous girl!"

He stroked the book cover and gently set it on his desk. He said, glancing at the closed door, "I think it's best, though, that you don't tell your brother, Lotte. You know how fragile he is. I've been writing to friends and relatives to see what they can offer him as a fresh start."

Bile rose in her throat. She thought bitterly, Oh God, always my brother! But she soon forgot that. All that day she was dazed, walking into furniture, tucking things into the wrong cupboards, running to the bookshelf where they had now set the first copy of *Jane.* Her brother would not notice it anyway, and besides, who was this fellow, Currer Bell?

She thought, How could I have done it? It's too personal. Now the world will know what I think. But they will not, of course. No one would ever think it was me. Oh, does it matter?

She walked out on the moor, through the drying late October, and told the sky, "I am so happy."

20

Emily

The first great snow fell in December, and the local newspapers when they could be delivered gave reports of lost sheep. For a few days no one could walk out on the moor, and they begged their father not to go on parish calls. Nicholls went instead with the horse and cart. A smaller publisher had agreed to bring out *Wuthering Heights* and *Agnes Grey,* though, as with their poetry book, the sisters had to bear most of the costs, as he doubted the novels would sell much, if at all. In the end, they paid more than thirty pounds. Emily gave in because Anne wanted it so much.

The snow on the cobbles turned gray with coal dust. People struggled up the street with cloth wrapped around their hands and clanking lunch pails to their factory jobs. The Haworth shops waited long for goods to come by train from London; word was that cargo ships unloaded slowly. On New Year's Eve, Patrick Brontë gave a Watch Night service to say goodbye to the old year and welcome the new one. At midnight, when the year turned to 1848, the church bells rang and people banged pots through the village.

In the parsonage, they tried to stop window drafts with cloth and paper, but still the cold forced its way into the rooms.

A few days before, she and Anne had received the first printed copies of their novels. Anne was delighted and Emily not happy that she had ever allowed such a thing. She would tell no one about it (they had agreed on that anyway) but one person. She gave the lad Charlie of the Black Bull's host a wrapped copy of *Wuthering Heights* to deliver to Jonathan if he could. The lad completed the errand and said the tall shepherd had given him a penny for his pains.

She thought perhaps he was angry with her, for she had stayed only one more night with him for fear of discovery. A week passed, and no answer came.

Curled newspapers and journals arrived from London in January and February with reviews of *Jane Eyre* and *Agnes Grey*. Charlotte's reviews were ecstatic. Anne's were complimentary, though not ravishing. But most critics did not like *Wuthering Heights*.

"A disagreeable story," they called it. "As a whole, it is wild, confused, disjointed, and improbable but with a strange power," and "the only consolation...is that it will never be generally read." Someone else felt differently and wrote, "This is a work of great ability."

"Which it is," said Anne wisely.

Emily cut out her reviews and took them to the cold church to read, wanting solitude more than warmth. The words seemed real and then again not. She reread with tears in her eyes because she could not let her sisters see that she cared.

Hearing the curate Arthur Nicholls approaching, she fled to the nearby path sparsely dotted with houses and walked up and down there. She did not want this dry, emotionless man to see her. Besides, any vague romantic future she had hoped he would have with Anne had dissolved. Nor did he like Emily, and as for Charlotte, he was so uncomfortable with her that he avoided her presence.

Emily was nursing her father and Anne, who were both sick with dreadful colds and did not walk out on the moors, but neither did she forget the shepherd. Since she had spent those nights wrapped in his arms, she longed for him. But what if he had loathed the novel?

The snow had stopped this February day an hour before dusk. The land hesitated between seasons. But with many things to do, she did not set out until later afternoon.

Emily held her waterlogged skirts up, crossing the stepping

stones over the black-silver water of moor streams, which held the fading light. All above her, low clouds covered the sky. One moved, and the sliver of moon glowed.

It was almost dark when she reached the hilltop above Jonathan's stone cottage. The air smelled of chimney smoke.

The colors of the heavy quilt on the bed warmed the room, as did the small fire. Jonathan sat at the table in his stocking feet eating bread and cheese.

"Emily," he said joyfully, rising. His face was open, warm, and tender. She rushed across the room as he stood, and they kissed. She explained, "I couldn't come—first my father, then Tabby…"

She felt the strength of him when he pulled her close and the strange feelings that arose bewildered in her angular body. He wanted to kiss her more, but she drew back and shook her head. She walked to the sampler on the wall near the bookshelf and blurted, "Did you loathe it? My story?"

"Loathe it? I have never read anything that captivated me more. How the characters are trapped, all in their own way. How complicated it all is."

"Oh, Jonathan! The world would condemn me utterly for writing such a story if they knew I was a woman. Some condemn me already."

He walked to her and held her against him. He said, "The world cannot know what to do with a brilliant woman. A brilliant, penniless one is worse. Do you know you are writing about me as I might have been?"

She shook her head. "If you mean my wild Heathcliff, you're nothing like him."

"I would have grown like him had I stayed on the island. I have made people very unhappy in my rages when they burst out. I wanted to be something different, to find a different world. They needed me in the place they wanted me, they wanted me to have a faith I did not. I became bitter. But here I've found peace and you."

"What can you see in me? The novel's failed. Most people

don't like it. I hoped to earn money from it for my family. I can't write the pretty redeeming things people want."

"I love that you can't."

He kissed her. She turned her head away. "It's dark," she said, brooding. "I should go back. But it's too late. I shall lie in your bed again and tell them tales. I knew coming this hour, I wouldn't return."

"But this deceit won't be forever. And I can't just let you go tonight. I have news." He spoke to her hair. He said, "My solicitor friend in Scotland has sent word that my wife desires to annul our marriage for desertion. I'll soon be a free man."

Emily walked some feet away, kicking the small shabby rug by the bed. She made her voice low. "What is that to me?" she asked.

He sat down by the table. She saw his unhappy face and hurried across the floor, dropping to her knees beside him, stroking his unshaven cheek, saying, "I didn't mean it that way. You want a lover."

He stroked her hair. "I want to marry you."

"Oh, that's worse!"

"Worse? Isn't that what your sisters and all girls dream of?"

"They may, but not me."

She kissed his cheek above his beard again, and then his mouth. "Very well then," she said. "I will say what I felt the first time I saw you when I was very young, for I *did* see you then. Perhaps it was a vision of the future. I didn't know who you were, but I think I wound the mystery of you into my childhood stories. I'm beginning to love you. I always did, but you were a dream. Do you see why I ended my novel so there could be happiness only after death?"

She frowned. "But in marrying, you'd own me in a way. My body wouldn't be my own anymore. I couldn't have my own thoughts. I'd cease to exist. If I had to choose, I'd rather be a lover than a wife. Marriage isn't the beginning but the end of love. Do you understand?"

He looked stubbornly at her. "No," he said.

"Though it was once for you."

"That was then. How lovely it is now! I long for you and you long for me. But I'm not keen to wait for happiness until death. I am not that selfless. I like being in the flesh now you're here with me. I never cared for it much before. But there is marriage and marriage. Consider it!"

Later Emily lay with him dreamily, feeling the rise and fall of his bare chest under her hand. His chest hair quivered by the firelight.

She loved the shape of his hand with the scar on one palm. She ran the backs of her fingers over his stubble and his lips. That night, more than ever before, all his life passed into her and hers into him. She felt him climbing the cliffs of Hirta. She felt his grief and rage at his loveless marriage and the strength of his arms as he rowed away through the fierce sea, weeping that he would never see his children again. And she knew that he had taken her feelings inside him: her grief about her brother, her worries over her aging father, her restlessness, her fear of being without people to love, the anxiety of being trapped by the needs of others.

Marriage meant arguments about money and tasks and neighbors and appearances. Being lovers was jealousy and suspicion. In both, a woman was never absolutely herself again.

Desire pulled you, ruled you.

But even holding that back, had it not already begun to invade her? Did part of her long for it while the other part disagreed? That ache between her legs and in her breasts? If he knew it, she would deny it. She suspected he knew.

"I'll stay until morning," she had said. "I planned it."

"What will they say at home?"

"I'll make up some story. As you say, I'm good at stories, though of all the stories I could tell, they'd never believe that I have a sweetheart."

In the darkest part of the night, when the moon hid behind

deep clouds, they were awake again and whispering. She said, "When I was a child, we'd watch great storms through the window. Branches fell, and once a tree was uprooted. My aunt said, 'Come away from the door!' but I opened it and didn't move. My hair blew loose, and the wind rushed past me and filled our hall with leaves and dry heather. I'd say, 'Stop, storm,' and eventually it would be still. I believed it stopped because I asked."

"So you have the power to stop storms?"

"I did it a few times. It hasn't come lately. I'm losing that power. I was told once that when I gave myself in love, my power would go."

Emily slept with her hand on his chest, feeling his heart, which beat so steadily. She could calm the storms and tell them to go back; she believed it and had done it. Her second wish had been to fly to arouse her eldest sisters from the grave, but she had doubted too much to try. The third she had to choose carefully. She had only three. She believed that.

She rose early next morning, slipping from his arms, kissing his sleeping face. She walked in the dawn with dim light rising on the horizon and quails and rabbits stirring, her skirt still muddy from last night. She made her way through the moor gate by the parsonage.

She remembered his promise. "I'll be here," he said. "The day after tomorrow if you wish to bring your sisters to meet me." She was so much in the memory of it that she was startled to find Charlotte standing in the kitchen, rushing up to her. "Where have you been?" Charlotte demanded. "I hardly slept with worry. Emily!"

No not both sisters, Emily thought firmly. Only one.

She waited until nearby bedtime, when she and Anne walked their usual nightly way through the parsonage rooms to make sure the fires were banked, and no candle left burning. Tabby was already upstairs asleep, and their father had wound the clock and gone to bed.

She heard Anne's skirt, with its few petticoats beneath, swish against the arms of chairs as they walked together, leaving each room in darkness. A cat's eyes shone from under the stairs.

They paused in their father's study between the dark shape of the cabinet piano and the desk chair. There Emily would have spoken but Anne felt for Emily's hand and spoke first in a soft voice. "It's not Mrs. Hawkins' house that sheltered you last night, Emily, is it? I think you were somewhere else."

Emily also kept her voice low. "I've been wanting to tell you, Anne. It's such a strange secret that it feels not entirely real and yet I must say something, or I'll burst of it. Do you recall the man in the stone cottage I spoke of a few years ago?"

Anne's voice grew wary. "Yes, that stranger. You promised you'd not see him again."

"I did. I wanted to see him. I'm a little in love with him."

Emily could feel her sister's start. "Dear Lord, who is he? Has anyone met him? This person no one knows, and now you tell me… It can't be." Anne dropped heavily into the desk chair.

Emily knelt beside her. "But it is," she said. "I never intended it to happen. He's unlike anyone else in the world. He's nothing to be afraid of. He's kind. He's good."

"Oh, Lord, have mercy, is that where you are all night? Is he your lover?"

"No."

"But you've stayed with him. What else can I think, Emily? This is worse and worse."

"It's not. I want you to meet him. He'll wait all day tomorrow for us. He told me. Charlotte wouldn't understand. You come, and when I'm ready to tell her, you can say it's all right. Darling, do come!"

Anne hesitated for a long time. Her voice was low and uncertain in the darkness of her father's study. "I will come," she said at last.

The late-winter day was cold but still and threatened snow. As they helped each other over rocks, Emily let the words and stories she had hidden for years spill out. She talked of Jonathan in a fast, excited voice. "He's first from the Outer Hebrides and then Glasgow, and now here."

Anne tugged back on her hand. "How do you know it's true?" she asked stubbornly. "Men say anything to take a woman's virtue and make her belly swell. Not you, for your menses hardly ever come. But he'd leave you with a broken heart...a shattered spirit, a disillusionment, Emily. You know what you write, not what is in the world." Anne pulled Emily's sleeve and stopped her. Her wet eyes pleaded.

"I know the world."

"You don't! You're a kind of child! A wise woman and a child, Emily!"

Sometimes there was a path and sometimes not. Older snow hid in crevices of walls and in patches of bracken. Emily held Anne's hand firmly as they climbed the hill, as if her sister would slip away. She understood the gravity of this day. Anne, who had been coauthor of the stories they had written together on tiny paper, tucked away in a box in Charlotte's wardrobe, would now know all of her.

On the hilltop at last, they looked down at the stone cottage. Anne was breathing fast. Emily said, "Wait here and I'll tell him you've come. You will like him so much."

The barn door below was open, and she reached over the stall door to feed the mare some windfall apples she had brought. Then she hurried through the small barren garden, calling, "Jonathan!"

No answer came.

Emily opened the unlocked door.

Over a chair hung the same shirt that had been there when she had left him. The same cups and plates they had used still sat on the table. That was unusual. He was very neat, washing things at once. But where was he? Had he gone away? And for what reason? He'd told her he'd wait the whole day for her.

His good shirt was gone.

"Jonathan?" she called.

The word echoed to the whitewashed walls and the faded framed sampler.

"Jonathan?" she called again wistfully, touching his dried socks before the extinguished fire.

Emily slowly climbed back up the hill, where Anne was waiting for her. It took her a moment to speak. "He's not there," Emily said at last, bewildered. And Anne put her arm around her and said with the greatest comfort, "He must have been called away. He'll be there next time. We'll make another time to come."

He had promised. He knew how important it was to her, this first attempt to bring the various parts of her life together. Her rage rose. She had long been angry at all the men in the world who did not make her sisters' dreams come true. And in the man in the stone cottage, she believed she had found one truly honest man.

In the morning, she tried to bake and burned the bread. She threw off her apron and glanced out the window. She drew in her breath. Jonathan was standing in the yard by the washhouse.

Emily ran out through the kitchen door and pushed at his chest with both hands. She felt the thick homespun wool of his shirt. He stumbled back at her ferocity. She exclaimed, "You weren't there!"

"I'm so sorry. Did you bring your sister to meet me? I forgot… Please forgive me. I walked out to see a friend. He's not been well."

"What friend? When we walked home, my sister asked if I knew one soul who knew you."

"What are you saying? I have some friends, one for a long time. Do you think I only wait for you? I'm not that solitary." He glanced at the parsonage disdainfully and said, "As for your father's house, I have not been invited in."

"No, not yet. Maybe not ever, now."

He was breathing heavily, one fist on his hip. "Oh, that

makes it easy to proceed with you. Then tell me: Who do you think I am? A chained convict somehow escaped? For what crimes was I in my prison ward? Murder? Abduction? Who am I? What do you think I do all the time when I wait so patiently for you? I visited my sick friend. You may believe it or not. Perhaps you think you can put me down like a half-finished book, and come back the year later and take me up again? That's how you've treated me. My first crime is that I left a place that stifled me. The second is that I love you enough to wait just for you."

She clung to her anger. "You keep so apart that no one knows you," she whispered, trying to keep her voice down. No one else was at home, but perhaps they would come. "You might as well be a dream."

"Your postmistress has seen me," he said insistently. "And those about your town and nearby. You are not the only person in my life, Emily."

They stood so close that she smelled the wool of his cloak, the scent of old fires from his house, and the books.

He asked, "Do you have a pencil in your apron, and paper? Give it to me and I will write something down for you."

Jonathan knelt to balance the page on a stone. She looked down at his golden rough hair and the anger in his neck and shoulders. "Here," he said, standing, giving her the paper. "My friend Michael Longfield has a small shop of books and sundries in Keighley by the river. I've known him a very long time. He'll tell you of me. The door's blue, weather-worn."

"I don't believe you."

"Then suit yourself and go or not. I will be waiting for you, but not forever. Remember that, Emily. I damn well will not wait for any woman forever. Not even you."

They parted abruptly, and when she looked back, he had gone. She returned to the house, listening to the silence. She was glad no one was home, though she would have preferred Anne to be there. She had never been in love before, and how she had challenged him in her anger shook her. Perhaps she would never see him again.

If this was love, it could stay in her mind. No, she would not go to Keighley. She would not give him that satisfaction. Then she became busy with things she had promised, and in the evening was sorry she had not gone after all. She felt the edges of the address he had given her in her pinafore pocket.

After sleeping badly, she set out the next morning with many conflicted feelings to walk the few miles to where she had said she would not go.

Emily heard the river before she saw it. The water churned green from the looming worsted factories. Her father said these factories with their mechanical looms were ruining the land.

She discovered some narrow side streets lined with stone boardinghouses, a few sinking into the ground. Workers lived here. She passed under laundry hanging between high windows and looked into the window of a shop that sold offal and another for old cloth. Some shops were shuttered.

Emily circled twice through a cul-de-sac with a boarded chapel whose sign was blurred by rain. When she reached for the address in her pocket, her fingers found only thread and cloth. For some time, she walked the streets but found no shop with a blue door. She thought she had gone one way and then another. Then it's true, she thought. I can't trust him.

She walked moodily home.

In the parlor, yesterday's newspaper lay on the sofa and a teacup sat on the table. Through the open study door across the hall, she saw the curate, Nicholls, reading to her father. The young man nodded to her and smiled slightly. Her sisters were washing their stockings in the great stone kitchen sink. She hesitated before the clock on the stairs, wondering which way to go.

Then, when unbuttoning her dress in her room, she noticed one of the older cats pawing at a paper beneath the desk. Kneeling, she discovered the address of the shop, which might have fallen from her pocket. Her anger softened. I will try once more to find his supposed friend, she thought. And if I do not succeed, I will never see Jonathan again.

The man in the stone cottage would become a dream, no more.

She was busy the next morning, but in the afternoon, she laced her mother's boots and walked out.

Fog had settled in Keighley by the river. The top floors of the worsted factories were lost in it, as were streets, which began and then seemed to fade into nothing. She could barely read the street names on buildings. Some had faded to illegibility.

Another narrow alley opened before her.

From it came an old woman with a heavy bundle of washing on her back. Emily asked, "Is this Dorking's Way? I am looking for Michael's Sundries."

"Walk through the alley. Knock loudly. He's a bit deaf."

Then it was there, as he had said.

The alley between two brick warehouses, wide enough for only one person to pass, opened to a small square. She made out a pub with dull lantern light through the window and heard the voices of a few men within. She walked farther past a shop for secondhand furniture and there, next to it, was a wooden hanging sign reading *Michael's Books and Sundries.* The words were so worn, she could hardly read them.

Emily walked down the few stone steps, put her hand on the blue door, and bent her head to enter the shop.

It was at first seemingly a small shop but then she saw it went on in turns. Chairs and piles of dusty dishes and pots were stacked high, while women's worn dresses floated disembodied from the ceiling. As she walked down one narrow aisle, she passed boxes and boxes of books. It was as if some great hand had opened the roof and stuffed everything inside. Having walked it, she saw it was small indeed.

One candle burned on a desk, where a man was reading.

His coat was wrinkled, worn, and made for someone bigger. From what she could see, he was twice the age of her friend. Tangled silky white hair fell to his shoulders, and he wore, on the top of his head, a deep purple cap, the sort she had seen on pictures of bishops. His face, when he raised it, looked kind and intelligent.

The smell of tobacco lingered in the crevices of the hanging dresses. She touched the edge of a bookshelf, and her fingers left a print in the dust.

"Young lady, are you seeking books or dresses?" the old man asked. "We have it all. A pot? A wig? But your hair is too pretty for that."

"I am looking for Michael Longfield."

He paused and struggled with a cough and then said simply, "I am he...and therefore you must be Jonathan's friend. He was here a few days ago because I was a little ill and he is careful of me, as if he were my son. I gave him a three-volume Shakespeare: all the plays, tragedies, histories, comedies. He put it in his rucksack; it was heavy. He talked of you, but I can't recall your name. He mentioned that one day he'd send you to meet me."

"My name is Emily," she said. "He said he's known you a long time."

"Indeed, he has. I watched him grow. We knew each other from Hirta. He felt a love with our island as I felt it and then the same heartbreak to leave it. You're fortunate you found this shop. I must write a sign on the wall at the alley entrance so people will take the proper turn. Look about. I have this letter to finish. I'll be with you soon."

He resumed writing, and she wandered amid shabby trunks, stopping to read their pasted labels. Paris, one said. Calcutta another. Who among the folk in the factory streets of Keighley took such voyages? But her body felt languid. The air of the shop was close.

Returning to him, she asked, "So, you're his closest friend?"

"I am. He doesn't trust people easily, but he trusts you and me. I do think we go about the world looking for a person meant for us. We are wanderers, and then we dare with that person to be known for who we are. We dare to stop wandering."

"Has he found this person?"

"He came a long way to do it. Look in that mirror and see her." She looked in the small oval tarnished mirror. Her reflection wavered a bit. She looked wary.

"Tell me about him on the island," she said.

Then in half sentences, interspersed with "you know," or "likely he's said this," he told her about Jonathan as a long-legged boy carrying the books found in the boat. He told her many things, some of which she felt she knew but did not know how.

Emily saw the reflection of the old man in his purple skull cap behind her in the mirror, nodding, smiling. "And now I have told you," said the old shopkeeper. "And now you know."

Emily, looking out through the dirty shop windows, saw darkness coming. How had it come so soon? Michael Longfield said, "My clock had stopped. Do return to see me, dear girl."

"I shall."

She walked home thoughtfully by the light of the moon, having no idea how long she had been away. She only wanted to be with Jonathan again behind the closed door of his cottage, her hand in his. She wanted to tell him how sorry she was she had ever doubted him.

As she approached the bridge into Haworth, the upper part of her mother's left boot split open from the sole. There was no more mending them—the shoemaker had said that. Tears filled her eyes. She walked as best she could, limping a little up the street on the icy stone cobbles, finding her way by a few lanterns in windows, for the moon had gone and the darker part of the night enclosed her.

Jonathan MacConnell was waiting by the cottage door the next morning. Emily hurried through the bitter wind of the moor and scrambled down the hill, to throw her arms about him. She felt the beating of his heart. "I'm here for you," she said breathlessly. "I'll always be."

21

Charlotte

But why do I feel so melancholy? thought Charlotte as she huddled in a chair by the parlor fire on this wretched day. Even her fingers were cold and moved a little clumsily as her neat little stitches followed one after another on the waistband of a new petticoat for Anne.

The truth was that the sadness had been coming on for days, perhaps before. It ached subtly inside her little body. Being alone made it worse. An hour before, she had heard the heavy front door of the parsonage close followed by steps on the path and voices. Anne and her father had sung out their goodbyes and braved the wind to go visiting. Emily had left earlier in the way she suddenly disappeared more often these days. Oh, that sister of hers! Even Tabby was away. The only sounds were the fire licking the logs and Anne's spaniel snoring lightly from her blanket bed in the kitchen.

Gradually Charlotte stopped stitching and rested her hand on the unfinished petticoat.

But why do I feel this way? she asked herself.

By some miracle after so many failures in her life, she had accomplished the task laid upon her when she was a small girl dressed all in black standing uncomprehending at the burial of her mother. There someone had leaned down to tell her that she was responsible for her family now: her weeping siblings, her devastated father who could hardly stand at the church service, and the unpaid bills.

She had done it. She had made the house secure. Had she ever imagined it would be from writing a story?

Open hand still laid protectively on the unfinished petticoat, she looked at her life over the past months since *Jane Eyre* had sold.

Because of her income (and more to come from new printing and translations), the family could afford house repairs and new clothing. They could afford candles. She had helped her father through his eye surgery, ensuring his work here was secure. Even Branwell was turning a corner, happy to be at home. A month or so ago, he had rattled on for an evening about his new plans to become a great essayist. He had spoken rapidly, brilliantly, about the writings of Samuel Johnson. He would see this through.

True, the banker always looked at her oddly when she deposited the drafts. Where did the money come from? Who was earning it? Perhaps Patrick Brontë's cousin had died at last and left the parson his fortune. Only Charlotte knew there never had been a cousin. Her father had confessed it to her after surgery. He had let them think it all these years so they wouldn't worry.

That was her father, so kind when you really needed it!

Little did he dream that his plainest, dullest daughter would rescue them.

Charlotte looked at the thread paper on the little table which was almost empty. She would put the petticoat away and go out to buy more thread from the little village shop to finish her work. Perhaps if she went out, she could shake her heavy feeling.

Taking her basket and drawing her coat and shawls tighter, she managed to push open the parsonage door into the wind. It had come suddenly, suddenly rising from the earth, rushing past the surrounding farmhouses, driving sheep into a huddle. She pressed down on her skirt to keep her ankles covered.

In the dressmaker's shop, the proprietress looked up from her own sewing and called, "You're out in the weather, Miss Brontë! Bitter cold, is it not?"

Charlotte bought thread, wistfully noting the bolt of yellow satin. Yellow satin was for brides. Anne would marry one day and leave them. It was just a matter of time. Charlotte would make the dress of course. She would manage that as well. She would manage a bright smile as she kissed Anne goodbye to leave them forever for married life far away.

Charlotte pushed outside to the street again.

The wind was behind her now, chilling her wool-stockinged legs under her petticoats. It pushed her so that she almost careened into one of the church members as he emerged from the stationery shop. They greeted each other and she slipped past him inside.

The smell of paper and book binding met her. It was the very same shop where she had first come with her sisters to buy paper when they were all small. Greenwood, who had grown old, sold and rented books now as well. He rose slowly from his stool, stooping.

"Bitter cold, Miss Brontë," said old Greenwood.

She replied, "Good day, Mr. Greenwood. Bitter indeed! I'd like fifty sheets of loose paper and two bound writing books, if you please."

But truth be told, it was not for paper she had come. It was more of a visit to herself for just to her left, tucked into a bookcase of volumes to buy or rent as she knew it would be, was a copy of her novel *Jane Eyre*. Charlotte touched it with the tip of one gloved finger.

"Ah, that book," old Greenwood said as he wrapped the paper for her. "Read it?"

"I have not."

"My wife can't put it aside. You can hardly peruse the news journals without seeing the author's name. Currer Bell. Six months ago, no one heard of him. That's the way fame comes, but I wouldn't know. Lucky fellow. A lucky thing to have a bit of fame, not that any of us will know. Not in this dull little town. No one in the great world will know when we pass on."

In the street once more, Charlotte hardly felt the wind. The touch of her book remained in her fingers. Oh yes, Currer Bell was lucky! So many strangers wrote letters to him care of her publisher, who forwarded them on. They praised his writing and invited him to literary gatherings and bookish teas to which of course he could not come.

Well, who was this man, Bell? She had imagined him as very tall, bone thin, and unmarried. He did not smoke and ate no meat. Over the months, since his name had appeared on her novel, he seemed so real it was as if he existed apart from her.

Glancing in a shop window as she walked farther down the street, Charlotte saw her small, severe face beneath her bonnet reflected in the glass.

Anne would fall in love and marry. Emily would do heavens knew what. But she, Charlotte, would remain alone. And when she died, the mourning card and church ledger would list her only as *Charlotte Brontë, spinster.* All she had bravely done would be attributed to this ridiculous man, this Currer Bell.

She thought, Dear God! Is this all there is for me? Is this all the world will ever know?

She did not understand, as she pushed up the street, if the wind made her eyes water or if she had begun to cry.

Part VI

Spring–Summer 1848

22

No coward soul is mine,
No trembler in the world's storm-troubled sphere:
I see Heaven's glories shine,
And faith shines equal, arming me from Fear.

—Emily Brontë, from "No Coward Soul is Mine"

Charlotte

She tried to put her feelings aside. She busied herself with her new book, but even as spring came on in Yorkshire, with its green fields and wildflowers outside the door, the feelings did not leave. Once she saw strangers in the village saying they had heard the brilliant Bell lived in this area and longed to meet him. Another visitor knocked on the parsonage door to inquire. "Oh dear, are you looking for Mr. Bell?" Anne answered him seriously. "I've never met him, but I hear he lives in York. Yes, he has rooms in the Cathedral Close." Afterward, she burst into rich laughter.

It was only when Charlotte gathered another packet from her publisher at the post office containing yet more letters from Bell's admiring readers that she knew she could bear it no more.

Taking all her courage in hand, she walked briskly into the kitchen where her sisters were drinking tea, dropped the packet on the table and dusted her hands together. "Well, I've thought about it a great deal! The time has come for us all to go to London to meet my publisher and tell him we are not men at all, but three gifted women from Yorkshire."

Emily turned from slipping an unbaked apple pie into the oven, her face alert. "What?" she demanded. "Charlotte, are you mad? Only Papa knows. Not even friends or relatives. You promised when we agreed to publish. And strangers can look and look and never be the wiser."

Charlotte shook her head. "Maybe I want them to be the wiser. Everyone is beginning to say that Currer Bell wrote all three novels. That takes the credit from both of you. It's time to meet my publisher at least and tell him the truth."

Emily said flatly, "For you perhaps. I don't want them to know that I am who I am."

"Listen to me!" Charlotte sat down on the bench, putting her small fists on the table near the teapot. "I am so tired of not being myself."

Emily set the pie in the heated oven and closed the door sharply.

"But, Charlotte, we only adopted male names because we wanted to be taken seriously," Anne said tenderly, stroking her sister's arm. "And because of not wanting Bran to know that we published without him."

"We'll ask my publisher to keep it the secret."

Emily turned around, face darkened, arms across her chest. Her voice was scornful. "And how long would that secret remain? A minute? An hour?"

Anne looked from one sister to another. Her face grew thoughtful as she took a sip of tea. She said quietly, "But in the end, Emily, it's not such an awful idea. I'd like to see London. I never have seen St. Paul's. There's a train from Leeds that goes overnight. We'd arrive in the morning. Nothing would change." She was smiling broadly, yearningly. "To tell the truth, I would love it!"

Emily remained with arms crossed. "You know very well we can't leave Bran! And I wouldn't want to leave Papa."

Charlotte took Anne's arm. Her words rushed out. "But… but Tabby and Martha can manage things for a few days. We'll tell Papa we're visiting my old school friend in London and that we'll shop for any books he wants. And Anne can see the city. Then we'll come home as quiet as mice, and I'll finish the new book and make more money to repair the roof. And no one will ever know but my publisher."

Emily looked at them both haughtily. She said, "Well, you two silly creatures may reveal yourselves, but I remain your brother Ellis and I will never change my mind."

Charlotte and Anne hardly slept on the all-night train from Leeds to London, evaluating every strange man who came into their compartment as likely to press a knee against theirs or not. The train did not contain a ladies' car. By the time they arrived midmorning, their clothes were wrinkled and their bodies aching.

They found a hackney coach which slowly maneuvered between more carriages and omnibuses. Huge brick buildings were darkened with coal smoke. How fascinating it is, Charlotte thought. And terrifying. How do people live here and find their way home again?

She reached for Anne's hand.

They stopped in one of the narrow city streets with an ancient building looming above them and the booksellers' lane called Paternoster Row to the left. The reception office of the Chapter Coffee House Inn was paneled with dark wood, and a laconic boy rose to guide them up steps to their room, where even the wardrobe, dresser, commode, and bed seemed strange. But Anne hurried to the window and cried, "Oh, Charlotte! Oh, my dear! Here's the dome of St. Paul's, all green and dirty, rising above everything. Just like the picture in the Keighley library."

Charlotte joined her. The window and its sill were smudged with the remnants of coal fires; coal dust hung in the air. Everything was dirty, even pigeon droppings on the windowsill, now a grayish white.

"Isn't it marvelous!" exclaimed Anne. "Never mind sleep! Let's go make our revelation to your publisher first."

The air was dirty, but the day was mild as they lost themselves a few times in the winding streets of this oldest part of London.

Finally, someone pointed to the hanging sign of *Smith, Elder & Co.* on Cornhill. Holding Anne's hand, Charlotte entered the outer office.

No one sat at the desk.

Opening a second door, she was almost driven back by the shouts of men in heavy, dirty aprons and the cacophonous sound of the presses. She gaped at the printers. One man with inky fingers shouted over the noise, "Where's Peter? Damn that lad! Devil and his bitches take you! Don't put that there."

Catching sight of Charlotte and her sister, he removed his cap.

"Can we help you, ladies?" he asked, glancing at the others.

"Will you kindly tell Mr. Smith that we wish to speak to him?" Charlotte's voice was so soft, he had to bend his head to listen. The boy who had been cursed nodded and raced up the stairs.

Presses clanked, jerked, and fell silent as the men stared at them. She was aware of the patch in her dress where it had been burned by the fire last month. Now she could feel the tiny stitches against her ankle. She could feel her rough-cut fingernails under her glove.

A carriage rumbled by outside.

With it, footsteps sounded from above. "Oh, heavens, here he comes," Anne whispered. "I feel it can't be him."

Charlotte looked up the stairs, expecting a heavy-footed fellow of sixty with a large belly beneath his waistcoat. Instead, a beautiful young man descended fleetly toward them, the tails of his pale gray coat flapping against his long legs. "Yes, may I help you?" he asked, his tone puzzled.

"Mr. Smith?"

"I am he."

"The publisher?"

"The same. May I be of help?"

If she could run from the door! She did not. Only her hands trembled as she removed her glove and drew his letter from her reticule.

He took it, reading the address on the envelope. "Why, where did you find this?" he asked, frowning. "This is to my author Currer Bell. Are you come on his behalf? Is he ill?"

She was truly struck silent.

"Is Mr. Bell not well?" he demanded again.

The words burst from her. "But there is no Currer Bell. It is I who wrote *Jane Eyre.* Here's my sister Anne, whom you know as Acton. Our brother Ellis couldn't come. We are three writers, not one. No one else must know this."

Mr. Smith looked from one to the other, astonished, smoothing down his oiled, neatly parted hair. Then he broke into boyish laughter. "But this is marvelous! My friend Thackeray bet me ten shillings that the author of *Jane Eyre* was a woman. He was right and I must pay. Come upstairs to my office, if you please! Well, I never… My dear woman. *You* wrote *Jane Eyre*? Do you realize all literary London is wondering who you could be? What is your name, the real one, please? No one will ever know it, on my life."

She raised her head. "It's Charlotte Brontë," she said clearly. "From the parsonage at Haworth in Yorkshire. But you know that. Your letters went there."

I am truly here, she thought.

Portraits of great English writers from the past, which hung on the walls, seemed to welcome them as she and Anne climbed the stairs.

23

Emily

Since Emily had hurried back from the bookseller in Keighley that day to throw her arms around her exiled shepherd, a new closeness had opened between them. Now when she left the parsonage, the distance between them was less. This day she did not even notice when she passed the factories, the stepping stones of the streams, grazing sheep, startled birds, rushing in her dark dress, a slender, eager form. She walked there every few days now.

Sometimes she felt she went from one home to another.

"I'm here!" he called down from the roof when she ran down the hill. "Birds got in the chimney. My shirt's all gone with soot to the shoulder." It was indeed, smudging his face and hands as well. He climbed down the ladder saying, "Don't touch me. What news?"

"Charlotte and Anne are in London to see her publisher. So they shall show themselves as women, whereas I remain their inscrutable, lawless brother Ellis, who walks about with a dagger tucked into the waistband of my trousers and writes obscene, immoral books."

She wound her arms around him. He drew in his breath and moved his hand to the small of her back; he always seemed shy and startled when she first touched him and then slowly became the confident, seductive, and yet strangely priestly man. Like her brother, who should have been a brown-cowled monk among the broken stones of a long-abandoned crumbled monastery. Surrounded by the sea, of course.

When she told him that thought, he laughed. "I would be no monk," he said. But now he said huskily, "Soot over your dress."

"I can wash it and dry it in the sun."

"So they're away in London for a few days? Does that mean you can stay with me?"

"Yes, nights. Papa's visiting York with our dull curate Nicholls."

"Poor fellow, such scorn. He sounds like a good man."

"But so ordinary! In a way, I'm glad my sister Anne didn't see you that day, or she'd have fallen in love with you. I have asked her to visit with me again, but she won't. Sometimes I suspect she assumes I am making things up, which I did as a child."

"Such as?"

"Old Celts walking the moors. I did see them."

She brought her lips to his. So sweet…like fruit sometimes mixed with many other things. She felt the kiss down to her stomach and lingered until the feeling made her wary. She turned her face but laid her head on his shoulder.

He sighed. Then gradually his breathing calmed. He whispered, "You've saved my life; sometimes I am so lonely without you. Yesterday I would have come for you if I'd had your permission. When will you give me permission to come and meet your family and claim you?"

She did not know what she felt then; the desire both to rise up and go and to move closer fought in her. She played with the frayed edge of his jacket pocket. "Soon."

"The annulment should come any day now, and then…" His voice was a bit strained; she saw his Adam's apple as he swallowed and touched it. "And then there is the question whether you'd have me. Whether you would say aye and be my wife. It's you I want. No one else."

She waited, holding on to his hand. She said at last, "I'd have to leave my home. It's always been there for me."

"Ah, your beautiful parsonage home! I have never been inside it. One day. My dear love, as I sit here feeling almost one person with you, I look at the years ahead. Time will move and things will change. We'll be married. Your sisters will marry too. And your father can't remain there forever."

Emily drew back. "You're wrong!" she stammered. She wanted to break away, but he gently held her. "Papa will remain! He will never die or give up his work. He'll be ninety and mount the pulpit stairs. You don't know this about me, but if I want it enough, I can make time stand still."

She pulled away from him and walked inside, arms folded across her narrow chest. "And there's Branwell," she added. "I can't leave him."

But even as she spoke, she felt that Jonathan had spoken true words. Change would come. Anne and Charlotte would marry and go away, leaving her in the parsonage with her father, who would eventually grow old. After he died and another priest moved into the parsonage, where would she go? Perhaps she might find a little room above the dry goods shop off Main Street where in the evenings she would pace it alone with a biscuit for dinner. There would be a locked drawer stuffed with new poems. And Branwell? He would marry his love. He would be well. No person who was loved as much as Emily loved him could fail to thrive in this world.

Emily stopped in the middle of this cottage with its low-beamed roof and crooked books on the shelf and blue smock on a peg, her breath shorter. "What will be?" she murmured darkly, staring at the floor. "What is certain?"

"What is certain is that I love you. When the annulment comes, I'll go to your father's house and ask to marry you. We love each other. We can't hide forever. I'll care for your family. I'll help heal your brother. What's dear to you will be dear to me. Your sisters will go to new lives somehow, and I am waiting for you. You must not be afraid of the future. My darling girl, it is bright."

Later, she took his hand and gently bit each finger. He said, "I'll leave this place. We could move closer to your family."

"No, I love this house. If I say aye to you, I will stay. No, I spoke falsely. I can't stop time. I can't make one perfect moment in time to hold all I love…because if I did get back the two older sisters whom I lost to death so young, you wouldn't be there. One thing goes, and another comes. I hate it. I hate it."

She stayed the night, and she cried about time passing and losing things, while he held her in his bed. They talked together deeply of everything they had not spoken of before.

She did not tell him that she had returned to the shop in Keighley and found it abandoned. The sign had been taken away and the proprietor gone. A woman who lived across the close said the old man had locked up one evening and not come back. Through the dirty shop window, Emily had seen the books, the fading dresses, the piles of chipped dinner plates and teacups. But the door would not open, even when the landlord came with his heavy keys.

Jonathan would find out soon enough. The world is like a sea, he would say, tossing you and your boat helplessly about, and we must be gentle with each other. But she knew he would take it hard, so she took the coward's way, as she told herself, and put off any news that his friend had gone.

24

Charlotte

Charlotte had never experienced anything as wonderful as her few days in London, so apart from her mend-and-make-do life. She and Anne stood under the great rotunda of St. Paul's, explored the city, marveled at the fantastic buildings of Parliament and the palaces. They had been taken to the opera, where most women wore silks and they had only their plain traveling dresses. They were moved almost to tears by the sounds of the orchestra and the singers filling the theater.

Above all was the guiding presence of her courteous publisher, George Smith, who entertained them and, with a wink, swore to keep their secret. He had even told his mother and sisters that Charlotte and Anne were obscure authors visiting from the north, hence their accents.

That Anne had also been thrilled moved Charlotte.

And now it was over, and she walked again into her father's stone parsonage with its dove-gray hall and, in the parlor, Branwell's portrait of her and her sisters above the fireplace. She walked down the hall calling, "Emily!" and a voice answered, "Here."

Emily was in the yard henhouse, throwing grain from a bowl. A few new chicks had been hatched and stumbled about, fluffy and yellow.

Charlotte kissed her sister's cheek. She said, "Did anything happen much when we were away?"

"I found another kitten. I call him Falstaff."

"Were you here?"

"Where else would I be?" Emily replied curtly. "How did your publisher take your revelation?"

"He swore he'd keep our secret, so Anne and I are the Bell

brothers to the world, and you, of course, remain our brother, Ellis. Bold, striding Ellis."

Emily smiled, put down another bowl for Anne's little spaniel and the big, loping mastiff. Charlotte sank wearily to a stool near the washhouse and the full wicker basket of laundry. The world of London was fading from her, with its galleries of great paintings, the silvery high notes of the opera's soprano, the courtesy of Mr. Smith.

Charlotte said wistfully, "Washday tomorrow, I suppose."

"Yes. Bran hasn't brought down his things yet. He keeps saying, 'I'll do it.' Which means he likely won't."

"How is he…Branwell?" Charlotte asked, almost unwillingly.

Emily frowned; she waited quite still by the open washhouse, which smelled of last week's fire. "One day forward and the next day back," she said. "It breaks Papa's heart. Some days he drinks a lot. We sat outside by the wall one night and looked at the stars, and he seemed so calm, so rational. But yesterday he went off and didn't come back. I've been thinking."

"Tell me."

"We could go into his room and clean everything. It would give him a fresh start, as they say. Perhaps you'd help, and Anne?"

Charlotte bit her lip and then nodded slowly. If someone had told her that Branwell had emigrated to far countries at this moment, she would not have minded. He so pulled her from the dream of all that had happened in London.

She was sorrier still that she had agreed when, the next afternoon, having assured themselves their brother was away, they opened his door.

Branwell's narrow room was scattered with filthy clothes and socks near bed legs; the papers on the table were stiffened with spilled beer and the chamber pot uncovered and full. The rancid smell made Charlotte want to retch. "Oh, my heavens," she gasped, covering her nose. Stunned, the three of them put down mops, buckets, rags, and polish and looked about.

It seemed months, not a day, since she had returned from London.

Anne said dully, "I suppose we must begin." She crossed the clutter and opened the window. Cooler breezes from outside filled the room.

Emily tidied papers on the table. The opened drawers below were full of more loose papers and bills. Pages of his writing were strewn over the floor with lists of resolutions and plans. They walked over torn newspapers with encircled help-wanted announcements. They trod on scribbled unfinished poems.

In the bottom drawer, she found several pages folded together.

Emily stood amidst the shirts and coats on the floor, reading. "So he's writing a novel," she murmured. "It seems good. Maybe if he finished it, he could publish and be happy with himself. I'm sorry we published without him!"

Anne replied sadly, "You know why we did. Besides, do you think he can finish anything? Anything he does?" She knelt and reached under Branwell's bed for dirty shirts.

Emily pulled off the bedding, keeping her face to the side to avoid the smell. "Oh, Lord, those sheets! They need to soak all night in lye before washing." Then her voice grew sharper, and she added, "Oh God, sisters, look! What's this?"

Charlotte and Anne gathered before the rusty stains on the sheets and pillowcase. They fell silent.

Charlotte whispered at last, "Lord have mercy! He's coughing blood like our poor sisters did so long ago. Where is he?"

"With a friend to Leeds to see if a portraitist there will take him on."

"What kind of friend? Does he ever speak the truth as he destroys himself and expects his employer's widow to love him? Emily, he's got to see Dr. Gregory."

"He won't."

"Does Papa know?"

"About this? No. About the rest, he tries not to know."

That night Charlotte lay awake until she heard her brother come in, and then she crossed the hall with her candle to his room. It was now perfectly clean and smelled of soap and floor polish. She took in Branwell's hunched shoulders and evasive face. She put her hand on his arm and looked into his eyes. They glittered back coldly. He would have pulled away if she hadn't held him.

"Welcome home from London," he said hoarsely. "Whatever the hell you were doing there. Whenever the hell you got back. It would have been nice to go. I could have chaperoned you girls, seen a few friends from my art student days. Not proper for unmarried women to go about like that. We all would have had a good time."

No, we wouldn't have done, she thought, but she bit her lip and asked as quietly as she could, "Are you coughing blood?"

He spoke calmly. "It's nothing. Just once, never again."

"There was a great deal for only once."

"Stop questioning me! Who asked you to clean here? It's mine, mine. I admit I came from Leeds and went straight to a tavern on the road to Haworth. Yet as I entered there, I felt a change of heart come over me. I made to go, very coolly. 'Where are you going, Brontë?' they called. I'm resolved to live in a new way, a new life. I did spit blood, but thank God, it was a warning I'm turning now. I'm making myself something. I'm taking up portrait painting again. I was good at that. But none of you asked what really was the matter."

"Tell me then," Charlotte said.

"Mrs. Robinson's marrying someone else, someone with money. The slut is marrying for money."

"Oh, my darling, I am so sorry. Did you really think she would be true to you?"

"I did, I did."

He was sobbing; he covered his face with his hands. She whispered, horrified, "Oh, you dreamer! What will you do?"

"Stay here and be your good brother again," he said. "Start again if I can. Write a novel. They're hard to do."

"I hear they are," she said sadly. "But yours will be a great one."

Later that night, Charlotte returned to watch him sleeping. His face was at peace. She sat in a chair beside him with her hands clasped. "Please," she murmured. "Nothing else matters, not fame, not love…nothing else matters more than my brother. He doesn't have to save us. He only must be well."

Despite that conversation, bills from the Black Bull were once more presented weekly at the parsonage door. Over the next months, Branwell pawned some of the silver spoons for money for opium and drink; she and Martha went stone-faced to the pawnbroker in the poorest streets of the town and redeemed them. A month later, they found their brother collapsed in an alley.

Then all talk of his writing ceased.

He was well for a day, perhaps two. He was calm that night, they later said. No, he was not. Anyone can tip a candle; anyone too tired can fall asleep with one burning and a wind through the open summer window.

Charlotte sat up in bed at the sharp, piercing cry of Anne from the hall and hurried from her door. Emily in her nightdress was rushing toward Branwell, who was hardly dressed. Behind him, flames leaped and consumed the bed hangings up to the poles.

He waited unmoving. "Bedroom candle! Knocked it over."

"How, by God?"

"I don't know."

"Stand away!" Emily had seized the full bucket of water they kept on the landing. Anne followed with a second. Charlotte ran down for more and struggled to carry it, back aching, bare feet leaving marks on the wet floor. In her brother's room, water flooded every crack in the floorboards. By then, their father had come with his own bucket.

"Why was the candle lit?"

"Fell asleep reading… Very sorry…" Branwell muttered.

The clock struck four in the morning by the time the flames were out. Branwell was naked to the waist, his thin ribs pressed against his strained skin, blotched with soot and some kind of crawling rash.

"You must believe me," he said.

As their father took his son back to share his own bed, the sisters remained shivering, white bare feet wet, hair wet. The sodden bed hangings from his room drooped down.

"Sorry." They heard the fragment of their brother's voice from behind their father's bedroom door and their father's voice sounding like it did so many years ago when they were very small. "Shh… God was watching… All's well."

Emily was silent. Then the words burst from her. "I wish he were dead," she said. Everything poured out then. With her fist, she struck the doorjamb again and again. She shouted and yelled. Her fierce brown mastiff rushed up and down the stairs again, barking and howling as if he could not stop.

In the floor below, water dripped through the ceiling, seeping into the crate of copies of gift books sent from Charlotte's publisher, dampening the pages, staining the cloth covers of the first few.

From that time on, their father made Branwell sleep on a cot at the foot of the paternal bed. Emily, now calmer, waited in darkness in the hall before her room. "Heal him," she whispered. Deep within her body, she felt the old power that would let her stop a storm. "Heal him and I will be Yours only again, you elusive God to whom my father has dedicated his life. That is the price of my returning to You." Charlotte came from her room and held her. They stood together, clinging to each other. Anne joined them; she had come softly, like a ghost.

25

Emily

Through the late summer they hoped. Every morning when waking, Emily prayed for her brother to be restored to what he had once been and some hours it seemed as if he might. Once again, she despaired. Now and then she raged.

"Miss, miss, your brother's making a great drunken noise in the Black Bull!" Tabby exclaimed on a warm midafternoon as she limped in with the shopping basket. Emily flung down her sewing and ran outside. The noise of the men drinking and boasting carried past the church and graveyard.

Reaching the public-house door, she pushed past the others toward her brother. He had heard her voice and crouched at his table, leering at her, wiping his mouth with the back of his hand.

Emily felt her father also at her side, shirt half buttoned, coat half on with the right sleeve dangling. Patrick Brontë never appeared like that; he was careful how he presented himself. Still, he spoke so firmly, and like an old prophet, that he filled her with awe and shame at her own weak rage.

"Come, my son," her father said. "I think today's work is done."

She felt her father's arms about her. He spoke in the same voice he had years before when he had come to that wretched school and taken her and her sisters back home. "Come, my children," he had said.

At home, Branwell got as far down the hall as the stairs, where he sank down on the first stair and wept. Charlotte who had come down from her room remained angrily at the landing near the tall clock, but Anne ran down and threw her arms around him. "Little one, little one," she whispered, stroking his filthy hair. "Now come to bed, darling! You're wearing yourself down, my brother."

When at last he slept above, Emily said, "He has consumption. Dr. Gregory told me this morning when I saw him in at the gate. God knows what else he has destroyed in his poor body." Her voice rose throughout the small rooms of the parsonage. "Destroyed, destroyed, while we build, and all our lives are washed away tending him as he falls uselessly…"

Their father's voice echoed in her mind as he had taken his son against him in the bed of new clean linens the night of the fire, saying, *O my son, Absalom!*

Part VII

September–December 1848

26

A dreadful darkness closes in
On my bewildered mind;
O let me suffer and not sin,
Be tortured yet resigned.

—Anne Brontë from "Last Lines"

Charlotte

On a day when he seemed to be healing, the three sisters put on their stout shoes to walk on the moors, though Emily never liked the new boots she bought after her mother's boots could not be mended anymore.

They proceeded cautiously, for curlews and golden plovers nested here in the grass and heather and over the past few months had laid eggs, many of which had hatched. They tried not to walk near and disturb them. There were smells of sheep and cow droppings, and the heather so sweet and brilliant.

They always went that way and then on to the waterfall.

Charlotte sat down on a low stone wall with her arms wrapped across her chest. "Can it be less than a year since we published our books?" she asked slowly. "I thought it would bring happiness. I don't know what happiness is anymore."

Tabby came toward them when they returned, face pale with worry, swollen fingers playing on her apron.

"Your brother fainted in the village," she said, sounding like an old person who cannot bear more. "Some men brought him home. The doctor's upstairs with him. He says he's dying; our lad is dying. Oh, my girls! My lovely little lad who picked me flowers and tried to help me when I broke my leg. My lad!"

It was a time between times. They all moved in and out of their brother's small room: the physician with his blood-letting bowl; Tabitha, who urged broth on Branwell; their father, who alternately stayed away or railed or wept openly by the door; and the three sisters. The room smelled of sickness: consumption and a body worn to nothing.

Passing each other, the sisters touched hands or wound arms around each other's shoulders, saying, "Courage, dear!"

September wind blew through the window. In the middle of the night, Charlotte heard Branwell's feeble call and weeping.

Emily alternately nursed him and raged, muttering between her teeth, "Don't you dare be sick, you bastard! Don't you dare!" The horrible hoarse sound of Emily crying from her room and her screaming "Get out!" when anyone knocked.

Anne was tender and bleak.

Their father sometimes retreated to his room, where his anxious voice called out, "Lotte, Lotte…I can't find…" He could not find his spectacles, which lay under his hand, or his book, fallen by his feet. At the sight of his only son's dying, he grew old before their eyes.

A few of Branwell's drinking companions visited respectfully, feet shuffling in dirty boots. The smell of sickness drifted all over the house. There was no word from the married woman whom he had loved, though they wrote her.

One of the pages of Charlotte's new book blew down the stairs, settling in the kitchen. She hardly knew where she had left off in the story. Her brother's sickness weighed down the house. The roof seemed to sag under it.

Arthur Bell Nicholls came twice daily. Before the sick and needy, he was tall and calm and settled. "He needs forgiveness," the curate said.

"Forgiveness?" Charlotte asked. "He willfully…he horribly, unjustly…he…"

She woke one night to the sound of running feet in slippers. Minutes later, Charlotte and her sisters gathered in their nightdresses and nightcaps around Branwell's bed. Nicholls was there; he had put on his clothes so quickly to come from his lodgings down the street that his waistcoat was not buttoned. Her father hovered. In the midst of them, Branwell reached out his pale, thin hand to grasp the air.

"Lad, there are good times ahead," said their sexton, John Brown.

But Branwell gasped, "No, John, I'm dying! In all my past life, I have done nothing either great or good."

Hours after dawn the next morning, Charlotte and her sisters found their father on his knees in church, rocking back and forth, his hands over his face, his thin, raspy cry rising up. *O my son Absalom, my son! Would God I had died for thee, O Absalom, my son, my son!*

Charlotte and her sisters washed the body and dressed it. Now her brother lay with closed eyes and white hands folded over his chest in the open coffin in the church. With his pointed nose, he looked like a dull schoolmaster.

Emily had cried until she could cry no more. She asked bitterly, "Why do people want to destroy themselves? Isn't life hard enough as it is? That's what God does…gives you situations and things you can't do anything about. And Papa wants us to sing respectfully to this Being?"

Anne gasped. "Do not blaspheme God," she said.

27

Emily

Mourning is endless, Emily thought as she sat in the kitchen drinking tea as dawn broke. And it has so many dark colors and layers. There are no words to speak, but piles of rubbish, and we sort them, trying to find a half phrase. And every pitcher and pot and beloved wooden spoon in this kitchen seems as if strangers owned it.

She thought, The house is not the same without our brother, sick as he was, nuisance as he was. The house has changed. We will never be the same again. There's Anne with her hands clenched in her lap, eyes cast down. There's Papa's curate Nicholls decently dressed, though he has not shaved, his face pale for lack of sleep. Outside, the birds have not heard the news, for they are singing, though timidly this September morning.

"Did we try hard enough to help him?" Anne asked. "I will ask that all my life."

A wind rose over the moors as they walked to the church. It tore early leaves from the trees and left the wall stones and pews cold for this time of year when the last of summer lingered. Dressed in black, they heard the burial service and waited by the crypt as the coffin was lowered among those of their late mother and dead sisters.

Emily could not stop shivering.

I have no power, she thought. He was not healed.

As they waited there, she turned her head and saw Jonathan MacConnell standing in the shadow by the church door. He looked at her with all the longing and tenderness in the world and clenched his right hand lightly over his heart. Suddenly, she only wanted him. Would the previous priests of all English churches mutter that her passion might have been punished by her brother's death? No, not even her father would believe that if he knew. Some Calvinist preacher might, perhaps, one who had railed from a chapel in the village two hundred years before; his bitterness had curdled milk and wilted wild roses.

And later from her father's window came the cry: *I will lift up my eyes unto the hills, from whence cometh my help!* And at dawn his pistol, which he kept for protection against the possible rioting from the desperate mill workers, was fired, reloaded, and fired again, and a struck rook fell from the church tower and splattered in black feathers amid the grave slabs.

But though Emily longed to see Jonathan, she could not. She had caught a cold at the funeral, and then they all were sick for some days; coughs echoed from room to room. Tabby alone remained well, and no one walked into the village for the newspapers. What was there to learn after their brother had died? Nothing. Did it matter how the rest of the country turned in foreign policies?

Tabby made broth and bread and tea. She went from room to room cosseting the girls, saying, "Here, my chicks." The pastor would not answer the door for his tea until Nicholls knocked firmly and turned the handle.

One day, Emily, standing at her own door, saw the solemn curate descend with her father's gun in his hand, to take it away for a time. He glanced at her stricken face. "Miss Emily," he said.

She dressed achingly and went downstairs for bread. Tabby said, "You've still a bit of a fever. Where are you going?"

Emily replied, "Out. I wish I could be as good a woman as you, Tabby. Honest and true for everyone."

The morning's rain had ended. Emily walked faster. She turned the other way at the waterfall and went over the moor. She had to stop every now and then to rest. Well, her weakness would be soon gone.

Jonathan was not in the cottage.

Emily curled on his bed, breathing in the scent of his warm body from his quilt, wrapping her arms and legs around it, then pulling it over herself. Sometime later, she awoke to his hand on her shoulder, seated on the bed's edge. He said, "If you hadn't come today, I would have come for you. Poor girl! The more I have you, the lonelier I am when you go."

"I lost my power," she said. "I thought I could heal him. I used to stop storms."

"My darling, whatever strength you have can't hold death back."

She was crying. She said, "Jonathan, there's no God. He's a fairy tale made up to keep children unafraid of the dark, but I'm no child and I'm very afraid."

"Poor dearest!"

"It must be enviable to be dead and not feel anymore."

"Not enviable," he replied. "Not for them and not for us. Their loss becomes part of us. We are changed always. We carry them with us, the ghosts."

"If you could have spoken to my brother…"

"But I did once, in Leeds. I followed him there and sat with him at a drinking house. He wanted to know who I was and why I cared very much. I couldn't tell him about you. I went away. I'm sorry. But look, darling, you've a fever; you're shivering. And that cough."

"Lie down with me again."

He looked at her frowning; with his hands, he measured her waist gently. "You're thinner, if possible!"

"Just grieving for him. I've had a little porridge and tea these past several days, nothing more. How did you know he had died?"

"I heard a few men talking."

She said, "I'd like to bring Anne again to meet you."

"Soon they'll all know about me. Wait until then. It's much too soon after your brother's loss."

"Too soon."

She looked into his eyes. By the gray light through the window, she could see every pore in his skin and his wheat-gold stubble.

She woke with the dawn; he was sleeping. Her body felt languid, and yet deep within it was a stirring to be with him. How easy to wake him and make love to him, but everything in her said, "Not yet." Everything said, "You must not, but soon. For once you give the last bit of yourself to this man, there is no returning."

And yet something urged her, like a hand on the small of her back, saying reprovingly, tenderly, "Emily."

He was lovely. What would it be like?

"I should go now," she whispered. "I stayed away all night again. They'll be frantic unless they think I stopped at Mrs. Hawkins' house, which is what I generally tell them. They thought I was too ill to go, but I'm not ill at all, just a bit feverish. You've cured me. Goodbye, my love."

"Let me get up and walk you."

"No, I need to clear my mind. My first wish was to quiet storms, my second to fly and bring my mother and sisters back from death, but I was mortal and afraid. My third was to keep my brother, to turn him to see his own strengths, but none of us could reach him. But I have another. I have granted myself that, and it is never to leave you."

Her vision blurred for a moment, and this kind, redeemed man also blurred before her as if he dissolved into the air and even his voice was from the deepest cave. Then he was there, slowly forming again, the rough unbleached wool of his shirt.

She felt a kind of panic rising and reached out and pulled him back to her.

She leaned into him, protected.

"You went away," she said.

"I never did," he answered. "And your wish is granted. You have four wishes. I say this. Where you go, I'll go. We will never leave each other. You've a fever and you're trembling. Are you going home? I'll go with you. Take my brown muffler. I've had it forever. My grandmother knit it for me."

Emily drank milk from his jug and ate some of his biscuits and cheese before she left, assuring him after a time that she was well enough to return alone. He turned back reluctantly, watching her go. Despite the chill, the early day was beautiful. The sun began to rise, all gold. The ground was wet under her feet. The sound of birds drew her along. The heart of autumn was coming, when everything would change color. And after the autumn, the first snows on the crags and the paths and the roofs and the backs of the white sheep and even on their black faces.

Time passed; you looked away for a moment, and it had moved some steps forward and you never knew, you never heard.

An uneven step and she staggered, losing her balance.

The coughing, which had somehow stayed away almost all night, began again; she had slept little and had begun to run fast because she had to get back to the house where they all were. If she imagined hard enough, her brother would be there too, neatly dressed, off to his offices in York, now a dependable much-loved bookseller, wrapping books neatly, making small talk, going home at night in his cap to his wife and children, having tea by the fire…

Her mother waiting also, saying, *Darling, you've been away so long.*

The world rearranged by your desires was an infinitely better one.

That strange pain in her side stronger.

Emily had come to the moor gate and leaned against it, looking up to see the tower of the church from which she had almost flown.

Charlotte and Martha surrounded her when she came in, exclaiming, "What's the matter? Where were you?"

"Walking. I need to lie down."

"Heaven have mercy!" exclaimed Charlotte, taking her hand. "You've a fever! Your pulse is racing."

Emily loathed the questions. She climbed the stairs slowly and went to her room, with Charlotte following her.

Her sister took up Emily's corset, which lay on the bed. "Hardly decent how you run about without it," Charlotte said. "I'll brew you something to bring your fever down."

Charlotte left, and silence fell once more in her room.

Emily gazed slowly about her bedroom, which now seemed strange to her.

I'm not well, she thought incredulously. Being not well happened to other people, not her. Jonathan would know she was not well if he were here. He always seemed to know everything about her. But he would not knock on the door to speak to her father until she gave him permission.

She was too ill to rise. Her brother came to her in her dreams, and she whispered in his ear, "I'm in love."

He smiled. He said, "I'll be back tonight; you'll hear my footsteps. Tell me about it then." She woke and listened for the footsteps. They did not come.

Days later she slowly made her way downstairs. Charlotte was waiting at the bottom step, holding something brown and limp in her hands. She took Emily's arm to help her down the last steps. She asked, "Where did you get this sorry muffler? It's full of moth holes."

"I found it on the path," Emily said.

"You're still a little sick."

"A little… How strange I feel."

Emily was ready to stare down her sickness. It was not her; she had always been strong. She carried in a half bucket of coal, which left her gasping. She pushed her way into the washhouse to help with the washing, scrubbing a spot in a shirt, thrusting it up and down through the soapy hot water as if that now-fading spot represented all she must overcome. Then that strange faintness filled her, and she leaned against the outer kitchen wall, and the pain in her side came.

Emily looked over the soaking laundry, breathing hard. The worn cuff of the shirt rose from the water as if taunting her. Where were Branwell's socks to be made clean and fragrant again when blown dry on the line? She cried, her tears running salty over her face.

"Come back, Bran!" she whispered. "See how soft and clean we've made your shirt! I mended the buttons."

Emily was seized by another spasm of coughing. What nonsense was her body doing? Another stained handkerchief. Only bloody because she bruised her throat in coughing.

Inside again, she looked vaguely from the window. The days had turned to late October, and she had told Jonathan she would be back soon. Once she saw him standing by the moor gate, but when she called his name, he didn't turn. She made her way toward him, but he was already striding away. Did he think she had broken her promise?

Later she left him a note under the stone, by the gate, saying she had been ill but was nearly well. It was their designated place if they should need to write each other. Two days later, someone had taken it away.

Her sisters assumed most of her work, and she agreed to rest and write just for an hour, or maybe two. She was writing more of a new novel, about a wild girl who eventually finds love. But it went slowly.

Emily finally summoned strength from every part of her body and walked through the moor gate. She thought, I love this world more than any world I can create: this moor, the cottage, the parsonage, the very air full of the seasons. In her mind as she walked to the cottage, she was all the ages of her life.

She reached the hill; she climbed it slowly and was half down when Jonathan ran up. He caught her against him and lifted her slightly.

The autumn wind blew his hair. He said, "You weigh nothing. Do you feed all but yourself at home?"

"I eat huge platefuls."

"That is hard to believe. When I took away your note, I hesitated for a time looking at the lights in your windows. I saw your father in his huge glasses. Emily Jane, when may I go to him? We would stand side by side and tell him of our love. I would accept his doctrines; I would marry in the church. I will not say, Then you'll be mine, because you don't like it. I will say, Then I will be yours, always holding you, always loving you. I had to come across the sea to find you. You are my dream."

She chose her words carefully so he wouldn't see how she had to breathe to make them come. "I'll tell Papa this week. I'll tell all of them. They won't believe it of me."

"Will you really?"

"I will. I want to. I forgot your muffler; this one Anne made." She moved her palm down his cheek. "Bristles," she said. "Awful to have to shave. It comes back every day."

"We become used to it. When you're a lad, you long for it."

"Why?"

"Lads long to be men, and then they long to be lads again. Come inside." He pulled her through the door, and she sighed. The fire burned. How she had missed this welcoming place of wood and stone when away for any length of time! But how long had she been away? She could not quite remember.

Jonathan said, "I've great news to tell you, but come under the covers with me! Your hands are so cold. I want to hold you and protect you." He lay down on his narrow bed, and she joined him and felt the beautiful warmth of his arm about her and the soft flannel of his shirt against her cheek.

She felt his kiss on her hair. He said wistfully, "Here you are! God only knows how I have longed for you."

"Has your annulment come?"

"It has. If you speak to your father by Christmas Eve, I'll walk over the morn of Christmas Day and meet him after the service. I'm free to marry you if you'll have me."

She was very still and then looked to her breath to form words. "Then that is what we will do."

He kept the quilt over them both. Some of the stitching had broken and a few feathers were escaping. She would mend it as she did the covers at home: open the stitches, spill out the drifting, wavering feathers in the sun to purify them, wash the cloth, and stitch it around the inside again. You had to do it on a windless day, or the feathers would blow away.

She felt his frown. "This day must be a short visit," he said. "You really aren't well. I'm taking you home. I'll stop a bit away so no one will see me."

"Come on Christmas Day and tell my family about us."

A few hours later, he gave her some food and tea, and she tried to make herself eat. "The day's so short," he said. "We want to ride in the light."

Emily rode behind him on his mare, her arms about him, her head on his shoulder, and gazed out at the moor. The few trees were bare, the rocks dull of light. The sky held snow, and though it did not fall, the light of it was everywhere. And through the fading light, she seemed to see white sheep's wool and hear on the faintest edge of her mind the sound of their calls.

"Your sheep," she murmured sleepily.

"I sold them. I told you."

"What happened to my lamb?"

"God knows; we would not know it."

"I love you," she said. "I love you with all that's in me." And she rode on, kissing his shoulders and winding her arms right about him. He said, "Emily," so softly she hardly heard his words.

Some few minutes away from the parsonage, he lifted her gently down until her feet touched the earth. They kissed again. Then she walked away, turning to wave. She thought, I will never be alone again.

Weeks passed; she did not know how. She heard Anne say soon it would be the darkest day of the year. Emily slept a little and woke to first light. She sat, feeling the pain in her lungs and side.

I want to go to the window, she thought. First, I must sit up and then put my feet on the floor. Then I must stand, holding on to the bedpost.

"Emily." Anne had knocked and was coming toward her with that sweet, tentative smile. She reached Emily, who was now at the window, and put her arm around her sister's waist, as they both turned to the moors. Snow was just beginning to fall.

"How beautiful it is!" Anne whispered.

Emily smiled and leaned into her sister. Snow would continue to gently fall and in time would bury the house. A hundred years later it would melt, and people would find it, astonished. They would find the little family just as they were now, Papa writing, the curate's knock on the door, Branwell marching into the house, calling, "Girls!" They would all stay here forever.

Night turned to dawn. Emily was lying on the parlor sofa under a heavy quilt, while outside, snow fell steadily. It would bury the house, but not yet. Not until Jonathan came on Christmas Day. Emily would have gone out, but she knew they would fuss. Ridiculous!

Charlotte was leaning over her. "I'm going to tell John Brown to go for Dr. Gregory," she said.

"I won't see him."

Her sister's eyes filled with angry tears; she stood little, upright, exclaiming, "There you go again! Always thinking that reality is only what you create in your mind."

"I'm going out," Emily said. But she only reached the kitchen when she began to cough so hard that she had to cling to a chair.

In the night, her family came with candles. By their flickering light, she saw her father's anxious face and her sisters bending over her. Her father was kneeling by her bed to pray and rising with a groan for his bad knees. The candle shone on the wallpaper and the white paper under the rock on the desk.

Emily looked away as they took her stained handkerchief from her hand. They would not wash them well; they never did. Soak in cold water with lye under the still-bright sun glistening on the melting snow. Tomorrow she would do it herself.

She spoke to Jonathan off and on in her mind. At night, she felt him lie next to her and touch her body in every place and in every way. She heaved toward him and fell away. Not yet, she said. And yet again. Her weak body fluttered so she cried out softly. Had she let him and forgotten? Had she remembered what had not been?

He had written her twice, leaving notes under the rock, which she sent Anne to find. "Darling, are you well? How empty is it here in my stone cottage without you! The sheets miss you, the dented pan, the cups…every stone of the house."

She memorized the notes and burned them in the small fireplace, watching them crinkle and curl to ash. She kept the folded cloth with the lock of his hair. She spoke to it. The day she had cut it, he had smiled and said, "You'll make a spell with it."

Emily closed her eyes tightly and whispered her old prayers to the stunted trees, which held the pagan spirits. Tabby's soup pot, which the potter had just mended, also held them, as did the blue sugar canister, the rows of sealed jars of vegetables and jams in the storeroom below, the cold apples laid in careful rows. Hold an apple in your hand and you touch them. On the cloth top of the blackberry jams were her initials, *EJB*.

Where was she? Books scattered through the house under beds, on top of wardrobes, on the stairs held her a little, but mostly she was outside, running among the wild sheep, stepping on the stones that forded the streams.

No coward soul is mine,
No trembler in the world's storm-troubled sphere…

She had written that years ago. She felt it again. If she could hide herself in that solid faith and wrap it around her, as she had once stolen her father's surplice and, dragging it behind the small height of her (she was eight, perhaps), crouched behind the pulpit of the church.

She closed her eyes; she was walking the moor, tall and swift, but the sound she heard was not the wild wind but the sea. She had never seen the sea in real life. There it was! And there was a boat just coming in on the great waves between the rocks, and the old keeper of the shop with sundries was rowing, and Jonathan rose, balancing, looking toward her. "Emily!" he cried.

She ran forward into the edge of the waves, her shoes and skirt hem soaked.

Then the fog came in fast and hid the boat and the men, and she ran along the shore's edge crying their names, saying, "Take me, too!"

"I think I will have the doctor now." She spoke the next morning and had to repeat it three times to be heard.

There was Dr. Gregory looming above her, and behind him Anne, hunched and subdued. Charlotte paused with clean linen in her hand coming across the room. Time tumbled. Emily wanted to tell her father it was nothing, that she'd be ironing his shirts tomorrow.

They faded. She was alone, and it was night and the snow still fell. Her sisters were small again and buying paper for their stories. Emily wanted to explain her thoughts to all of them, but words did not follow. There was the other world, and it went by different names. There was a map that appeared in her dreams, but as soon as she tried to memorize it, it faded. Follow me, the voices said.

28

Charlotte

Charlotte sat by Emily's narrow bed, her sewing on her lap. She had not slept much the last several nights. On the shelf were Emily's childhood books and that large ancient one. Charlotte had read several of the loose pages with translations, but some seemed to have disappeared. She had looked around the room for them.

Emily was fading; all the flesh seemed to have left her thin arm that lay outside the bedcover, and dark sunken smudges deepened below her eyes. Her walking dress, still unbrushed from her last moor walk, was draped over her chair. Her mother's boots, long too broken to wear, sat side by side by the bedroom door.

Charlotte looked at the window. Because she was dazed with sleeplessness, she did not know, when the light faded, if it was dawn or dusk. Anne had gone to sleep, as had her father. Mr. Nicholls came now and then with a tray with two cups of tea and flaky slices of meat pie. Martha's cooking. Martha had faith in meat pie.

Emily stirred in her bed and murmured, "Open the drawer; there's part of a novel. I can't finish it. I want you to burn it."

Charlotte turned her back so her sister would not see she was crying. A few pages at a time, she fed the novel into the low fire.

Emily lay back. "Charlotte…there's something I want to tell you."

Then Charlotte, who had gone outside to stand shivering in the wind, saw a tall, strongly built man standing still outside the graveyard, his face in his hands. Now and then his shoulders shook. It is him, she thought. Her secret.

She began to walk toward him, but he turned and strode away much faster than she could go. She stopped, blown by the wind into which he had turned, hearing a bare tree branch blow back and forth outside her sister's window.

Part VIII

Winter–Spring 1850

29

Can spirits, through any medium, communicate with living flesh? Can the dead at all revisit those they leave? Can they come into the elements?...What are all those influences that are about us in the atmosphere, that keep playing over our nerves like fingers on stringed instruments...? *Where is* the other world? In *what* will another life consist?

—Charlotte Brontë, from *Shirley*

Charlotte

Through the rooms, there was silence. It hung in the air. It lingered over the empty chairs, above the wardrobes with the clean dresses, in the shoes by the beds, in the unfinished book with a sprig to mark the place the reader had left off. It was broken then by Tabby sighing and muttering in the kitchen, and her father's faint, sharp call from his bedroom, "Daughter..." That faded to a murmur. Nothing then. A bird fluttering against the window. A tree moving. Seasons changed.

She waited with her hand on her chair as snow fell against the window.

Then it was spring.

Past the fragrant spring wildflowers someone had gathered in a vase on the dining table, she crossed to her father's study door, knocked, and entered. The Reverend Patrick Brontë was at his desk, which was so covered with books that there was little space for the letter he was writing. His white, bristly hair rose up. He paused for forgotten words.

The books were mostly gifts from her publisher; he said he would not read the novels, yet she suspected he did. She had caught him once engrossed in a romance.

Her father moved back so she could place the cup of tea on the desk before him. His hands trembled a little as he brought the cup to his mouth. Drops of milky tea landed on his trousers. He muttered, "Just answering a letter here from the warden. Is the work too much for me? he asks again. I know what they mean. They want more than ever to remove me. I'm seventy-three… Then to the poorhouse for us. Who'll look after poor Tabby?"

"They've been sending those letters for years. Besides, we're not poor anymore. Everyone looks up to you, Papa."

"Hmm! Did you send your new novel to your publisher?"

"It's called *Shirley*, and I sent it last week. I told you, Papa. It's not quite as intense as *Jane*." She added softly, "I've been a bit used up this past year. Now, shall I call Mr. Nicholls?"

"Nicholls! Useless fellow."

"He does very well for you, Papa! I'll see you both at breakfast soon. Porridge is nearly cooked."

April morning a few days later. When she stepped outside for the dairyman to fill their jug with new milk, the softer wind blew against her stern face. She thought, It's still early and already Papa is worried about his work, money, and his very able curate. Really! I must tell my sisters. Papa's the same as ever!

Charlotte held the jug in her arms, chill creeping under her light wool dress. *I must tell my sisters*—there was not a day when she didn't think that. You could not put aside the habits of a lifetime. She still felt if she opened Emily's door quickly enough, she would find her sister in the bed by the window with her portable desk. Most of the times when she slipped inside the room, she knew she would find no one there.

It had been a year and a half now nearly, and the edge of pain was not as sharp as at the beginning. Then she would collapse in her own bed fully dressed and wake with her corset biting into her side. Where were her sisters? First Emily succumbed to consumption and then, five months later, Anne. At night,

Charlotte walked around the house with her candle, and the floor creaked as always. Was it her footsteps or theirs? They had walked up and down together so often.

Branwell's scrubbed and newly papered room now belonged to Tabby, who hung her worn dresses from hooks, her prayer tracts on the shelf with torn journal articles about the royal family and ghosts. The other rooms were untouched. At night she heard sometimes what seemed like the piano playing and voices singing, but no one played now.

Charlotte brought the milk to the kitchen, where Martha was stirring the porridge, and mounted the steps, opening Emily's door again. Her eyes moved from the white coverlet to the wardrobe to the desk with its locked drawer. She had opened that drawer some months after Emily's death and found it almost empty. Charlotte thought, If I do it again, she'll rush into this room in fury at me. Keeper will growl and show me his sharp teeth.

But no one rushed past her, nor did Keeper growl and bark. He was no longer here. They had given him to the blacksmith, for none of them could manage his truculent ways.

Yes, the drawer held only the remembered bits of diaries, letters from a few friends. *Made bread today… We are all weary here; Branwell has been bad…*

How had her life been since Emily had left? Somehow, Charlotte had finished her own new novel. Each day was the same as the ones before. Walking to town, buying sugar, buying thread, passing the bookseller and the shop where they bought their paper still.

Wherever she went, she felt her father's needs. In the past year he had slipped into increasing fragility, his voice peevish, his balance uncertain, rages shaking his thin body, and then the return to the calmness of his faith.

Most Sundays he walked slowly to church on the arm of his curate and preached in a voice first weak and then growing in strength. His preaching at least restored a sense of order in the world to himself. How many times over the past year and a half had he whispered, "Charlotte, you must bear up! I'll sink if you fail me."

Now from downstairs she heard voices and, descending the stairs, saw her father coming into the dining room holding Mr. Nicholls's arm for balance.

Nicholls also appeared to mourn Anne, though he did not say so. He seemed, as always, a little wary of Charlotte. She had made it known what she felt about curates who simply quoted scripture at you, passages she was not certain they had thought about. But though Nicholls had no imagination, he had a sweet smile and some warmth in his brown eyes. Sometimes it touched her. There was the calm of his always being there.

"Good morning, Miss Brontë," he said formally.

The morning sun poured through the windows as the three of them took their places at the table and her father said grace. Breakfast was the only meal her father ate with her; the rest he took in solitude.

"Charlotte, my very dear, I'm wondering if you might want to go to London for a week or so," he said. "Your publisher invited you to stay with his mother and sisters a few times. You must be lonely here."

Her father's kindness brought a swelling to her throat, but she spoke over it. "Do you think I should go, Mr. Nicholls?"

The black-bearded curate looked at her thoughtfully and said, "Yes, you should go. They'll introduce you to other writers." For by now, more people knew that the Bell brothers had been the parson's three gifted daughters.

She crumbled a bit of Martha's bread onto her plate. It was always too heavy in texture.

Her father touched her hand. He said, "A week only, daughter! I can't spare you more. Oh God, that I should live to be so old and have but one child of my six left to me!" Now his thin shoulders slumped.

How can I go when he speaks to me like that? she thought. But I must go. They are unbearable, dull, the lot of them! In

London there are authors, opera, galleries, people discussing great ideas. I converse with no one here. Not really.

"You must have new dresses," Tabby said at once when Charlotte told her of the visit. The old woman leaned on her cane, but her mind was alert with excitement. "My cousin went to London once fifty years ago. All the women dress like princesses."

Tabby was rarely loquacious, but the idea of dresses brightened her eyes.

Charlotte bought a train ticket from Leeds to London, and having found her seat, settled down to gaze through the window at the passing fields and towns. At her feet was her trunk with two new walking dresses and a modest one for the dinners or theaters. All the fabric was gray or deepest blue for her mourning period. At first, she had worn only black.

The long spring day still held as they came toward the city with the brick houses crowded together. Finally, the Great Northern Railway engine pulled into its temporary wooden terminus in Maiden Lane. Charlotte peered anxiously through the crowds for her publisher's reader, Mr. Williams, who had offered to meet her. "Look for a pale man about fifty," he had written. "With spectacles."

But no such person was there. Instead, a tall youthful man walked toward her in swaying dark coat and top hat; the crowds seemed to part as he came. She had not seen him since her trip to London two years before. For a moment she was afraid he had not recalled how plain she was, how simple.

"What a pleasure to see you again!" exclaimed her publisher.

"Mr. Smith," she said.

Within minutes, they were both enclosed in the leather-padded interior of a horse-drawn carriage. Charlotte remembered first meeting him in his publishing house. He had been a little bewildered then, bluffing his way through his new role as head of his firm. Now he seemed to have settled into a masculine capability. There is nothing I can't manage, he seemed to say.

"Good journey?" he asked briskly. "We're happy you've come! My reader, Mr. Williams, always inquires of you. I am afraid the rumor that the author of *Jane Eyre* is a woman has spread even further. Everyone in publishing knows, and soon will your readers."

Charlotte did not reply. She gazed through the smudged carriage window at the crowded streets outside. Barefoot boys dashed into the street to sweep up horse manure to be sold for fertilizer, and hundreds of shop signs rose two or three stories on the brick buildings. Everywhere, even on the sides of horse-drawn omnibuses, were advertisements for tea and soap.

But the noise of the wheels on the cobbles was too loud, and they both remained silent as the carriage mounted into the winding streets of the historic city and stopped on Fenchurch Street before a white-stone private house. His mother and sisters emerged to greet her, wearing bright dresses, saying one after the other, "There she is! Ten hours' travel for such a delicate woman."

The younger sister, who was still almost a child, asked, "Do you want to rest?" Charlotte remembered them from when she had visited with Anne; her publisher's sisters had awed them in their elegance.

They led her upstairs to a guest bedroom papered in a pattern of violets, the bed high with a soft coverlet. "We'll send up tea," they chattered. Their voices retreated down the stairs. "The guests will be here by eight…just a handful of writers and friends."

Dusk fell outside in the London street. A maid came in with a curtsey, followed by a kitchen girl, both carrying closed brass pitchers of hot water and then cold water to mix it. With repeated visits, and after filling the brass tub a third of the way, they left. At home, she and her sisters had bathed once a week in the kitchen behind a screen. Her father always sang Irish songs while bathing. Branwell also sang German lieder and splashed water everywhere, leaving wet footprints as he mounted back to his room.

Had George Smith said there would be guests? This was bad; she had not expected it. Charlotte sat on the edge of the bed, so anxious her stomach hurt. She had refused the help of the maid; it would have appalled her to reveal her plain chemise before a stranger.

Time passed until voices from the rooms below drifted up the stairs. The sound of a waltz on the piano mingled with laughter. Oh God, people had come in. Who were they? What could she say to them? And now the bathwater was cold.

Standing barefoot, she looked at her new evening dress, which was laid on the bed. She remembered an evening a long time ago when she had been a governess, instructed to sit outside in the hall of the parlor while piano and harp played. When she had been called in briefly by the mistress to go upstairs and check on the children, no one else had looked at her.

Would these guests also be so condescending?

It had been a mistake to come here, and she must leave at once, but how? The back steps perhaps, past the scullery and the kitchen, out into the alley. She could not carry the trunk; she would have to go without it. She could find a hansom cab and huddle inside it until she reached the station for the night train to Leeds. She would leave a letter of profuse apology on the undisturbed bed in this guest room of the Smith family.

Yes! If she went quickly, quickly, her whole family would be waiting for her at home: she knew it, she knew it. She hadn't lost both her sisters; they were there, saying, "Where were you?"

Charlotte covered her face. She whispered hoarsely, "Anne."

During the five months that followed the laying of Emily in earth, Anne had mourned, exhausted and ill with grief. Her strong cough came more often through the house. Charlotte wrested Anne's handkerchief from her one day and saw the bright blood. "It's not much; it will pass," Anne had said. But it did not. Like Emily, she had denied she was ill. Then her clothes began to hang on her and their father was too stunned to see it.

"Charlotte," Anne had said one day. "I'd like to travel to Scarborough on the coast, to the sea. You must take me there. Maybe it will heal me."

They hired a private couch. As it rolled down the Haworth streets, so many people stopped their work and looked after them.

Within an hour of arriving at the boardinghouse, they walked slowly down the sand to the edge of the water, noting the patterns and the shells at each renewing wave. Charlotte gathered shells for her sister. She vowed, "You're the last; you can't succumb. I've got to heal you."

Anne replied, "That's not possible, beloved! But it's all right, really." For some time after Emily's death, Charlotte had felt strongly that Anne knew their sister's secret, but she had said nothing.

They had a handful of days in the little room overlooking the sea before Anne died, saying, "Take courage, Charlotte!" Charlotte did not have the strength to bring her body back to Haworth but buried her sister at Scarborough, leaving money for the sexton to tend the grave.

And now the Yorkshire parsonage was full of things no longer needed. Chests full of extra bed linens folded with sprigs of lavender remained unopened. The larger cooking pots were seldom used. In all the rooms were only the spinster writer, her elderly father, and Tabby. Martha Brown came up the path early each morning from her own father's house to start the fires and the porridge. Old Tabby, who could still mend and cook a little, fretted over everyone. And Mr. Nicholls came four times daily to walk Anne's grieving spaniel.

On the large bed of the guest room at the Smith family home in London, Charlotte curled very small and fell into helpless sleep. Later, she woke with a start. Where was she? She had thought she was home in Haworth. What was this room? Where was her family? Was her father sick?

Then she recalled her journey and the party. She made out the clock hands at two in the morning. All the guests had likely gone home. The guest of honor had fallen asleep and ignored them all. And she could not remember being so hungry since those years as a child in that desolate school.

Perhaps she could find the kitchen and pantry and discover some bread and cheese. In the morning, she would leave. She never should have come.

Charlotte pulled her dressing gown from her trunk, tied it on, creaked open her door to the landing, and looked down the stairs to the parlor.

George Smith was sitting alone at a desk in the corner, writing, forehead resting on his hand. He had thrown off his jacket, and his sleeves were rolled up and his shirt open at the neck. She had to pass him to go down. Still, he had heard her. "You're awake," he called up softly. "My mother says you must have been so tired."

"I missed the whole party! I'm so sorry."

He shook his head. "It was madness to expect you to meet a dozen strangers when you'd traveled all day. My sister Sylvia left you a tray of covered dishes in your room. She went in very quietly."

"I didn't see it…"

"Here's some cake. Shall I bring it up or will you come down? An odd way to meet my favorite author again, I must say! Alone in the middle of the night. Not done! Shall I wake my sisters to chaperone? I'm up late because I have some work to complete."

"I'd like cake," she said, descending. Oh, she thought, his favorite author…did he say that? How lovely.

He fetched a plate and seated her near the tall clock some feet from his desk. She ate ravenously. He smiled and went away, bringing back thin slices of ham and cold potatoes in a white sauce.

The gloomy house where she had earned thirty pounds a year as governess faded, and she was here in a pretty parlor.

George Smith sat again, rubbing his blond mustache with the edge of his finger and smiling in his crooked way. "We all spoke of you tonight," he said. "I don't know a single person who hasn't read *Jane Eyre.* They're all surprised a rural parson's daughter could write it."

He continued, shaking his head. "You've known more than your share of losses, poor woman! Your sisters were also so gifted. I intend to take over the publishing of their books. Anne's sells modestly, and, I'd say if I might, your sister Emily's tale is strange. *Wuthering Heights.* Never in my reading have I seen a character like Heathcliff!"

"Emily had a great imagination," Charlotte said.

"That she had, poor girl! But now that you're here, I want to show you more of London. We all do; my family will take you when I must work. Concerts, museums, the Tower, the Abbey, where medieval kings sleep. And bookshops with your novel, of course, soon to be joined by your new one. But no more great dinner parties…one stranger at a time. I forget what a quiet life you lead."

Later, she could not remember all they said in that hour, though most of it was about books. His hand on the desk was large, with a heavy ring on his finger, which he told her had belonged to his father. Eventually, she climbed to her room and slept amid many pillows for a long time. She wondered until she saw the cake crumbs on her dressing gown if it had only been a confused dream.

Charlotte returned to Haworth on a cold spring day, water dripping from the roofs of the houses. Main Street hardly deserved its name after the great streets of London. Rooks called down from the trees.

She removed her bonnet in the parsonage hallway and walked through the rooms, touching the dining table and the wicker box of sheet music on top of the piano.

"Emily," she said.

There was no reply.

On a train platform she had seen a woman with a narrow back, her face turned away. Charlotte had pulled open the train window, scraping her hand, but the woman was not her Emily.

Now she mounted the parsonage stairs. In her sister's empty room, Charlotte sank onto the bed and pulled the pillow against her face, shaking with sobs, which had been rising in her the whole week.

"Listen, dearest," she managed. "I've been to London. I've met many people who praised me. I've met famous authors who stared at me. I've seen so many things, but they weren't worth an hour with you. At least Anne told me of her hopes and dreams. I knew her, but you… *Who* was the man I saw weeping outside the house the night you died? *What* did Anne mention to me about a watercolor of him, and *where* did she say it was?"

She held the pillow in her lap. "Oh, Emily!" she whispered wistfully. "Did you have a lover?"

She suspected the man lived somewhere on the moor, but where? She thought, I can't walk the whole moor asking for someone whose name I don't know and whose likeness I have never seen. Perhaps he lived in the village or Keighley or even Halifax. Who is he? Where is he? Anne knew, but never said.

Tears came again.

"Oh, dearests!" she said. "All I want is to be where you are."

Charlotte had never had real friends in the village; she demanded a lot from friendship: intellect and an iconoclastic mind, wit, wryness, devotion. She was a bit of a heretic; she believed in women's suffrage. No other woman in the village was like her, and as the parson's daughter, she must always be discreet. Discretion had silenced her. Her sisters had been her closest friends and near them two school friends. One had emigrated to New Zealand but the other, Ellen Nussey, still lived in England and had never married.

Though she wrote them regularly, she felt terribly alone.

Her father withdrew more and more into himself.

But the daily mail brought bright letters from some other new writers she had met, including Mrs. Gaskell, who was making her name as a novelist. There were also her publisher's sisters and kind Mr. Taylor from the publishing firm. Life seemed less here and more outside the village. Some weeks after she returned from London, Charlotte told her father she was visiting there again.

"Go," he said. "You're too much alone."

But it was not London that drew her.

It was her swift, urbane publisher who had fed her cake in the small hours of the morning and brought to life ideas of which she had not spoken since her conversations with her French professor, who, though he had been frightened of her passions, had felt her mind equal to his.

On the speeding train to London, she looked at her rash, brief dreams with a frown. How could she allow a flurry of attraction for her publisher, George Smith, who was some four years younger herself? He was twenty-six, a man of business who moved in cosmopolitan circles. At the small dinner party that his family had given her on the last evening of her visit, the few other young women were entirely beautiful with their perfect complexions, sweet lips, and bright eyes that needed no spectacles. They lived carefree lives of dances and theaters. They were flowers and she a bramble bush.

George Smith had written that he would meet her at the London station. It was difficult to meet someone when you have thought of him in such an impossible way.

But there he was. He came striding toward her on the train platform and lifted her trunk with the two new dresses. "You must come home to rest," he said. "And tomorrow afternoon, let me show you more of the old city; and perhaps we can know each other more, since I intend to be your publisher all your life. To tell the truth, I think about you a good deal."

I should not have come, she thought. I have only imagined he wants to really speak with me, imagined it because I want it very much.

But the Sunday after she had arrived, he took her for a walk to show her the old city of London, where he lived and where she had first visited him at his publishing house. It was midsummer. She wore one of her newer dresses and felt pretty in the many yards of blue linen.

After a time, they sat down on a bench in the gardens of St. Paul's Cathedral. He said, sincerely, "I've wanted to know a little more of you since the fascinating conversation we had that night when everyone else had gone to bed."

She was startled. "What can I tell you?" she replied. "I am a parson's daughter. We keep very little company. I live in books."

"Indeed, there's much more. You read, you think, you write compelling stories. I suspect what you think is compelling. Women are cautioned not to think, which is nonsense. Tell me about Haworth and how you see it. I can't imagine a place without theaters and huge shopping streets."

Charlotte took off her spectacles. She knew she looked less severe without them though the cathedral was now a blur. She said, "It's a strange, uncivilized little place; you would be bored to tears in one hour. No one speaks of anything but the price of grain and wool. I suspect they think London is decadent in thought and morals."

He said, "And from this barren place and the parson's daughters came these wild novels. I imagine Rochester and Heathcliff striding around the moors and Arthur Huntington from your sister Anne's second novel."

"I assure you that you wouldn't want to meet Heathcliff or Arthur; they are immoral and heartless. I had urged my sisters to make them kinder." I sound prudish, she thought.

Trees shaded them, and innocent pigeons pecked around their feet. George Smith's face was sad and tender. He said, "I cannot imagine what it would be like to lose so much of one's family! Such loss can never be remedied, never! Still, my dear Miss Brontë! One must have friends of the heart, friends who share your thoughts and your intellectual curiosity. Did you ever consider a life in London? I know a woman novelist who lives with a companion and has literary evenings. My friends and I go monthly at least and talk flows like wine."

She shook her head, aghast. "Move to London? I would be so alone!"

"What's this? Miss Brontë! You wouldn't be alone! Why, you'd have an intellectual circle who'd visit you every day. I'd come as much as you'd have me. You'll see what a delight you'll be at our dinner party tomorrow. It is intimate."

"I won't know your guests."

"You will charm them!"

She fumbled for her spectacles again. Looking through them, Paul's Cathedral seemed huge and forbidding even in the loveliness of the first summer days.

The night of the dinner party arrived. In her bedroom in the Smith town house, Charlotte pulled her best mauve dress from the wardrobe where the maid had hung it. Sylvia, the older sister, came in smiling to help. "Pinch your cheeks," she said, standing behind Charlotte before the oval mirror. "There! And bite your lips to redden them. Everyone is waiting for you. Only the family and three guests. You look beautiful."

Charlotte's full skirts and crinoline rustled against chairs and bedposts. Her hands were cold with anxiety. Oh, why had she allowed so many people to learn her true identity? She could have pretended to remain a poor relation—then when people talked of her book, they could attribute it to the mysterious Currer Bell.

All the guests turned their heads as she descended the stairs. Dinner had been called, and an embroidered dining chair at the long table was pulled out for her; she was seated.

She thought, I shall talk about politics and literature as we used to do at home when we were all happy and Papa was not so frail. Still, with everyone looking at her, she could barely begin.

The hearty man next to her burst out in a voice that rang to the chandelier, "Damn my soul, but it's Jane Eyre."

She murmured, "No, I am not Jane but her author..."

She drank her first glass of rich French wine for confidence and at once felt her body and mind soften. Then she spoke of literature, not daring politics yet. The second glass of wine encouraged her. Everyone disliked the sending of convicts in exile to the penal colony in Australia, and she knew the history well. Raising her voice a little on a subject she had always spoken of with her sisters, she said clearly that to send young women on scant evidence of lack of virtue was barbarous.

Everyone was looking at her with admiration. "And if they lack virtue, it is men who make them so..." she continued in a loud voice. No, she would never be silent again. Now they were all talking so loudly, they did not at first hear the clanging of the house doorbell until the maid flew through the room to answer it and voices came from the hall.

The girl hurried back, holding out something. "A telegram has come, sirs, for Miss Brontë," she said.

George Smith went at once to his desk to find the night train schedule, and the butler ran outside to the hackney stand three streets away to ask for a carriage to come round at once.

Charlotte rode the train north all night through the darkness, alone in her compartment, too anxious to have more than a little tea from a porter who came around with a tin. She heard other porters chatting about pony cart races and, some compartments away a baby crying. Her hastily packed trunk sat at her feet. She changed to the local train.

"Keighley!" called one of the porters, and she heard the wheels slowing with a scraping of iron wheel against iron track.

Wildflowers crowded the edges of the tracks. The day was fresh at just past eight in the morning when she stepped onto the platform of the new stone train station and saw Mr. Nicholls in his long, dark coat walking toward her. He looked as if he hadn't slept. "Oh God, how's my father?" she burst out.

"His heart is better. The doctor has been here many times. The pains have ceased."

"Is he resting?"

"For now. He works too hard. I wish he trusted me more to

do most of the visiting, but he doesn't want to let anything go. My father was the same. A man works hard to gain his place in the world, and it's hard for him to admit he's tired. Your father is a force of nature. But you know that."

"But he'll live!" She seldom let herself cry before anyone, but she cried now with relief. "I thought…I couldn't bear it if…"

Mr. Nicholls said gently, "Your father will live many a year."

She thought, Oh, my father!—his goodness kept like snuff in a box, his fingers and beard tinged with it. His hand shaped to the turning small staircase banister leading up to his pulpit. *The word of the Lord…*

This was so far away from London conversation.

Arthur Nicholls shouldered her trunk, tipping the porter, and the train began to move away. A child on the platform was staring at her as she dried her eyes.

She said as they walked, "How grateful I am to you! You've stayed here all these years. Everyone's fond of you. You could find a church of your own with a much larger stipend. But what would Papa do without you?"

He directed them to his cart. All her fright and lack of sleep had left her weak, and she was glad he gave her his hand to help her up. "Walk on!" he said to the horse, and when they were steadily on the path toward the parsonage, he answered her.

"I like the people here even though it's a little place," he said. "They're family to me. I don't take to change easily. I'm not an ambitious man. I have enough for my needs and send some money home. My family in Ireland is safe, thank the Lord. With so many bereft, it is a miracle for me. The land's desolate now from the great hunger but I have faith the crops will grow again one day."

He hesitated a moment and added a little wistfully, "You, on the other hand, are remarkable. In spite of all your obstacles, you've become a real writer. I found your novel in your father's room. The name on the title page wasn't yours, but he said you wrote it. It's beautifully done. I never read a novel before."

"Really?"

"No, never."

Summer dust rose from the dirt road. He continued, "Your father said your sisters also wrote books. I miss both your sisters and your brother."

"You're very kind."

"I?" he asked. "I try."

Later, when she thought about it, she realized he had said a great deal; she never heard him talk much but to her father about parish affairs or to any man, woman, or child who needed him. But within days after making sure of her father's recovery, her mind turned back to London.

The train to the city became a frequent thing over the next many months; Charlotte would settle herself comfortably with a book, needing only bottled cold tea and a bit of cheese on bread wrapped in a cloth. She tried to find an empty compartment so she could read without the chatter of others.

She rode in her dark traveling dress, with Emily's shawl over her shoulders. The compartment smelled of train smoke; the engine roared, pulling them on. She was no longer simply going to see London. She was going to meet George Smith, though neither acknowledged it. He would be waiting at the station for her, top hat on his carefully oiled and brushed hair, his hands slightly extended as if to make pleasant the air around her.

Sometimes he worked long hours at his office, and she was left at his lovely townhouse with the tedious chatter of his mother and sisters over hat styles, fabric, and the betrothals of others. That neither of George's sisters was yet settled was a problem; that George was not yet settled either was less worrisome. He would have so many opportunities, his mother said.

She told Charlotte solemnly, "When we lost my husband, we thought we'd be out in the street because my son was hardly from school and the business nearly bankrupt, but he worked and worked. He revitalized everything."

When Charlotte could bear no more talks of hats and betrothals, she pleaded the need for some fresh air, and rambled through the fascinating streets passing ancient churches and the guild halls, through a London which now felt comfortable. It had been many months since she had first come to visit. She always ended up on Cornhill and the redbrick house with the sign painted above the door that read *Smith, Elder & Co.* Alexander Elder, the partner, was out of the country.

George Smith always welcomed her as he had the very first time, briskly descending the stair when told she had come, smiling. "Shall we go out? Shall we ramble?" he always asked. "I will fetch my umbrella in case it rains."

Once he took her to have her portrait painted. She was a famous author now, he said. She protested at first. He escorted her to the studio of the painter Richmond on York Street. When the artist had finished after several sessions, she cried because her face in the portrait looked like Anne's.

George Smith dried her cheeks with his fine-linen handkerchief; she felt its hand-embroidered monogrammed initials brush her cheeks. GMS for George Murray Smith. His mother had stitched it for him.

In Yorkshire again for Christmas, she felt the familiar wind blow against the church and howl as the parishioners sang carols. It circled the bells and made them sound slightly as dim warning from above. Then snow fell over roofs and fields, covering flocks of sheep kept warm by their thick unshorn wool. Her father's hacking cough and roof leaks and Tabby's illness kept her home.

George Smith wrote her regularly. At first, he had addressed her as *My very dear Miss Brontë*, and signed it, *With most sincere regards, G. Smith.* Some weeks after, it became *My very dear Charlotte (if I might)*—and *Yours sincerely*. He signed it, *GMS*.

Then he scrawled, *George*.

He wrote quickly, somewhat illegibly. *Dear Charlotte, Are you coming to London soon? My mother and sisters anxiously ask after you. They miss you. I miss you.*

Part IX

March–October 1851

30

Long ago I wished to leave
"The house where I was born;"
Long ago I used to grieve,
My home seemed so forlorn.

—Charlotte Brontë, from "Regret"

Charlotte

Charlotte had been quite busy for a few weeks with her father when she received two envelopes on the same day from George Smith's company: one with another check for her new novel, *Shirley,* and the second from him, scrawled and personal.

> My very dearest Charlotte, I must go to Edinburgh on business and am bringing my sister Sylvia. She has made the marvelous suggestion that you come as well to keep her company while I work. It's only for a few days. If your father can spare you, dear Charlotte!

She pushed aside the floral plate with its remaining bit of cheese from her solitary lunch. To go anywhere, anywhere but this dull parsonage and the repetitive caw of magpies asking, *Why? Why?*

Edinburgh was more than 160 miles away, where the doomed Mary of Scots, had lived. But that was little or nothing. He had written "Dearest Charlotte." He had asked her to take a journey with him and his charming sister, who had decided she wanted to write.

It took a time to make sure her voice was steady and then she went into her father's study to tell him. She was certain he would cough a bit more to show her he was unwell. He did not. He looked over his piles of desk papers and barked, "Of course you must go! Nicholls will be here. You do nothing but mope anyway."

She answered George Smith that she would come, and his response arrived almost at once.

> Dear Charlotte, You have made us very happy. Will you meet us in York station in the ladies' waiting room? Our train from London will stop there for an hour at four before going on to Edinburgh. Sylvia will bring some of her writing, as you agreed to read it.

She breathed anxiously and yet was relieved. In Scotland something would be settled between the two of them.

Charlotte walked alone to the Keighley train station, sending on her trunk by the carter. She wore a dark blue bonnet and her new blue cloak against the April chill. It looked like rain. She boarded her train to York and descended there. Someone directed her to the ladies' waiting room, a jumble of benches with mothers and children and solitary elderly widows. A map of England and a portrait of the queen and her prince consort hung on the walls, with various framed pastels of churches and the countryside.

Just as the train from London was announced, she looked up to see George Smith standing at the door near the woman selling barley water from a lidded pottery jar. Charlotte saw the great sweep of his tweed coat to his knees and that his smile was both shy and eager.

She rose to her feet and said, "There you are, George. The porter will put my trunk in the baggage car. But where's your sister?"

"Ah, poor Sylvia! Felled by an awful cold. She's so sorry. There was no way to let you know. I could take you back to Keighley. It's a clumsy thing to happen...traveling without a chaperone for you. Not done."

For a moment Charlotte wondered if Sylvia had ever intended to come with her brother. She hesitated and then spoke in the silence. "No, I'd like to go on with you," she said. "To see Edinburgh."

The train was called, and they boarded. He had brought a plaid traveling rug for her and draped it over her knees.

There were many echoes in her mind of voices since girlhood about what a proper woman might do; certainly, Charlotte's late aunt would have frowned at the very thought of a good woman traveling alone with a man not of her family. But being a modest woman had gotten Charlotte very little in her life, and she knew George Smith was a gentleman.

As the several hours of the journey passed, they sat across from each other speaking of writing and authors. Calm settled within her small body. Her hand lay open, unguarded, on her dark skirts.

In Edinburgh, they climbed into a carriage to ride to the enormous Waterloo Hotel and Coffee Room, where he had reserved two sleeping chambers. Night fell on the mysterious streets, with gas lamps shining through the fog. They ate in the dining room, and he ordered expensive French wine. She became tipsy, and they both laughed a lot. At the end of the meal, he escorted her to the door of her room. He leaned down and lightly kissed her cheek, then left.

All the next day they walked about, seeing the brownstone houses of the enchanting city, stopping in little restaurants and visiting Holyroodhouse, the palace of Mary of Scots. When they found a tea shop down one of the narrow closes of the Royal Mile, Charlotte was glad to sit down.

Across the plates of crumpets and jam and ham, George Smith laughed nervously and gestured openly, showing his soft hands, the hands of an intellectual who turns pages of books. He ordered whisky with his tea. Slowly, like something emerging from under a cloak, his face lost defenses. She was enthralled.

He said, "We're Scottish, but you know that. My father started the business. During his illness…bad stuff, bad stuff, all our interests in India suffered. And then he died. I was under twenty-one and had to wait to take over the firm until my majority."

He poured more golden whisky into his tea. His polished boot was very close to her buckled shoe under the table.

He said, "My family…well, you've seen them. May I speak honestly?"

"Of course!"

"They adore me and wait on me, and yet still…they stifle me a bit. Surely you've seen it. It's not only that I must earn them a good living, which, of course, as an honorable son, I do. Only they want to direct me… My mother wants to make sure I am on course, as she says, as if I am a ship and she at the helm. I love them, but a man can't be ruled. I sometimes think of making a fortune and leaving the business in my partner Elder's hands and going off for six months about the world. See the whole world. Or buy him out, chuck him out. He stifles me too."

"I'm so sorry! You do everything. You saved the firm."

He reached past the plate of ham and took her hand.

"Where would you go?" she asked, hoping he would not notice how her pulse was rushing. If he did, he made no mention of it. Perhaps he was too absorbed in his own story.

He answered, "Where would I go? Egypt to see the pyramids. France and Italy for the art. They're digging up this classical city called Pompeii, buried eighteen hundred years ago in hours by a volcano. I'd like to see the islands of Greece. The Parthenon, of course. I'd like to get drunk in the moonlight and call up the ghosts of the old philosophers. And India. Our business is strong there again."

He hesitated and looked deeply at her; he was now, she could see by his eyes, a little drunk. He spoke as carefully as he could. "Dear Charlotte! I'd like you to come with me everywhere."

Charlotte's throat was dry. "How could I? We are merely friends, I think."

How much whisky had he had? She wasn't sure. He smiled

and pushed his cup to her, and she drank some. It went to her knees. She was aware of the other empty tables and portraits of great Scotsmen on the dark papered walls.

"Things could be settled between us," he said. He held her hand still. "We could find a way to…settle things. Make them regular."

She thought, Dear God! Is he asking me to marry him in such a strange way? Men are strange, I know. What does he mean?

"I'm so hemmed in," he said starkly. "Never had a chance to know myself, and here you are, so free. You went through terror, and you made readers feel it. I have never met anyone like you. I cannot cease to be fascinated by who you are and what you can do."

He rose and motioned for the waitress. He finished his tea and said, "Come, let's walk."

Outside in the narrow close between the buildings, now shadowy with the fading day, he took her in his arms and kissed her mouth. Charlotte threw her arms around him, returning his kiss.

He passed his knuckles over his lips. "Too much, too fast," he muttered. "I'm so sorry. I'm just a man, you know, beasts that we are. I like to think myself better, but I feel so much and it's all honorable, very much so. I just felt…but you know."

They returned to the hotel hardly touching, glancing shyly at each other. They met again for dinner, and neither ate the lamb.

"I'll walk you to your room," he said.

At her door once more, he hesitated, clearly fighting something within him. He peered into dark corners of the hall, away from the lantern he held. She didn't care. Nothing matters in the world until now, she thought. Oh, do come in. Let's forget the whole world and be just together, you and I. My nightgown will slip to my feet. You'd show me how it's done. I am so sick of waiting. Don't you think women can desire this as much as men? That under our modest looks, we are also ravenous?

She waited, door key in her hand as he gazed down, and then at her. "Tomorrow," he murmured.

Charlotte undressed and slipped between the sheets of the canopied bed in the paneled room. The air smelled of snuffed candle. Her feet were cold. She listened to the church bells, which rang each hour. Three o'clock.

He had kissed her with passion; he had spoken of world travels together, of her coming to London. He urged her to come…but no word of marriage. But perhaps he needed to buy the ring to ask her. That was his hesitation.

Charlotte pulled on her dressing gown, walked to the window, and opened it.

Cold air blew at her, and above, the sky was filled with stars. It was the same sky she and her sisters had seen when they'd walked out a little on the moors by lantern one night when they were young women. They had lain on the scratchy grass, arguing softly about which direction heaven lay. And Emily had whispered scornfully, "Heaven's not a physical place! Everything that happened once happens again and again somewhere right now. You mustn't tell Papa. There's so much he wouldn't understand."

Her mind turned again to George Smith.

Charlotte thought, I could go down the hall to his room. He'd be asleep, his hair rumpled. I could slip into bed with him and ask him to hold me. Things would follow, of course, and then I would know what I'm sure Emily knew. Her sister would lie about it, but Emily knew the body's full ecstasy.

She thought of Emily's words of ordinary love. This was magical, and she could do as she wished.

But she did not go.

George Smith appeared to have slept badly when he came down to the hotel breakfast room in the morning. He bent down, and she felt his kiss on her cheek. "How are you?" he asked.

"Oh, very, very well, thank you."

"Come, I need several cups of tea without whisky. If they bring any, make them take it away." And he took her arm carefully, as if she were fragile, and led her to a table near a large window. Rain fell on the glass. "Scottish weather!" he muttered.

"No worse than Yorkshire."

She glanced at the other people eating there and wished they were alone. She would have liked to tell him that her door was unlocked last night and that she had worn nothing under her nightgown. But he looked so guarded over his porridge and bacon that she leaned forward and asked, "George, what is it?"

He stirred his porridge and muttered begrudgingly, "I found a letter in my luggage from my mother. She must have tucked it there before I left. I'm here with you and so happy…but I have a life. It's all been planned for me since my father died."

He stirred again. Charlotte sat quietly and straight.

"It's all been planned," he said with a sad laugh. "She doesn't know you came with me here, so the letter was about…about something else. About someone else."

"She doesn't know?"

"I was evasive at home."

"Did your sister ever intend to come?"

"She would have, had I asked her."

Charlotte looked down at her untouched porridge. She murmured, "Who does your mother mean, dear George?"

He shrugged as if his coat were too tight for him. "My intended is called Elizabeth. She comes from a socially prominent family, and that would help my work. Damn that letter! It reminded me that I can't get away. None of us can get away. I have to take care of my mother and my sisters, Charlotte. Since my father died, I'm not free. We're not engaged, the young woman and I, but everyone expects we will be."

"I didn't know that."

"I've been mortgaged since my father died young. You're precious, Charlotte. I've never known anyone like you. You have a quiet loveliness, and I'm so drawn to you."

She murmured, "But you kissed me."

"It was wrong of me."

"I'll never regret it." She now stared at the sugar dissolving in her porridge.

He reached out and held her hand, clinging to her. He exclaimed, "It's not as if you'll lose me, Charlotte! We'll be dear friends. We'll write. You'll be more than a sister. You're part of me."

Her words spilled out, though she kept them low because the room was crowded, and she was angry now. "She's beautiful and young, besides, I imagine," Charlotte said. "All her life she's been loved and cared for and protected and knows just what to say in every circumstance. She's socially acceptable. You said you liked me for what I am, and now you reject me for it. I am pleasant. I write well."

"More than well. You're a genius. When you move to London, Charlotte, I'll visit all the time. I'll make sure."

"But still, you'd be with her, and I'd be alone. And when you visit, you would always want to ask not if I were lonely or frightened (oh, you'd care about that, truly), but the most important thing would be: Are you writing any more wonderful novels, Charlotte? Because I need to have novels to be a great publisher. And you are a genius, Charlotte. Go and be great, Charlotte… Loneliness will make you write more intensely."

"I think we should walk," he said, putting his napkin on the table.

"Why should we do that? Or anything?" Her voice rose and then broke. An older couple had turned to stare at them.

As they walked down the street together, she could see he was ashamed by his hands deep in his pockets and his covert glances down at her. He was removing himself the way men do; men buckle armor about them and hide within it, untouchable. The softness in their faces grows stern; they have retreated to a place where a woman can never reach.

"I should return home," she said.

"Must you? I have to stay some further time on business."

"But certainly I won't stay with you!" she said, appalled.

She had resolved to be silent, but as he walked her into the train station late that morning, she burst out, "Why wasn't I born into a wealthy home instead of fighting my way?"

He smiled sadly. "But if you had been born otherwise, Charlotte, you wouldn't have written *Jane Eyre.*"

"Oh, that wretched book!" she murmured. "It's paid the bills but not brought me happiness. I expected both would come together. I was wrong."

The train pulled into the station, filling the air with smoke.

Charlotte cried on the train home. What would she do now? Be alone, of course. There would be no more chances—she knew that. Even if there were, she wouldn't trust them. It had almost been, in the end, that glory shining far down upon us from heaven. But it was not.

Everything was her decision from now on. It was her life. She would stay home to keep her father company, but after he died, she could travel. If she wanted, she could visit Paris, Rome, the Alps. She could sit by lakes and mountains alone. Another parson and his family would move into the parsonage, and she would leave Haworth forever and never meet the man her sister had known.

The compartment door opened and an old man with one small carpetbag felt his way in. "Is this place free, madam?" he asked courteously. She nodded, and he took a seat opposite her.

He had touched his odd purple cap to greet her, and the sun through the window glistened on his thick white hair, which flowed to his shoulders. He looked like a painting she had seen in one great house where she had worked, which had hung at the end of a dark hall. He seemed frail, reaching out to grasp things with a tremulous hand.

"A long ride," he sighed. "I need to change trains."

"How long have you been traveling, sir?"

"A week…boat and train but I couldn't reach where I wished to go. The weather was too bad. Where do you go?"

"Haworth…my home."

"I know your village. I lived near there, in Keighley. I had a shop by the river full of unwanted things, but I've grown too old. It was too much for me; I had to close the doors. Michael's Sundries. Perhaps you've heard of it. No? Pity! Now I search for tenth-century poetry and translate it. I collect it. My best book was old. I lent it to a friend; he lent it in turn. Alas."

"But where are you now?"

"I came from St. Kilda long ago. I may return. It's an island, very far away from everything. All my friends there are gone. The sea is a fierce, fierce thing. I hear it calling to me in my sleep. A dear friend left and was not seen again."

"What happened to him?"

He did not answer. The train rocked her; her eyes closed against her will.

When she awoke, the old man was gone.

As weeks went on, Charlotte who was home again looked at her life. On her bedroom desk before her was a copy of her second book, *Shirley*. Some critics and readers said it didn't have the immediacy of struggle in it, which had made *Jane Eyre* so exceptional. Moving to London and holding literary evenings was also a dream. If there, no one would notice her. She was such a plain little woman. Her portrait, now on the dining room wall below, mocked her.

She touched the cup of quill pens, rubbing its edge.

Write me another *Jane Eyre,* Smith said wistfully in his now-formal letters. Even if she could write again, she knew there would never be another book just like that. That was an outcry of a woman shouting against her obscurity. She could, of course, continue to write novels of lonely women.

Loving George Smith had always been a fantasy.

If only her sisters were here!

Charlotte opened the door of Emily's room quietly, as if she might disturb something. Sinking onto her sister's narrow bed, she gazed out the window on the moor and drystone walls below.

"So, you're back," her father said on the day of her return when she came down for tea. His hand trembled more these days, and the tea sloshed a bit to the sides of the cup when he lifted it.

"Yes, Papa. I was supposed to meet friends in Scotland, but they were detained. I'm back to stay."

Patrick Brontë stroked his white beard. "Well, I'm very glad to hear I'm not to be entirely deserted in my old age. There are troubles with Nicholls, as I always knew there would be. He came to me when you were away and told me the most extraordinary thing. He said he was thinking of going to Africa as a missionary. And today he told me he had changed his mind. A most inconsistent, flighty fellow."

"That is unusual!" she said. "But he's served you for these years. That is hardly flightiness, Papa."

"There's a woman in it somehow, Charlotte."

"He's never mentioned any woman," she replied. "I thought he liked Anne, but he made no move. He said he was going and now he's not? How very strange."

As the weeks at home passed that summer, she felt Mr. Nicholls looking at her now and then. She heard his voice more outside the house; sometimes he laughed. He seldom spoke directly to her. He never asked her about her trip. She felt somehow that he knew what had happened to her in Edinburgh. Mr. Nicholls would surely think the worst of her, having put herself in a compromising situation with her handsome publisher who was to marry another woman.

Seasons changed again, first to late summer and then autumn. When she raised her head from her writing, she could hear the wind blowing over the gravestones and against the stones of the parsonage. George Smith's letters had once more become notably formal, as though they had hardly ever been more than friends. Surely he had not kissed her so passionately in the narrow close in Edinburgh; surely he had not almost spoken the words to make her his wife.

His life was full and hers empty.

Charlotte fastened her cloak tightly and struggled to the library in Keighley, where she borrowed two books and fought the wind home again up Haworth Main Street.

She read in her room or the warm kitchen. As long as there were other people's words, she didn't have to face her own disappointment. One day, Smith's mother sent an invitation to her son's wedding. Did Charlotte want to come? Her son so admired his favorite novelist.

Charlotte threw the letter away.

She was sewing in the parlor a few evenings later with the wind moaning in the chimney when Arthur Nicholls came in. "Am I disturbing you?" he asked.

He advanced a few feet and stopped. He ran the palm of his hand over a chair back again and again as if measuring it. He bit his lip. He pushed back his hair. She had not known him to look so unsettled since the blacksmith's son had died at the age of twelve last year; he had adored that child and grieved for weeks.

"I'm not disturbed, Mr. Nicholls," she said.

"Miss Brontë. May I sit down?"

"Of course! My father's gone to bed. It's past nine, quite late. You're also asleep by this time most evenings."

"That is true," he said, reflecting on it. When he could rub the chair back no more, he sat down and studied her fixedly in silence, hands on his knees. He swallowed several times.

He said, "I've come to ask you to marry me. I've thought about it for a few years. I love you."

It took her a time to find words. "But that's extraordinary!" she said, flushing. "A few years! That shows me one never knows what another person is thinking. I never dreamed you'd… What is this? I heard you were going for a missionary, that you again thought of that. You were, then you weren't, and now once more you are."

"It was only because I hadn't the courage to ask you. I

thought you were moving away for a time, but now you're back. I had to make sure you were staying. I should have spoken when you were just the parson's daughter and not a famous writer who travels to London. I've loved you for a long time."

Charlotte sat more deeply in her chair, hands clutching the arms. Had he been drinking? But, no, he didn't drink. "But this isn't possible," she said, bewildered. "You loved Anne. We thought you took your time to ask."

"I liked Anne. I was uncertain if I'd stay here or if I wanted a wife. Then I realized it was you. But you're difficult to approach, you know. If I might be honest, you throw out disdain for all around you."

"Disdain? I never… I am not disdainful."

Arthur Bell Nicholls rose to his feet, stern and tall in his dark beard and gazing down at her from his great height. "Will you think about it?" he asked. "If your answer is no, I must go away. You see, I left my family and became devoted to yours. I grieved the loss of each of them; I do every day. I admire your father and could never be the preacher he is, but things have happened, and here we are, both alone. I know if I went off and found a better position, I would earn more money and easily afford to marry, but I stayed. Steadfastness is a dull virtue, I am sure, even though in the Bible, we are told to 'hold fast to that which is good.' I'm not certain if it means the one good thing you have found, not looking for other good things, but this is how I am."

Charlotte felt compassion softening her. "You never should have stayed so long," she urged. "There's little for you here."

"There's you."

She focused on the bookshelf and not on him. "Arthur (if I might call you by your name), I'm a strange woman. I have loved, but nothing came of it. In one case, I was foolish and almost did something I'd always regret; the other I think you sense. After that, I locked up my heart."

He replied, "Did you find a better world in London?"

She said sadly, "No. I thought I would, and I didn't. If you took so long to ask, perhaps you'll give me a time to answer you! I don't mean to disrespect you. You've astonished me."

When he left, she recalled a conversation with Anne when she and her sister had gone down to the sea in Anne's last illness. They had been walking slowly on the shore when Anne said, "Mr. Nicholls is fond of you, not me." And Charlotte had answered, both haughty and incredulous, "Mr. Nicholls! He's not fond of anyone. Besides, I'd never marry a curate."

They had walked slowly by the sea, the spring salt wind whipping her dress and her bonnet strings. Anne had said, "He's very kind and faithful. And his heart's good."

"How would I know what sort of heart he has? He never talks but to the poor and dying. He understood Branwell. He was caring of him when we gave up."

Still alone in the parlor, Charlotte began to cry at the memory of her sisters; she wanted them there to giggle with, to discuss wryly, to dismiss this strange offer. Why did she need it? She had them. But, no, she didn't have them anymore. And as for her father, the only other living family member, she hardly saw him for days. And one day he too would go.

Charlotte steadied herself in the chair at the thought of it: If her father died, she would be quite alone. To do what, as she had planned? Travel about the world, writing a book about it? *Travels of a Spinster…* No, not a good title. She rose and walked quickly up the stairs, where she knocked sharply on her father's door.

Patrick Brontë was sitting up in bed reading, the flame of the candle reflecting in the window. She closed the door and stood with her back to it. "Papa, I'm beyond words," she said. "Mr. Nicholls has just asked me to marry him."

"What?" her father asked. His eyes grew dark and feral; his white beard trembled. He sputtered so a thin arc of spit flew from his lips. "What? How dare he? What answer did you make?"

"I said I needed time. He just asked."

"Then you have had enough time to refuse him. A poor curate who hasn't made his way anywhere in the world. A man of no family and no prospects."

Her father was now trembling so much that he knocked the book from the quilt to the floor. She rescued it. "It is no, of course," she said. "Of course, you're right, Papa!"

Charlotte returned downstairs to turn off the lamps. She had told her father, knowing exactly what his reaction would be and taking the burden of the response from her. Still, as she lingered in the parlor with her hand on the table where she had written much of her books, she thought of kissing Nicholls, this man in his worn brushed suit who was a favorite among the children and old people of the village.

Before eight in the morning, she was dressed and downstairs. The house smelled of Martha's porridge. She could see Nicholls through the window walking Anne's forlorn spaniel, letting the little dog sniff where she would.

He saw her and came shyly into the kitchen with the spaniel in his arms. She was laying down spoons for breakfast porridge. "In reply to your kind offer," she mumbled with difficulty, "I think I must say no. But you've been generous with Papa and… all of us! I will miss you if you go to Africa."

He blinked several times and nodded. She gazed up at this big incomprehensible man, the dark beard and stubborn, square face. She said, "You're a good man for all your six years here, but I can't be a parson's wife. It's not the life I want."

His long face darkened. "I am myself before I am a parson, and I love you."

"You don't understand. I may go back to London. I may travel. I have money now. I can do what I like."

He carefully hung Flossie's leash on the hook and said, "Well, there it is. You move in the world of great men. Men of letters write ecstatically of your work. I visit the sick and teach children. I love children. You have more money than I'll ever have and much more fame. Why would you want to become

Mrs. Nicholls?" He added stubbornly, his lip stuck out, "Yes, you're right. What do I have to offer you?"

"Nicholls has given me his resignation," her father said at tea later that day as he munched away at his crumpet, a crumb falling into his beard. "No, he's not going to Africa. He's accepted a call to a church fifty miles away. Good riddance, that is what I say. Let him sniff out the daughters there."

Within a week, Arthur Nicholls was gone.

Part X

April–May 1852–Winter 1853

31

Then let my winds caress thee;
Thy comrade let me be—
Since nought beside can bless thee,
Return and dwell with me.

—Emily Brontë, from "Shall Earth No More Inspire Thee"

Charlotte

Several months passed. Spring of 1852 came round. Charlotte baked and ran out of things to iron. Martha was absentminded and Tabby had a time getting down the steps. Patrick Brontë vowed to have no more curates, so half the work did not get done. Sometimes he forgot to wind the clock.

There was no danger of their having to leave for financial reasons, however; the old man was beloved by many. And she was famous. Even the church wardens deferred to her. They would not risk the scandal of a good priest and his famous daughter set out on the road. Of course, if it happened, Charlotte could buy them another home.

All is well, she thought. Only I am not well. I am unhappy.

Each day Charlotte moved her portable desk from her bedroom to the parlor to the kitchen, hoping to find inspiration. Sitting motionless with pen in her hand, she thought, Now that I have all the leisure and public interest to write my books, I no longer want to create them.

It shocked her. She had been one way all her life and now she had changed. She did not reply to the polite letters from George Smith's kind reader Mr. Williams inquiring when they could expect her new novel.

Maybe they would not.

I need my sisters, she thought.

Charlotte left the house and walked down the steep village street. The shop bell of the stationer tinkled as the door opened. On the shelves were the same dusty boxes, and the same lamp hung over the counter as it had when she and Anne and Emily were young and where, a few years before, she had seen a copy of *Jane Eyre* on display.

Oh, but it was not the same! The man behind the counter was now young Jack Greenwood. His father, who had worked here, was no longer well enough to come in.

"What will you do with all this paper, Miss Brontë?" young Greenwood asked, though his smile said he knew. More and more people knew. Strangers came to the town asking where she lived. Now many approached the parsonage door. A few showed up in church on Sundays, staring at her for half the service.

She searched the corners of the shop.

The little girls she and her sisters had been were no longer there.

Even a letter in French which arrived last week from her beloved French professor lauding the translation of *Jane Eyre* and saying he always knew she was highly gifted only made her smile wryly.

Charlotte climbed slowly back up Main Street. A young curate visiting here passed her and tipped his black hat. Then what she had tried to push away came flooding back so intensely that she ceased to walk. It was now months since she had refused Arthur Nicholls, and she sometimes wondered if she had made a mistake. "What's done is done," she muttered under her breath as she turned past the public house and through the gates to go home.

And then he returned.

He sent no word; he just appeared. Through the newly washed kitchen window, she saw him standing in the garden. She wanted to rush out and cry, "Arthur!" but she did not. She went to the door very coolly and walked slowly to him. He saw her and gazed down at her.

"Why, how nice of you to visit!" she said. "Papa's inside. I'm sure you've come to see him."

"You know I have not," he said, turning his hat round and round in his hands. "Charlotte, I love you so much. I feel I'm dying of grief away from you."

"But, Mr. Nicholls, no one comes fifty miles to say he is dying."

"I lay my feelings bare, and you answer with acerbic wit."

She replied, a little ashamed, "I've never known how else to defend myself."

"You've defended yourself against strangers since you and your sisters were children. But whatever you may think, I feel I'm part of this family. I love you. I decide things slowly and don't change my mind. You've made fun of me for this. Are men who smile at you and leave better? The only ones worthwhile? The handsome ones? In which case, there's no hope for me. I've read your sisters' novels too, now. All of you write of heartless men. Is that what you want?"

"Of course it's not what we ever wanted. We were writing fiction. We wrote the impossible, especially Emily."

"If I may paraphrase a touching moment in your first novel, Do you think, because I am poor and obscure, I am soulless and heartless?"

"Mr. Nicholls, you may not speak to me this way."

Her throat filled with tears as she walked back into the kitchen. From the window she saw he had not moved but remained, still holding his hat. She hurried upstairs and passed her sisters' rooms, saying under her breath, "Tell me what to do!"

Reaching her bedroom, she paced the few steps between the desk with the pages of her new novel and the wardrobe with the dresses she had worn in London. Could she love this curate? He had always simply been there; it was only when he had been gone these past months that she realized she missed him a little.

Charlotte sat on her bed. Was that best then, to come home to someone who loved her steadily, even if she never wrote another book? He had loved her before she had published her first novel, before strangers came to seek her. At least he said he had.

Likely, he had gone away.

But when she descended the stairs, he was still standing in the garden, wistfully surveying the moors. Cautiously, she again opened the kitchen door and walked out to him. It was some time before either of them spoke.

"Arthur, I think we should be married," she said. "Come inside for tea."

"I should like that," he said, though his words were a little stunned, and she wanted to ask if he meant the marriage or the tea but felt he was so serious that she ought not say that.

An hour later, Charlotte walked into her father's study and told him.

The Reverend Patrick Brontë rose from the piano stool where he was playing an Irish melody; it was only recently that he played again. Now he let both hands crash discordantly on the keys. "What, are you mad?" he cried. "You wish to marry a nobody? Desert me too, I suppose. Go and live in his new larger church, leaving me alone in my aging years. I knew you would do it. I always suspected it."

She kissed his hands. "Oh, Papa! Not that again! Arthur wants to return here to assist you."

"You marry because you're lonely! Very well. You must live in the one room above the sexton's quarters, because I will never have another man in this house."

"Now that I'm able to have some happiness, you deny it! I'm lonely. Did you think I wouldn't be lonely here, alone with you speaking to me a half hour a day?"

"I'll write to the bishop. I'll have Nicholls thrown from the church for seducing my daughter."

"Papa, I am thirty-six and earn my own keep. I am allowed

to direct my life in some ways, though it would be easier for me if you agreed. I wish never to leave him."

Patrick Brontë did not come downstairs for three days. After each meal, Tabitha brought the untouched tray down the steps again. At last, Charlotte ran up the steps and flung open her father's bedroom door. He sat in bed, so frail. She exclaimed, "Do as you will, Papa, but I will marry Mr. Nicholls. If you won't have him return, I'll go to the church he serves now, and you may stay here alone."

A few days following, Arthur Nicholls walked into the parsonage and into the study. Charlotte heard the men's voices through the door. Arthur's was full of emotion. He said, "Do you intend to keep Charlotte with you unmarried until you die and then leave her alone in the world without a soul close to her? Is that what you wish?"

She could not quite make out her father's begrudging reply.

Within a few weeks, Arthur had taken up his position again as curate in their church of St. Michael and All Angels and moved back to his former rooms upstairs in the sexton's house. Charlotte climbed the stairs to help him put his books back on the shelves. Among them were her two novels. By the wardrobe, he bent down and kissed her lips. She took his hand and put it on her bodice over her breasts. He smiled.

Those days, Charlotte began to write once more. She wrote very slowly, but at least she wrote. Sometimes she felt she would never finish a book again. She made herself write at least a page and then went to find Arthur. She waited by the moor gate for him to come. They walked a bit; she held on to his arm.

The autumn days grew colder, the wind cut hard, the drying heather bent before it. In that time, she reflected on everything. Recently she had thought of the last days of Emily's life, and her words. *I want to tell you something…*

Emily had entered her mind again fully, and with her memory of those last days came also the thoughts of the nights her sister didn't come home and the letters that Tabitha said she believed were left under a rock. But you couldn't trust Tabby's memory much anymore.

Charlotte thought, I must know. Did she hide those letters somewhere?

Emily's room was still, the way a place is when intense life has been lived there and is now gone. Charlotte walked to the bookshelf and pulled out the ancient volume of Gaelic poetry. To hold a book handwritten many hundreds of years ago! She had read some of the loose pages of translations.

Those pages were gone leaving only the book whose language was incomprehensible.

As she was puzzling over it, she noticed that the side edges of the last pages were stuck together. Carefully, Charlotte broke the glue. On the last page, which had been left blank by the scribe, Charlotte found herself gazing down at a watercolor portrait of a thoughtful, masculine face with badly cut, wheat-colored hair. Emily's painting, of course. Words were written below in the unsteady handwriting of her sister's last illness: *Beloved Jonathan,* and below it, *With my body I thee worship*—those words from the prayer book's marriage sacrament.

The stranger had a name. But "body" and "worship"?

A good unmarried woman did not write those words.

Emily's keys were in her pocket.

Charlotte had opened the wardrobe drawer years ago to find Emily's hidden poetry and the second time under her sister's direction to retrieve the unfinished novel to burn. She could still see the bits of the manuscript within the fire. After the novel was burned, the drawer was nearly empty but for notes and scraps. She had looked through those a few years ago.

She opened it for the fourth time.

It was no longer empty.

A folder lay at the bottom with a dozen or so poems in Emily's hand which Charlotte had never seen before. She looked at the first and quickly flushed, tucking it away, biting her lip. Beneath loose papers, written in an unknown hand, was a rough drawing of a lamb. "Dearest Emily," it said. "It's your birthday today and as usual I won't be there, but my heart's with you. You remember the way! A half mile past the Graham farm, turn left, and go up and then down the hill until you see my cottage. I think you've forgotten since you don't come. I long to have you in my arms again. I enclose a map, for I know you've forgotten. I am teasing you; you would not forget. Especially the yellow door. Ever yours in love, Jonathan."

So, this was it then! Emily truly had had a lover. And for how long? A few years? How could her sister have not confided in her? Perhaps she had confided in Anne. Again the clench of sisterly jealousy, as if she were now entirely unloved. But the drawer had been nearly empty before, or so she had thought.

Charlotte understood then that this was the man who had wept outside the house when Emily died. She shivered. Oh God, what did she know about her sister, really?

She understood one thing. She had to find the house and that man if he was still there.

Charlotte set out the next day; the wind tore at the paper in her hand. She walked until she reached the uneven ground, her feet aching. It would be like Emily to go this way and not stay on a path! The directions on the page weren't clear. She lost her way twice; a stranger pointed the direction and then said he wasn't sure.

Finally, in the distance, she saw the Graham farm. The family were not churchgoers and might only know her from passing on market days. She was tired now and felt foolish as she approached the woman who was hanging laundry on the line, two small children clinging to her skirts. Charlotte said, "I'm a little lost. I'm looking for a stone cottage with a yellow door."

"Go farther to that hill with the large rock and climb; go down again and you will see it, but it's empty as far as is known to me."

"Have you lived here long?"

"No, this house belonged to my brother, and it came to us when he died a year ago or more."

"I'm sorry for your loss! I'm looking for someone who lived in that cottage before your brother's death—a man with fair curly hair. Did your brother talk of a man there?"

"Not a word, miss. My son went that way months ago and said the house was empty. There was crusted porridge in the pot and a bit of milk in the jug, long dried, he said. Very odd, he said. Barn empty too. Signs that a horse had been there and sheep once, but a time ago."

Charlotte walked on, climbed the hill, and, looking down from the top, saw the stone cottage with its slate roof. The sheep pen was, as reported, empty.

She descended carefully and crossed the grass to the cottage, where she put her hand on the unlocked door.

No one had been there in a long time. There was a heavy cloak, a dented kettle, but mice had eaten part of the quilt. Books on the shelf were half ruined with rain from a leaking roof; she touched them gently, making out they were eighteen-century sermons and the classical authors in translation. In each of them was inscribed the name Jonathan MacConnell. There were mouse droppings and an empty bird's nest. A bird must have flown in through the glassless window, stayed a time, and flew away again. Someone had left the shutters open.

But on the dresser was her sister's handkerchief and a piece of paper in Emily's writing. *Think of me until then*, it said. Charlotte dropped down on one of the unsteady chairs and burst into tears. She took up the handkerchief and buried her face in it, though it smelled dirty, and then folded it and replaced it on the dresser.

She closed the cottage door carefully when she left.

It took her a time to stop crying.

She had to put it aside; she was preparing for her wedding.

There was the white gown, ordered from the local dressmaker, and the bonnet, which Tabby would trim. There were the invitations and preparations for the small reception. A few friends would come and some people from town. Arthur had some friends as well.

Her love was not a glory shining from heaven but some small patches of light, lovely, warming. And perhaps there would be more.

As the marriage came closer each day, she cried, sometimes inexplicably. She went for walks. Mostly, she was clearing her things away. Rooms would be changed: her bedroom enlarged for a marital bed, the coal room moved to a shed, and that space scrubbed and papered, transforming into Arthur's new study.

In all these renovations, she remembered the box that had been made for bottles of men's hair oil and had held their childhood writings. After Branwell's death, they had moved it to his room under the bed and when Tabitha took the space, Charlotte had removed it once more to her wardrobe. She thought she would look at it in a few months, but the night before her wedding, when she couldn't sleep, she carried it down to the kitchen in her white wool nightgown with her hair down her back.

She placed her lantern and the box on the table and stirred the ashes.

The box was scuffed and deep. She opened it to the many pages of small writing, even a whole tiny book, the pages handsewn together. That story she had written long ago. It fit into the palm of her hand.

Tabby appeared at the kitchen door, her long face under her sleeping cap with its floppy white brim. "I thought I heard you, child!" she said. "Many a bride's up late before her wedding. The master's asleep?"

From above came Charlotte's father's snores. She could see him as she had earlier through the crack in his door: large peasant hands on his chest like a stone figure of a Celtic saint.

Charlotte said, "He's sleeping; tomorrow he'll deny it."

"Yes, he declares he hasn't slept in months. How can a clergyman refuse to marry his daughter in his own church where he's been these thirty years? Letting some other parson read the vows! I'll weep during the service, I'm sure. For him and your sisters. They should be here tonight."

"They should indeed! But my father will relent in time."

"Good night, then, my child."

Alone again, Charlotte sat with her eyes closed, her hands on the table. The wind was in the chimney. It blew across the vast craggy Yorkshire moors, past the high wild grass, through the broken roof of the abandoned cottage she had found.

Then the question that had haunted her since she had seen it returned to her mind. She had read the letter the stranger had written to Emily, she had seen the sketch and the map, she had gone to the cottage and found her sister's handkerchief. But how had the letters appeared in the drawer, and when had the drawing with watercolor in the back of the book of Celtic poetry on Emily's shelf been made?

Charlotte could see his directions, the sweep of the *J* of his name in the letter and the great space he left between lines. She had walked out near the house again and asked in other houses. One old woman said she recalled a thin young lady coming over the hill at first light one morning years before.

But who had been in the cottage when her sister went inside and closed the door? There had been smoke from the chimney at times, the neighbor woman had added. Vagrants perhaps. But where was the man? And *who* was he?

Charlotte sat for a time. I must put this away from me now, she thought. Later I will try to find out more, or maybe not. Maybe I will forget about it.

She closed the box of writings and took them upstairs to store away in the bottom of her wardrobe.

In the morning she was married to Arthur Bell Nicholls; and that night, in a roadside inn, the first night of their honeymoon, she went into his arms. She had no idea what it would be like after all her fantasies, but he was gentle, and she found it beautiful after it ceased to startle and ache. She lay awake fingering the end of her braid, smiling in the strange inn room. Love does startle, she thought.

They traveled on to Ireland by train and carriage and then boat, and then farther by train and carriage to the north and County Antrim, where Arthur had been born on a farm outside the village. The famine had ended, and men and women worked in the fields, though Arthur said the churchyards were fuller than he had remembered.

It was very moving for him to go home; he had to bend his head to enter the thatched cottage where he had been born. Relatives came down the road to see them, though quite a few were missing; some were dead, and many had gone off to America.

She saw the humble world her husband had come from; her father had come from the same world of a two-room cottage. But Charlotte understood. They had quarreled because her father would not admit his younger countryman now had the strength that had once been his. Of course, he would come around in time.

Weeks later, when they walked back into the parsonage, they found her father well if disgruntled. "It's like you both to leave me with all the work," he said. They had, of course, made sure an assistant helped him when they were away.

Arthur Bell Nicholls moved into her enlarged room.

He was busy then, as much had not been done in his absence. He never said it to her father; he was very kind. And she did not write then; there was too much to do. It was such a change to be married that she hardly remembered her work.

So it was many weeks before she began to think again of the empty cottage and the man who had disappeared.

I'll go again and take away Emily's handkerchief and her note, at least, Charlotte thought. Why had she left them when she went there before? Any memory of her sister was precious. It had been more than four years, and the immediacy of Emily's presence was slipping away. Some days, she could not quite recall her voice. So on a lightly windy morning, the kind they all had loved so much, she set out over the moors.

She lost her way and was tired by the time she climbed the hill and at last looked down at the cottage.

The stable door was open, but inside as empty as before. Charlotte walked down the hill balancing and hesitated at the house door. She touched the scuffed yellow paint, and still she knocked and called. No answer came.

But inside there was a small pocket of heat from the coals and ashes of a fire. The pot held some fresh porridge, still a little warm. A blue-covered book lay on the bed, and there was a declivity in the pillow, as if someone had slept there. There was no sign of mice.

She heard footsteps on the path and the barking of a dog. She crossed to the door.

A tall blond man, hands swinging at his sides, was coming toward her, so absorbed in his thoughts that he didn't see her until he was only a few feet away and his dog growled.

He blinked and walked slowly up to her, hushing the animal, gazing at her intently. He said at last, "I think you're my Emily's sister."

That so startled her, she took a moment to find words. "Yes, I'm Charlotte Nicholls," she said. "Mrs. Nicholls. I recently married."

"My congratulations. I'm Jonathan MacConnell."

"I found your picture. I thought you had left."

"I did go away for some time. Let's sit down. I thought eventually we'd find each other."

"I'm glad we have," she said.

Charlotte looked up; the roof seemed to have been patched since she was last in this place. She sat down slowly and then murmured, "You're really here. As I walked today, I had the strangest feeling that you'd never been here at all, as if she had made you up."

He shook his head. "Made me up?" he asked. "Here I stand. She found this cottage one day and liked me. I don't know why.

I wanted to marry her, you know. Ah, perhaps you didn't know that, by your face. She wasn't certain she could leave any of you, and then she said I might speak to her father for her hand on Christmas Day."

He turned to the bookshelf and his face filled with sorrow. "But she became ill. I knew how ill she was the last day she came here."

"I saw you outside the house in her last illness."

He held on to the rough stained table, which appeared as worn as if it had sat outside in all weathers, but the bed and plates and chairs were also like that, as if the poorest jumble shop would sell them for a few shillings at most.

His voice was low. "I can't describe the grief of it. She knew about my life and understood it all, where I came from St. Kilda, far out in the Hebrides. And you lost another sister. Anne. I never met her."

"So Emily really came here? Then it's true."

"Yes, she came many times. We hid away and talked. A remarkable girl with so much love inside her." His voice caught, and he covered his eyes. "If you had heard me crying at night, you'd know. I wanted her as my wife. I wanted her forever."

"She never wanted to be a wife."

"Not *a* wife, but *my* wife," he said. "There's a difference. I would have let her be free as she wanted, as long as she came back to me at the day's end or even the week's end. I knew we likely couldn't have children, but we didn't have to have them. She stayed here some nights in my arms. I loved her."

Charlotte bit her lip and said in a low voice, "Before marriage. You did this before marriage."

He stood tall. "Oh, you people with your church rules!" he said scornfully. "Does it matter what we did or didn't do? What do you know of love? Do you think it's from a contract?"

"But this is shocking to me. Can't you understand it? Because I knew my sister; she may have said I was judgmental, but I knew her, and I loved her. If she is as you say, I never knew her. And I know what love is."

"But there are different sorts of love."

It was a few moments before she could speak. Then she rose. "I didn't expect to find you. I came to take her handkerchief, and some note she wrote for you."

He said, "It's my note and I need whatever she left. I don't have much of her except her presence. She comes to me. I call her when I'm too lonely, and she always appears in the door. I leave it open. She lies down in my arms and tells me it's not over, that she's waiting for me."

Charlotte wanted to be out the door, but she spoke with compassion. "I could send you some things of hers. No, wait. If you come to the parsonage moor gate tomorrow morning, I'll leave a basket outside for you. I think we have your old glove."

In parting, she took his hand. It was warm.

That night, Charlotte took their worn wicker basket from the cellar. She walked through the house, gathering one of Emily's shawls, a few of her drawings, and some jars of her blackberry preserves marked with her initials on the cotton top. She dropped in her sister's recently discovered new verses. She turned the pages of the book of Gallic poems with his picture before adding them and closed the canvas top of the basket, securing it with twine. On a tag she wrote, *To be called for by JM.*

Her husband, who was upstairs a little sick with a cold, had gone to bed early. She walked to the moor gate.

In the morning, the basket would be gone. The man would take it away. Charlotte doubted she'd see him again, but she hoped her sister's spirit would go to him; if anyone could do that, Emily could indeed.

In the night, snow fell. It was still falling lightly when she woke beside her husband, wondering what the hour could be. It was that strange snow when you felt yourself between worlds, when you wanted just to lie in bed and watch it tumbling. Spirits were there. Somewhere in those flakes were her sisters. Lying near the warmth of her husband, she dared think that.

She lay listening to the sounds of the house. Nothing but her father's snores. Charlotte squinted at her watch on the table. Two minutes past six. Martha would come in an hour. She sat up slightly, feeling the length of her husband beside her. He had wound the hall clock as her father always did, taking over that work. That was a great step in her father's acceptance of his son-in-law.

If she put her feet on the floor, they would be cold. She must pull up her bed socks and put on her wool lavender dressing gown, which had belonged to Anne. First her spectacles, though. Wretched eyes! And then she fell back onto the feather pillow and watched the snow. There! Now, through her lenses, she could see the world outside the window more clearly.

Charlotte rose slowly and opened the window a little. Still, she could make out nothing but the back of the house and the kitchen garden. She could not see the gate. Charlotte opened the bedroom door and walked down the stairs. She was glad her husband had wound the clock; if it stopped, there would be no more hours in the world.

Writers and poets realized how our world opened and closed like a blowing window curtain and, for a moment, revealed the other worlds beyond them, too quickly closed to put your hand out and touch them. Her sisters and brother had played at that when young, knowing if you did touch another world and hold it fast, something completely wonderful would happen. The tiny world would find its strength and, in less than a breath, grow until it was big enough to enclose you.

That was how they started to write.

That other world had formed about the four of them. Closing their eyes and holding hands, they had floated in it above the rooftops of Haworth. They floated up at night into the stars, far away, each daring each other to keep the moment. And Branwell would whisper, "Look!" and there were all the places in the world below them and about them, a thousand stars. "Hello, dear children!" said the stars.

And then Branwell would shout, "Now!" and they would

float gently down again. The world fell away, and they stepped into the dining room. They were tired and longed for toasted bread and prayers before bed.

"Where have you children been?" their father would ask. "Down to the shops? Did you see widow Miller? Did you?" Sometimes they thought to tell him, but he wouldn't understand.

Martha would come soon, footsteps on the flagstone floors, rushing and muttering into the kitchen toward the stove to light it and let the warmth fill the kitchen. She would not pass the gate where Charlotte had placed the basket for the stranger.

Charlotte opened the door. The snow was not deep, but she sat on the bench to pull on her boots and then stepped outside. Her heart beat a little quicker as she walked, leaving her footprints in the snow, toward the gate where they used to run out to the moors. The basket would be gone; she had sensed Emily's love come last night and take it away in the darkness.

But he had not come.

The basket sat there still in the snow.

Charlotte held on to the gatepost, peering out toward the moor. Of course, she thought bitterly. She had imagined him. He had never existed. But that can't be, she thought again. I saw him. I touched his hand. He will come. There were the books, the letters, the handkerchief.

That day it snowed on and off, and the night was cold. In the early morning she went again, but the basket was untouched, and the snow had leaked through the wicker box. She unfastened it and looked inside. The shawl was wet from a thin layer of ice, and the pages of the letters were half frozen. Some of the ink had run. Some of the words were gone.

That day when Martha brought dinner into the parlor, she asked why a basket sat by the moor gate. "A neighbor who lives on the moors is coming back for it," Charlotte answered. "He needed to leave it as he was carrying so much."

"A neighbor?" asked Arthur, drinking his ale and frowning. "Who? We know everyone about here, Charlotte, and if we didn't, we wouldn't want him at the gate. What a strange thing! Maybe he's one of the poor vagrant travelers Emily would feed. You know how she was."

"I met him in the street; he seemed a decent sort."

She tried to put the threads together between lies; fortunately, her husband did not know that part of her. But of course, he couldn't know it. There was such a difference between her and him. He could never enter the world of her sisters and brother. But I can't go there entirely, she thought. I'd lose him. They are only in my heart now and he's here.

Still, the next morning when light woke her, she descended to open the kitchen door and walk through the moor gate.

The closed basket had not moved.

For seven days it stayed there, and then deep snow came again. She untied the twine once more; everything inside was cold and sodden. More lines had run from the poems. She had not copied these; they were the only ones. The sensual content had disturbed her.

Bending over the basket, hearing the children recite their lessons in the school close by, she thought, I'm being silly. The stranger had gone away; he had forgotten. Perhaps he had gone back to his island far off the coast of Scotland; perhaps he would get word to her. But he didn't write, and winter came and soaked the basket, and all the lines of the poems were gone.

She wrote signs describing him, asking if anyone had seen him; she drew him from memory and the watercolor in the poetry book. She hung the sign in the tiny post office and tacked copies on moor signposts. She never went to the stone cottage. She was not feeling strong. She understood she was with child.

It was the last of the winter then, and he had not come.

Charlotte began to forget him. She forgot just how he looked and what they had talked about, but then she was forgetting so much. She could not quite recall what it was like when they were children and enclosed in their own world, away from all troubles. If she walked softly down the hall to the parlor, she might hear the four of them sitting around the table whispering games…and earlier than that, when there had been six of them and their mother's singing had drifted through the house.

More, she was forgetting the despair she had felt when writing *Jane Eyre*; it was now apart from her, that longing to belong that had created the book. Maybe the stranger also longed for that, but the truth was, she thought of him less and less. She was sleepy and her belly was swelling. She was married to a practical, ordinary man. She served her own father in his many needs.

I can't hold on, Emily, she thought. I was always more earthbound than the rest of you. Yet one time I believed that the things we imagine are as real to us as the things that everyone else can see; if we love them enough, we give them life.

But I can't live in both worlds, and I can't stay in the one we shared. Now I'm married and I'm going to have a child, maybe more children if I'm not too old.

Charlotte took up the basket one morning, or what was left of it. Chewed fragments of a handkerchief and shawl, stiff paper with a few words left smeared here and there. Gently, she dropped the whole basket into the fire and watched it burn. The last bit of a man's glove seemed to reach out to her, the last bit of empty paper.

Goodbye, my Emily, she thought, but not for always. Even when I'm old, our worlds and the people we loved will come to me. Then from my bed, I'll hear the gate open, and a whistle, and the restored basket will be taken up. "There's a stranger at the gate," my husband will say sternly, bewildered. Oh, my husband, Arthur, who will be old then too! And I will smile a little and say, "I know it, but he's gone now," and then he will sit by my bed and give me his hand and fill me with his love.

But for now, she had a new novel to finish.

Charlotte took her little portable desk into the parlor and uncorked the ink. For a little while she listened and then began to write.

Author's Notes

All historical fiction is speculative, particularly when the characters are based on real people. It is speculative in small ways, as we don't know just what sisters would discuss having tea in the parsonage kitchen when the cold wind from the moor rattled the windows and the cats slept by the fire. And it is speculative in their larger personal lives. We know of three major loves/infatuations in Charlotte's story: her Brussels teacher, her publisher, and the man she finally married. We believe the lovely Anne was much taken with a curate who died young. But much of Emily, including her possible love life, remains a mystery.

History has given us glimpses of these complicated young women, all of whom are still but shadows on the wall. Emily left one novel (a second unfinished manuscript was supposedly destroyed), many poems, and a few letters. She was fiercely private and possibly had agoraphobia. However, she took long walks alone on the moors and, in this story, met someone secretly. The question has often arisen as to whether she could have written the tormented love of Heathcliff and Cathy without knowing love. But suppose she did love someone very much and trusted him, but he was nothing like Heathcliff? Suppose her love was tender and simple...because we don't necessarily want the wild bad boys we dream of. Or suppose her love was safe because he existed only in her mind, but so intensely that he was entirely real to her? Or was he a phantom? Perhaps the truth was somewhere between these things.

Some dates of certain historical events have been changed for this novel.

The book Jonathan lends Emily is an ancient handwritten copy of some of the poems in the famous *Book of Exeter,* such as "The Wanderer" and "The Seafarer." The original book, dated approximately 960–990, can be found in Exeter Cathedral Library. It is possible there was more than one copy, now lost. Maybe one day someone will clear out a long-forgotten attic, like the secret one in Westminster Abbey. And like the lost treasures found under the Abbey's floorboards, there the book will be.

The few lines from *The Wanderer* which appear in this book are by the great Princeton translator Charles W. Kennedy (1882-1969).

Charlotte's real story ends early. She died in March 1855, likely from hyperemesis gravidarum, a complication of pregnancy. Her husband, Arthur, remained with his difficult father-in-law some years, until Patrick Brontë's death, and then returned to Ireland. He kept many of Charlotte's things, including Branwell's family portrait, which Arthur folded away so long that creases remain in it today. It hangs in the National Portrait Gallery in London.

Do go to the Brontë Parsonage Museum in Haworth. Stay in one of several B&Bs in the village if you like and climb the steep cobbled street past the little shops to the church gates. Walk past the church and the gravestones. I went first at dusk and heard the magpies in the trees. Find the inside of the house pretty much as the family left it. They even have Charlotte's wedding dress and the very scratched parlor table at which the children wrote their first stories. All the family but Anne are buried in the crypt. Walk out on the moors, but unless you are a very good walker with a strong sense of direction, go with a guide. A hiker friend went out by herself and barely got back to the village by dark.

For nearly a hundred seventy-five years, the literary world has been fascinated by the Brontë sisters. Everyone sees their story a little differently. This is how it came to me.

ACKNOWLEDGEMENTS

As always, writing books is not possible for me without my generous friends and beta readers whose comments and corrections and, most of all, encouragement, are priceless.

For reading drafts or/and long talks and e-mails to bolster me, I thank Judith Ackerman, Pat Barry, Amy Baruch, Christina Britton-Conroy, Linda Aronovsky Cox, Christine Emmert, Karen Finch, Jane Gardner, Sandra Guillard, Rhonda Hunt-Del Bene, Mitchell James Kaplan, Katherine Kirkpatrick, Pamela Leggett, Judith Lindbergh, Kathleen M. Rodgers, M.J. Rose, Andrea Simon, Anne Easter Smith, Sanna Stanley, and Ali Tufel. And to Susan Dormady Eisenberg for her daily cheering e-mails and sharing thoughts on the writer's life. Thanks for the wonderful comradery of the Historical Novel Society and its New York City branch, my zoom Historical Novelists' Wine and Chat group, and the love and support of clergy, musicians and parishioners of St. Ignatius of Antioch. Sincere apologies to anyone I have forgotten!

For copyediting extraordinaire, thanks always to my lifelong copy-editor friend, Renée Vera Cafiero. And greatest thanks to my sustaining family: my sons Jesse Cowell and James Nordstrom, Erica Langworthy, my sisters Jennie and Gabrielle, and granddaughters Hanna and Emma Nordstrom.

I am grateful to the Brontë Parsonage Museum in Haworth, Yorkshire, which keeps the house of the Brontë family pretty much as they left it and thanks to the docents, particularly Rory, who welcomed me so warmly and answered all my questions with such patience. Alas, I have forgotten the name of the kind woman who when I was in my twenties took me walking on the moors and showed me the house that may have inspired *Wuthering Heights.* I greeted sheep and ruined my pretty blue pumps as they sank deep into the moor mud during our climbs.

I have a few shelves of books on the Brontë family and as I have been reading them for years, I cannot say which influenced me most.

Last, I am so grateful to Regal House Publishing for choosing to publish this novel: to editor/founder Jaynie Royal, managing editor Pam Van Dyk, and all the gifted small staff. Thank you!